NIGHT PREY

NIGHTHAWK SECURITY - BOOK SIX

SUSAN SLEEMAN

EDGE OF YOUR SEAT BOOKS, INC.

Published by Edge of Your Seat Books, Inc.

Contact the publisher at contact@edgeofyourseatbooks.com

Copyright © 2021 by Susan Sleeman

Cover design by Kelly A. Martin of KAM Design

1

———————

Just the sight of this man curled Malone's stomach and sent a bead of sweat down her back.

Horrendous memories that she'd battled for seventeen years came rushing back. Sickening, terrible ones. Suddenly she was there again, smelling his rancid breath, aching under his grip on her wrists. Thank God she'd managed to avoid the worst, but only just.

Acid rose up her throat. She planted her feet to keep from bolting from the ballroom filled with round tables draped in white cloths, each anchoring colorful balloon bouquets reaching for the ceiling.

She forced herself to look at the offender, Gilbert Flagg Jr., otherwise known as Junior. He hadn't grown even a fraction of an inch since she'd last laid eyes on him at high school graduation. Now, fifteen years later at their reunion, if his high boot heels were any indication, he still had an issue with barely clearing five feet in height.

She glanced at his fingers. No wedding ring. He'd been desperate all through high school for a girlfriend, but very few girls were his height or shorter, and he'd been too self-conscious to date a taller woman. Drug and sexually assault one? Sure. That he could do. Namely her, but date one? Nah.

Chad Williams crossed in front of her and headed straight for Junior. One of their meaner classmates, who now played professional football, had his arm slung around a slinky woman, looking up at him with hero worship.

He strolled past Junior, cockiness oozing from Chad's pores as he nudged junior out of the way.

"Hey, shrimp," Chad said, his tone raised for others to hear. "I see you're still a junior version of the old man."

Chad's rumbling laugh filtered through the crowd, causing the others to shift uncomfortably.

Junior gritted his teeth and fisted his hands.

Normally, Malone would feel sorry for a guy in such an uncomfortable situation. She might even call their class-mate out for calling him Junior Shrimp. But not with Junior. She was just thankful that Ian Blair had come along that horrible night at the football field, or Junior would've finished what he started.

"Lay off, Williams." A deep voice took control of the crowd and burned a path through Malone's heart.

Ian. He was there. Sticking up for the underdog, as usual. Even a creep like Junior.

Malone wanted to turn. To drink in the sight of him, but she couldn't. Wouldn't. No way she would risk him seeing that she still had the same stupid crush on him that she'd had in high school. Maybe it was more like he was her hero, but no matter. She was a grown, thirty-plus-year-old woman, and she didn't need to be infatuated with anyone. Especially the class bad boy, Ian Blair.

"Still sticking up for the wimps, I see." Chad cast Ian a challenging look.

"And I will be as long as there are bullies like you in the world." Molten iron ran through Ian's tone, and she could remember the fire in his eyes, the same fire she'd seen when he'd pulled Junior off of her.

"Chill, dude." Chad lifted his hands and backed away.

The others in the room let out a collective sigh, and Malone had to grip the back of the chair next to her not to turn and look at Ian. She heard footsteps, and Junior materialized in front of her.

"I need to talk to you," he said, his tone demanding. "Alone."

She gritted her teeth to keep from telling him off in front of the whole class. "If you think I have anything to say to you, you're wrong. And I'll never be alone with you again."

He inched closer. She jerked back.

"You'll want to hear this." He leaned in close, his voice low. "It's about your parents. Their car crash wasn't an accident."

"What?" Her voice rose, drawing attention from her former classmates, and she had to work extra hard to control the pain that rose up at his comment about her parents' crash that had killed them back in the nineties. The sheriff's office had ruled it an accident, and Junior was just likely blowing smoke to get her attention. "How dare you even talk about them after what you did to me."

She glared down at him and tried to ignore the other guests' questioning stares.

"I was young. Stupid. I'm sorry." He looked like he regretted his actions, but an *I'm sorry* for attempted rape didn't cut it.

"Please leave me alone." She gritted her teeth. "I can barely look at you."

"If you want to know how they died, I'll wait for you in Ballroom D." He marched off.

Feeling her classmates eyeing her, she concentrated on taking deep breaths and trying not to flee. She'd never told anyone about the assault. She was too embarrassed, and she worried the authorities would take her from the foster home, and she hadn't been willing to risk being separated from her older brother, Reed. She'd had to swallow the pain to be sure they would remain together and stay with the loving foster family they'd been placed with. She knew that this family was a blessing from God. God had watched out for her and Reed after the car crash that had killed their parents when she was six and Reed was eight.

And now this guy, this creep, was telling her the crash wasn't an accident? She'd done a report in her high school psychology class about the crash and the influence it had on her life, but Junior wasn't in her class. So how did he even know about it?

"You think he really knows something?" Ian's voice came from behind her.

Startled, she spun and locked gazes with those large eyes the color of rich sapphires, forgetting all about Junior for now. She freed her gaze to run the length of his body, taking in his black zip leather jacket, white button-down, and V-neck sweater in a cashmere gray. Deep navy jeans and suede chukka boots rounded out his attire. All of it fitting a body that he'd kept toned since high school.

"Like what you see?" He grinned, revealing his even white teeth.

She hated that he caught her ogling him, but it wouldn't be the first time and perhaps not the last. He'd been a fine looking teenager and was an even finer looking man. Partially due to the fact that he carried himself with an air that said he couldn't care less what anyone thought about how he looked. It was intoxicating.

"I do, actually," she said. "You're still something to look at, and you know it. Though you work very hard to pretend you don't."

4

He snorted. "Still the outspoken Malone, I see."

She nodded. What did a grown woman say to a man that she'd followed around with a huge puppy dog crush her last years of high school?

"You look quite nice yourself," he said. "I always knew you would be a stunner as a woman, and I wasn't wrong." He gestured at their classmates. "The guys can't take their eyes off you."

She waved a hand, though she had indeed caught a few of the guys studying her when all she wanted to do was fly under the radar until the ceremony. "I'm surprised to see you here."

"Why's that?"

"You never took any interest in fitting in. Always the loner and happy to be one, if I'm right. So why hang out with people you spent two years avoiding?"

"I saw your name on the invitation and had to see if I was right."

"About what?"

"About if you turned out to be a stunner."

"Oh, that." She shook her head. "Here we are talking like we're back in high school. That how we look is *so* important when it's not a big deal at all."

"Sure, there are more important things, but isn't seeing how people age the biggest reason for coming to a reunion?"

"Maybe." She looked around the room, searching for Junior now, trying to decide what to do about his comment. "I wasn't planning on coming until they promised to donate to my favorite charity if I attended a brief ceremony."

"I like that the reunion has a purpose. Says a lot about the committee that they took what we're going through in our country right now and decided to focus on outreach and how we can make a difference."

She nodded. "I hope our classmates give generously to all the causes the committee is highlighting."

His eyes darkened. "I see the need every day and have the same hope."

She didn't know anything about the current-day Ian Blair, and as much as she was thinking of going after Junior, she wanted additional details about Ian too. "What do you do for a living?"

"I'm a detective with the Portland Police Bureau."

"You're what?" She gaped at him. "That's the last thing I would have guessed."

"Yeah, me too." He grinned.

She had to swallow hard not to lean closer to that magnetic smile. "How did you get into law enforcement, if you don't mind me asking?"

"You remember my parents are loaded, right?"

She nodded.

"My dad made his fortune in the movie industry before we moved up here from LA. Their lifestyle was—actually still is—such a waste. Parties. Living for social standing. Superficial."

Memories came back from high school. "Their parties were legendary at school."

"Yeah, and I wanted no part of it. When I graduated, I knew I had to do anything but what they were doing. I wanted to make a difference. So I got a degree in public administration, but I figured I needed to live the life of service first before taking charge and making changes."

"And being a cop was the route you chose."

"It kind of chose me." He focused on his feet, uncharacteristic for this take charge guy. "We had a situation with my mom. An overdose. A veteran cop showed up and handled it well. I was impressed with him and told him so. He said they were looking for good men, so I signed on. I thought it

6

would be a short-term gig. I didn't expect I would really like the job and stick with it."

His decision fascinated her, and she needed to know more. "What do you like about the job?"

"I encounter people on their worst days. Many of them are just misunderstood and need someone to advocate for them. Touches a nerve with me." He took a long breath. "I was misunderstood in high school. When we moved here in my junior year, it didn't take long for my parents' partying ways to get around. Everyone expected me to be a Holly-wood party guy. But I wasn't—I'm not—and I wouldn't pretend to be one just to fit in. That's all kinds of freak show in high school. Everyone couldn't get why I turned my back on the lifestyle they would love to have. But I wouldn't pretend to be anything to fit in, and no one knew how to classify me. So I kept to myself."

"Except for that night when you intervened on my behalf." She swallowed and searched the crowd for Junior but didn't see him.

Ian ground his teeth. "I can't believe you didn't press charges against the little creep."

"I couldn't." She explained about staying with Reed. "And after all my work with runaway teens, I think I might've been right, and I would've been moved to a new home."

"I wish I could say you were wrong, but I could see it happening."

"It doesn't matter," she said. "It really doesn't. Not anymore. It's all in the past now. In a way, his attack was a good thing."

Ian snorted. "How can that be?"

"It helped make me want to do what I'm doing now, and my underserved clients benefit from that. And it also helped me learn to forgive."

"So you've forgiven the little creep?"

She glanced past him at the group and wondered what they thought of her outburst with Junior. "It was either that or let it eat me alive. My youth leader helped me see that wasn't a good option. I still don't like him or what he did, and I don't want to be around him. But I *have* forgiven him and moved on."

Ian tilted his head and studied her. "I'm most impressed, Malone Rice. You're not only something to look at, but you've developed into quite the person too."

She felt a blush crawling up her neck and heating her face. "It's no biggie."

"But it is. I mean look at that." He pointed across the room at the displays set up to highlight charities where her picture was posted outside the office of *Teen Solutions*. "You're a charity rock star."

His tone held respect, but his gaze was playful, and if she wasn't mistaken, he was flirting with her. She couldn't hold her own in the flirting department. She had little to no practice, and she was sure Ian had fully mastered the skill in grade school.

She pointed at the door where Junior was exiting the room. "I need to decide if I want to hear what he has to say."

"I remember when you did that report in school. You said the crash was an accident. So do you think he's right? That there's more to it that you don't know about?"

"Doubtful. There was never any question that it was more than an accident. He probably has something else up his sleeve."

"But you don't know what he's playing at?"

"No," she said. "But, heaven help me, he piqued my interest enough that I have to find out."

"Want me to come with you?"

"No." She pulled her shoulders back. "I'm a big girl now,

and I won't drink anything from an unknown source tonight. I can fight my own battles."

"That, I don't doubt one bit."

Those eyes, with ever-changing shades of blue, lit with humor, and his face was alive and tempting. Now, there was a battle she was losing.

"Excuse me." She forced herself to walk away before she decided to linger in the warm, calming, and yet exciting effect Ian still had on her.

She strode out the door and down a long hallway in the posh hotel to Ballroom D. Why he'd chosen that room she had no idea. Could just be because it wasn't booked for the night.

The smaller ballroom held a stage at the far end of the room. Tables and chairs were stacked near the side walls. Junior sat on the stage swinging his legs. When he caught sight of her, he stilled. His gaze lit up, raising Malone's concern. He jumped down and rushed toward her, the sound of his boots rustling over the carpet, bringing a tinge of fear to her heart.

She planted her feet and pulled her shoulders back. She would make herself look confident even if she didn't feel it.

"You came," he said. "I didn't think you would."

She eyed him with her best *federal prosecutor* stare, which could strike fear into the toughest defendants—and sometimes defense lawyers. She held up her evening bag. "I have pepper spray in my purse, and Ian knows I'm here with you."

"Your knight in shining armor." He fairly spit the words out, telling her he might not really regret what he did. Or he was just jealous of Ian's height.

She resisted the urge to get into an argument with him. "We're not here to talk about Ian. We're here because you

9

said my parents' deaths weren't an accident. But there was never talk of anything else. Do you have information?"

Before he could answer, a door for staff along the side of the ballroom opened, drawing their attention. A man wearing a black ski mask entered. Around six feet tall, he was slender and wore all black. His gaze locked on Junior. He lifted his arm and aimed a gun at Junior.

She gasped.

"No, no, please!" Junior cried out.

"You messed with the wrong person." The man planted his feet and fired two rounds.

The retorts erupted like explosions. Malone jumped with each bullet that struck Junior. They pierced the linen fabric of his shirt, and blood spread across his chest.

His eyes wide, he collapsed on the carpet, lying spread-eagle on his back.

Her breath trapped in her chest, Malone lifted her gaze again to the gunman. She couldn't just stand there. She needed to do something. But what?

She wanted to move. To act, but her body remained frozen.

Did she check on Junior? Try to talk the shooter down?

The gunman marched across the room toward her, his gun still aimed, now at her, the firearm glinting in the overhead light.

She took a step back, dropping her purse and putting her hands up. "Please, don't shoot me. I don't know what's going on. Junior didn't tell me anything."

He stopped in front of her with a thump of his boots and eyed her for a long time, those dark, almost black eyes burning into her through the opening in the mask. Keeping his gun trained on her, he dropped down on his knees and dug through Junior's pockets until he found a phone. He pocketed it.

He stood and stepped toward Malone.

She lurched back, but he grabbed her raised hand with his gloved fingers. She wanted to jerk away, but he still had the gun trained on her. He placed the weapon in her hand and wrapped her fingers around it.

After a long look, some sort of warning in his eyes that she couldn't decipher, he turned and walked away.

"Stop!" she shouted, cupping the gun and lifting it.

He kept walking.

She checked the safety to confirm it was still off. She aimed the barrel at him. Dropped her finger to the trigger.

No. This isn't right.

She wasn't a killer. She couldn't pull the trigger. Couldn't shoot a man in the back. Was that what he was counting on when he'd handed her the gun? That she couldn't shoot him?

He stepped over the threshold, and the door closed behind him with a solid thump.

Should she run after him?

No. Junior. She dropped down next to him and felt for a pulse. Nothing. But she shouldn't be surprised with his eyes open and rolled back.

No. If there was still hope, she couldn't let him die.

She laid the gun on his belly, started CPR, and screamed for help.

The front door burst open.

The shooter coming back the other way?

Malone grabbed the gun and pointed it at the door, her hands shaking.

"Drop it, Malone." Ian stood in the doorway, his own weapon drawn and pointed at her.

"He..." She looked down at Junior and lowered her hand. "I think he's dead."

The sound of two gunshots, as crisp and clear as could be, had Ian calling for backup and running for the room down the dark hallway. Finding Malone leaning over Junior with what was likely the murder weapon in her hand. No. He'd never imagined he'd find that. Never.

He crossed the room, gun still trained on her, and eased the gun from her hand. He kept his gaze on her in case she decided to run and holstered his firearm. He put on gloves he always carried in his jacket pocket, and popped out the clip on the gun he'd recovered from her, surprised not to find any bullets. He shoved the magazine back into the gun and tucked it in his belt.

She stood, eyes trained on Junior, shock creating a tight mask on her face. He couldn't tell what she was really feeling as he kept his focus on her but squatted down and checked Junior's pulse to be sure he was dead.

"I didn't shoot him," she said.

"No?" He tried not to sound disbelieving, but it sure looked like she was the shooter.

She shook her head. "I didn't even bring my gun tonight. I left it at home. It took up too much room in my evening bag." She pointed at a sparkly little purse lying on the carpeted floor a few feet from Junior's body.

Ian stood, evaluating the size of the bag which could hold a gun, but not along with other essentials. "Then where did the gun come from?"

"The shooter had it." She lifted her trembling hand to point at the side door, her focus following along. "He came in that way. Shot Junior twice and then crossed the room to steal Junior's phone. Then, he put the gun in my hand."

Ian didn't think the Malone he knew would lie about such an important thing, but if she did kill Junior, she might.

Nor did he think she would commit murder, but her story of a shooter handing over his gun stretched credibility. "You don't think the guy was worried you might shoot him?"

"He didn't seem to be." She finally looked at Ian, and her haunted eyes were like a physical punch to his gut.

"I thought about it," she said. "But I couldn't shoot a man in the back. Maybe couldn't shoot a man at all. He must've been counting on that."

"Maybe that's why there were only two bullets in the gun."

"Right, yeah. That makes sense." Her eyes cleared. "Either way, you have to go after him. He's getting away."

"I called for backup on the way, and officers will seal off the hotel, but I suspect we might already be too late. I need to stay here to preserve the murder scene and keep an eye on you." He took a breath. "Describe the man so I can tell the officers who they're looking for."

"He was wearing a black ski mask so I couldn't see his face. He was six feet tall or so. Slender. Dressed all in black."

"That describes half the guys in our class, but I'll still put out an alert." Ian took out his phone and shared the description, but he sounded skeptical.

"You know I didn't do this, right?" she asked when he ended his call.

He didn't answer.

"Seriously, Ian. I might not have liked Junior, but I'm not a killer."

He wanted to assure her, but he had to consider the evidence in front of him, not how he felt about the person. "Look at the incident from my point of view. The point of view of a police officer. Two gunshots are fired, and I enter the room where they were fired to find one person deceased from gunshot wounds and one living person with a gun in hand, the living person having recently argued with the deceased. What conclusion would you draw?"

"Not the one you're drawing." She crossed her arms. "I'd take into account the character of the people in the room. In this case, it would be clear to me that someone is trying to set me up for murder."

2

_____

Malone watched. Listened. The rasping sound of the body bag zipper razored into her brain and stayed there while the medical examiner and her assistant loaded the body onto a gurney. The body of a man who'd been murdered right in front of Malone. Unbelievable. Could she have done something differently? Saved him?

She gritted her teeth to keep from crying and willed the sound from her mind to focus on Ian. He'd taken charge, escorting her to a chair on the side of the room and telling her to stay put. As soon as patrol officers arrived, he'd assigned a young guy, Officer Yeager, to search her and cuff her, then stand watch over her.

Ian had called in the ME and forensics staff and made copious notes in his small notebook. He'd also dispatched officers to the other ballroom to take witness statements from classmates who'd heard her arguing with Junior. That didn't look good for her at all, but it didn't really matter. She *had* argued with him and wouldn't dispute it.

Ian occasionally glanced at her, his expression blank when she wanted him to empathize with her. To show her he believed her. To help her deal with seeing a man gunned down. But all she received was a blank, professional stare. She'd asked to call her brother, Reed, an FBI agent, for support, but Ian said no phone calls. Not yet, he'd said.

He walked to the door with the ME, who was pushing the squeaky gurney holding Junior's body, the pair in deep discussion. At the door, the ME shook her head hard, and Ian glared at the woman, who was petite with a lush silvery head of hair that seemed to have a mind of its own.

What were they talking about? Her? Did Ian really think she'd murdered Junior? What did he think her motive might be? Junior hadn't gotten a chance to explain about her parents. And the attack back in high school? That was in the past, and she'd come to grips with it. She didn't like Junior, but she'd had to forgive him or it would've eaten away at her. She'd just told Ian that so he would know her heart and know she hadn't come in here to kill Junior in revenge.

Her youth leader at church back in the day had urged Malone to report Junior, but it was hard enough living every day, waking up in the morning and wondering if something would change that day. Would her foster parents decide that was the day that she and Reed had to find a new living situation? That uncertainty did something to a person's psyche, and she'd already had plenty of issues without stewing over Junior.

But now? Now it would all come out. It didn't matter. She was a mature adult. She could handle it. Reed would be upset when he heard that she'd kept it quiet all these years, but he would support her.

But would Ian or would he just assume she was a killer until he'd proven otherwise?

When the doors closed after the ME, Ian spun and marched across the room toward Malone, purpose and determination in each step. His expression just as tight. By the time he reached her, his expression had flattened, and he looked mildly angry.

"Problem?" she asked.

"Nothing I can't handle." He squatted in front of her. "I'm finished here."

She took a long breath. "Which means now's the time you either arrest me or not."

"There's no either. I have to arrest you."

She'd expected him to respond that way, but having a man she'd once had a crush on arresting her for murder still cut her to the bone. "I need to ask a favor."

"What?" His eyes narrowed.

"Your forensic people did a GSR test on my hands and will probably take my clothes to do the same thing."

"Yeah, gunshot residue tests are typical in this kind of situation."

"I held the weapon, so we know the tests will be positive. Doesn't mean anything. I could even have residue from moving my own firearm from one purse to another. Or just by stepping near a gun when it was discharged because it lingers in the air."

"Your point?" His tone deepened as if he was getting upset with her.

She paused to draw in a long breath. "I told you there was a shooter, and I can tell you the approximate location where he took the shots. He'll have left GSR behind. Can you have the forensic team do a GSR test on the carpet in that area?"

He let out a long breath. "Not sure what you hope to accomplish there. You could've taken the shot from across the room and had plenty of time to run over to the body before I arrived. The test won't tell me you didn't fire the gun."

She wanted to grit her teeth in frustration, but swallowed instead and tried not to snap at him. "But it *will* confirm the bullets were fired from a distance. That at least confirms what I'm telling you is possible."

"I don't need GSR for that. The ME will tell me if the gun was fired from a distance." He looked like he wanted to sigh but stood instead. "Give me the exact location."

Shocked that he'd agreed, she nodded that direction, and he strode that way until she called out to stop him in the right place. He waved over a forensic tech and gave him detailed instructions.

When he returned to her, she smiled at him. "One more favor. I'd like to call Reed."

"Sorry. No can do."

His negative response added salt to her open emotional wounds, but it wasn't surprising. Her prosecutor days told her that if a detective thought the arrestee would ask the person called to mess with damning evidence, they often didn't allow a phone call. Did he really think she would involve her brother in something illegal?

"I don't normally do this," Ian said. "But give me his number, and I'll call him for you."

Malone rattled off her brother's phone number before Ian changed his mind. He tapped the screen on his phone and looked at the ground instead of her.

"Reed Rice?" Ian asked.

Malone heard her brother mutter a response.

"I'm with your sister." Ian brought Reed up to date on the incident. "I'll be taking her into custody, and we'll determine if charges will be brought."

"This is ludicrous. She would never shoot anyone." Reed's raised voice carried over to Malone. "I'll have an attorney meet her there."

"Sal Sutherland," Malone called out. "Call Sal."

She expected a dirty look from Ian. Sutherland was the

top criminal defense attorney in the city and not popular with detectives. But Ian just ended the call with Reed and stowed his phone. "Yeager will take you in."

He glanced at Officer Yeager, who was still guarding her. His smooth face and apple-red cheeks made him look fresh out of high school.

"Ms. Rice is all yours," Ian said, his tone devoid of emotion.

"Stand, please," Yeager said.

She complied but kept her gaze pinned to Ian. "You know how humiliating this is?"

"I'm sorry. I have no choice."

"Can you at least take me out the back way? I'd prefer not to be perp-walked in front of our whole graduating class."

"That would be up to Officer Yeager."

"I can do that," Yeager said. "But I won't take any short-cuts that could jeopardize the investigation."

Exactly like when he'd searched her earlier. Another humiliating experience. Yeager was thorough and by the book. At least it hadn't been Ian searching her like a common criminal. That would've been worse.

And now she barely controlled her tears while Ian read her rights. Didn't he see how much seeing Junior gunned down cut her to the core?

She locked gazes with him, remembering the night he'd come to her rescue, unlike tonight. Wishing that guy were here instead of this one.

"You believe me, don't you?" she asked. At the tightening of his jaw, she felt vulnerable and wished she hadn't needed to ask.

"Doesn't matter what I believe," he said. "It's what I can prove in my investigation that will decide your future."

Ian watched Officer Yeager lead Malone away, and Ian swallowed hard. His job required him to put his feelings in check and do what he was called to do. Look at the leads. Forensic and otherwise, and find Junior's killer. Be it Malone or the masked man she claimed had been there. And to do that, Ian had to dig deep to put on a mask of impartiality with her. He knew he'd hurt her, and he hoped if she was cleared of charges, she would understand.

Shaking his head, he headed for the manager's office and spotted a sign by the door that named Arden Vandyke as the operations manager. Ian poked his head inside the small room containing a desk, credenza, and two chairs. Vandyke, who'd been wringing his hands outside the ballroom earlier while he'd waited to talk to Ian, was sitting behind his desk and had his hand plunged into sandy-brown curly hair. On seeing Ian, Vandyke shot to his feet.

Ian held up a hand to encourage the guy to relax. "I need to see any video footage for the staff hallway outside Ballroom D and for the main entrance too."

Vandyke plopped back down on his chair. "We only have cameras in the lobby and at all the exits. None in the hallways."

"Then I'd like a copy of the footage for the lobby and the exits for the last twenty-four hours."

Vandyke frowned. "I'll need to have security pull that together for you."

"I also assume you have a camera on the front desk, and we have classmates from out of town who are staying here."

"Yes and yes."

"I would like that footage as well."

"Um, well, there's a problem with that if you want to

catch everyone. We did recent lock upgrades, and not all guests will have stopped at the front desk to check in."

"Upgrades?" Ian asked.

"We've installed door locks for our rooms which use Near Field Communications. A guest can use their smartphone with NFC enabled to check in and check out without ever stopping at our front desk."

Ian had heard something about the technology being used but hadn't encountered it and didn't know the details. "How does that work?"

"When a guest is due to check in, our hotel sends a code to the guest's smartphone that will unlock their room door and any of the outside doors that we keep secured."

Ian shoved his hands into his pockets. His murder had to have occurred in a hotel with upgraded features that made his job even harder. "Do you have a list of guests who are here for the reunion?"

Vandyke shook his head.

"I'll need a complete guest list for tonight to cross-reference against the list of reunion attendees."

Vandyke poked his narrow chin up at Ian. "I'm sorry the guy died, but my bosses would have me require a warrant before I give you anything."

"True." Ian was losing his patience. "If we wait for a warrant, I'll have to keep your ballroom cordoned off longer. I'm sure you'd like to expedite the investigation. And even more, I'll bet you'd like to get our crime scene seal off the door so your upcoming guests don't have to look at it."

He lowered his chin. "If I give you what you need now, you'll give me a warrant to show my supervisors?"

"Yes."

"Fine." He grabbed the handset for his desktop phone and ordered security to compile the video. He hung up and tapped a few keys on his computer before his printer spit out a few pages. He grabbed them and shoved them at Ian.

The pages held guest names, just as Ian had hoped. "I also need you to send the video for all of the exits and the lobby at the end of each day until I tell you otherwise."

"But why?" Vandyke asked.

"I need to look for any guests who might not have checked in at the desk but checked out that way."

"Okay."

"Don't make me come looking for these files."

"I'll send them each night at ten, which is when I get off."

"Thank you," Ian said. "While we wait for the video files from security, you can show me the staff area that feeds into Ballroom D."

He got up, his face a blank mask. "Follow me."

The guy skirted around the end of his desk and nearly fled into the hallway. He was slender and fast, and Ian had to hurry to keep up with him. At the far side of the lobby, he pushed open a door marked Staff Only and led Ian down a dingy hallway to a large open area with lockers and benches. The area smelled like roasted meat, and Ian's stomach grumbled.

Several uniformed staff members stood by a computerized time clock, and a few others were gathering their belongings from bright aqua lockers.

Ian faced Vandyke. "Do all employees sign in and out here?"

Vandyke nodded, and Ian looked around for cameras but didn't see anything. "I'll need a list of employees on duty tonight and their sign in and out times."

Vandyke's eyes widened. "You can't think one of *my* people killed him?"

"We need to be thorough."

"Fine. This way to the ballroom." Vandyke started across the room. He continued on, and they passed a large commercial kitchen with big stainless steel appliances and prep tables.

"Door at the end of the hall leads to Ballroom D," Vandyke said.

Ian studied the area. "Means if my guy exited this way, he would have had to pass by the kitchen and any employees in the staff area. Maybe someone saw him."

"I asked around before, and no one saw a guy wearing a mask."

Ian assumed the suspect put on the mask right before entering the room and took if off the moment he stepped into the hallway, so what Vandyke asked or didn't ask was irrelevant. Ian and the officers that he assigned would be doing the questioning. "I'd like to talk to the kitchen staff to see if they noticed anyone out here."

"Sure." Vandyke took Ian into the bustling kitchen, where the staff were plating up cheesecake slices and drizzling fresh strawberry sauce over the top. The reunion had ended abruptly, and since the only other group booking a ballroom that night was a gathering of Realtors in Ballroom A, he had to assume the dessert was meant for them.

"Let's talk to Chef." Vandyke strode toward a rotund man dressed in a white chef's coat and hat. His face was flushed, his coat stained with red sauce, and he snapped out orders at top speed.

"Chef," Vandyke said. "A word."

Vandyke led Chef to a quiet corner and introduced Ian.

"I hoped one of your staff might have seen the man we are seeking," Ian said.

"Hold on." Chef spun and crossed the room where he let out a high whistle. Suddenly, silence filled the room save the hum from the running refrigerators. "Did anyone see a guy come out of Ballroom D about an hour ago?"

Chef received shaking heads in response. "Okay, back to work. I want desserts on the table in five."

Chef turned to them again.

"Is this everyone?" Ian asked.

"My staff, yes, but not the wait staff who are in and out of here too."

Ian fished a business card from his pocket and handed it to Chef. "If you remember seeing anything, call me. My team will be back to interview everyone individually."

Chef looked like he wanted to groan but nodded instead. "I'll make sure they're available."

"Thank you for your cooperation." Ian avoided giving Vandyke a look saying this was the attitude to have when a detective was investigating a murder.

Chef didn't wait even a second to cross the room to oversee his workers.

"He runs a tight ship," Vandyke said and started for the exit.

Ian followed him back in the lobby and to his office, where the security file was waiting for them. He gave Vandyke a business card too. "Workers are bound to start talking. If you hear anything, no matter if you think it's important or not, have them call me."

"Will do." Vandyke creased his eyes. "How long will your team be in the ballroom?"

"Forensics will finish tonight, but I'll want the room cordoned off for a bit longer."

"I have an engagement party booked for the room tomorrow night."

"We should be done by then."

"Not to sound unfeeling, but I'll need time to get the blood cleaned out of the carpet."

"You might want to plan to replace it."

He opened his mouth to argue but gave a sharp nod instead.

"Call me if you hear anything." Ian left the irritating man behind and strode toward Ballroom B, where the reunion had been in full swing not more than two hours before. His classmates having fun and catching up while he looked on. Now, the only people left were the committee members packing up their items in shocked silence.

He approached Janice King, chair of the committee, who'd sat by him in algebra.

"Did you catch him?" she asked, a hand clutched to the chest of her revealing black dress. "The guy Malone saw, I mean."

Not a surprise that she'd heard what happened. Not with how gossip traveled at a crime scene, and one connected to a class reunion would add fuel to the fire. "I was hoping you could give me the sign-in book for tonight, along with a list of the RSVPs."

"Sure, sure." She thankfully ignored the fact that he'd sidestepped her question and hurried to the welcome table, where she gathered the information Ian needed and handed it to him. "You need anything else, let me know. I'm more than happy to help in any way I can. Junior wasn't...well, let's just say he wasn't the friendliest of guys, but he didn't deserve to be murdered. And Malone sure shouldn't be set up for it. She's like this saint, helping battered women and kids and runaway teens. I know she didn't get along with Junior, but she would never kill him."

"Can you think of anyone in our class who might have wanted to kill Junior?"

"Want to?" She tapped a red fingernail, which matched her lipstick, on the table. "Sure. Plenty. But do it? Hmm. No. I don't think so."

Ian handed her a business card. "If you think of anyone who might or anything that could help, give me a call."

"Is that all?" She smoothed back brassy blond shoulder-length hair that had replaced the mousy brown he remembered from high school. "I mean, is that all of your questions. I thought like on TV you'd have much more to ask me."

"Real life investigations rarely happen like you see on TV." He held up the folder of information. "Thanks again. You'll get it back after the investigation concludes or after the trial if the information is vital to the case."

He tucked the folder under his arm and headed for his truck. On the road, he ran the information he'd collected through his detective filter. He knew Malone, and if he took off his detective hat, he believed her. She wouldn't kill anyone. Though, he suspected if she ever became homicidal, it would be with Junior.

Ian flipped on a blinker and turned the corner, memories coming back from one Friday night in high school. He'd recently moved to town and had been invited to a party at one of the football player's houses. He'd gone on a whim, even though he'd had no intention of trying to fit in with the crowd Chad Williams ran with. Shoot, Ian had no intention of fitting in with any of the crowds at that school. He'd planned to do his time and move on.

At the party, he'd seen Junior hitting on many of the girls, and they laughed at him. But when he hit on Malone, she'd been kinder. She made it clear that she had no interest in him, but she'd done so in a softer way. Problem was, Junior didn't take it too well. He got all sullen and brooding and started drinking up a storm. Ian saw the guy escort a very tipsy Malone away from the house.

They were a few blocks from the high school, and Ian trailed Junior and Malone as they made their way to the

26

school. Junior had taken her out back to the darkened football field and started pawing all over her. She tried to fight and begged him to leave her alone, but she soon became silent and dropped to the ground.

Ian waited for Junior to back off, but instead, Junior had taken her limp body as his cue to fall on her and take advantage. Ian couldn't let that happen. He jerked Junior to his feet and pummeled him, telling him that if he ever saw Junior near a girl again, he'd report him to the police.

Once Ian dispatched Junior, he helped Malone up and took her back to the party and left her in the hands of her older brother, Reed, who escorted her home. Ian figured Reed told her that Ian had brought her home, because that Monday at school she introduced herself and offered her thanks. That was when she formed a crush on him. If he'd had any interest in dating, he might've pursued her.

Even back in school, Malone had a way of looking at him that resonated with him. As if she saw right through the façade he'd created, the one that said he didn't care. He thought he'd imagined it all those years ago, but, dang if he wasn't surprised tonight to see that same look.

And what did he do about it? He put her in jail, and now that he'd put her behind bars, he doubted she'd ever look at him the same way.

3

_____

Ian settled in the chair in his supervisor's small office, surprised he could find a place to sit in the room filled with stacks of case files and boxes holding more, all containing information about an ongoing murder investigation that the department had been working for six months. Lieutenant Zane Hoffman stared at Ian across the desk, searching and appraising, as Detective Londyn Steele came into the room behind Ian. After Ian texted Hoffman about the murder, he'd come in to work.

"Have a seat, Steele," Hoffman said.

Dressed in a black suit and a white button-down blouse, she dropped into the chair beside him and crossed her legs. Ian had always thought she had a strong cop demeanor, including her muscular build and her tough, rugged vibe. Still, she challenged that appearance with feminine blouses and manicured fingernails, often painting them in the pale pink she sported today. A big contradiction that kept people off guard—her intention, he was sure.

"Now that you're both here," Hoffman said, his gaze pinned to Ian, "I'd like you to update me and read Steele in on the reunion murder."

Only two reasons Ian's boss could want this information. He planned to give the investigation to Londyn, or he planned to have her partner with Ian. Either way, Ian didn't like it. Not when they rarely partnered on investigations. Like Malone had said, he was kind of a loner. But he would have no choice in the matter, so he provided succinct details about what transpired earlier that evening.

"I notified Junior's parents," Ian said, "but neither of them had any thoughts on why someone might want to kill him. The father was stoic, the mother fell apart. Not unusual. But I got the feeling that they weren't very involved in his life."

Hoffman narrowed his eyes. "I was hoping you had more evidence than you do. And a solid motive."

"If Malone shot him, it could have to do with what he told her about her parents," Londyn said.

Ian shook his head. "He never got a chance to tell her anything other than that their crash wasn't an accident."

"Or so she says." Londyn raised one eyebrow, giving him a pointed look.

"Yeah, you're right. She could be withholding information, but my gut says she was being forthcoming. Initially, when I asked her, she was in shock and not thinking clearly, so I doubt she was trying to blow smoke my way." At least he prayed she wasn't.

"And what's your gut tell you about the shooting?" Hoffman asked. "Did she do it?"

"I doubt it, but only the forensic evidence will confirm that," Ian said.

"Exactly," Hoffman said.

"The supposed shooter took Junior's phone, so I had it pinged, but no luck," Ian said. "Shooter must've destroyed the phone or he took the battery out."

"You knew Malone in high school, right?" Hoffman steepled his fingers.

"We weren't friends or anything, but I knew her and her brother, Reed." Ian left it at that for now. If more was needed later, he would share it.

"You're not going to like this," Hoffman said, "but I just got off the phone with the DA. He's choosing not to file charges at this point."

"He what?" Ian shot up in his chair. He might not think Malone was guilty, but there had been sufficient evidence to arrest and charge her, and the DA was ignoring the department's recommendation.

Hoffman held up his hand. "He's not ruling it out in the future, but he doesn't think we have enough to hold Rice on."

Hoffman leaned back and clasped his hands behind his head. "Honestly, I think she has friends in high places who advocated for her release. She's well-respected in the community. A former federal prosecutor too. Means the investigation will get a lot of press and attention from up top, and we need to make sure we don't drop the ball. Which is why I'm assigning the pair of you to the case. It's still your investigation, Blair, but Steele will assist." He snapped his chair forward and ran his gaze between them. "Any questions?"

Ian shook his head and glanced at Londyn. She followed suit, her shoulder-length auburn hair swinging over her shoulders.

"One thing you should know, though," Ian said. "Her brother doesn't know about the DA's decision, and he's called in Sal Sutherland to represent her. The DA might not charge her, but she'll remain a suspect and Sutherland will likely tell her not to say a word."

Hoffman groaned. "Usually I'd say if a client hires the

most expensive defense attorney in the business, you gotta wonder if they're guilty. Not this case, though. I remember reading he was her mentor when she went into private practice. The hire's likely more about that."

"And we also need to remember that her brother's an FBI agent," Londyn said. "My parents are good friends with the Byrd family. The Veritas Center's forensic expert, Sierra Byrd, is married to Reed. If Malone wants to investigate this on her own, she'll have unlimited forensic and investigative help."

"We can't stop her," Hoffman said.

"Too bad they can't work with us," Ian said. "They have top-notch experts at the center."

"We don't have the budget for outside help." Hoffman clapped his hands and stood. "You'll want to get over to Junior's place to check things out. We don't need a warrant, but I'll still request one. No way we want bereaved parents or attorneys contesting our search. Should have the warrant to you by the time you arrive. I'll text you when I do."

Law enforcement had every right to access Junior's items. Fourth Amendment rights gave people privacy protections while alive that didn't extend past their death, but the public, who was all about people's rights these days, would look more favorably on the search if the warrant was obtained. And if Ian could prevent grieving parents any additional turmoil, he was all for it.

"And by the time you finish with the condo," Hoffman continued. "Rice will have had a few hours in lockup, and interviewing her before we kick her loose might give us one detail that can lead to this mystery man. *If* he exists."

"Understood." Ian got up and let Londyn file out before him. He didn't need to tell her that he wasn't excited to have a fellow detective on the investigation. She would know. They were all used to working alone. Having to read someone in on every development would be a hassle. But even more disconcerting was delegating work that he would want to do himself to be sure it was done right.

"Hey, I get it," she said, stopping at the edge of their bullpen of detectives, where only a few guys were working that late on a Friday night. "I know you're not happy having me tag along for this. I wouldn't want an assistant either, and I don't much like being one. But I'll take directives from you as long as you give an honest listen to my opinions and suggestions."

"That I can do."

"On the bright side, I have all the time in the world for the job right now, and you can work me to death."

"Life change?"

"Breakup." Her matter-of-fact tone said the breakup didn't bother her in the least, but the anguish in her eyes held a different message.

He didn't know her well enough to ask for details. "I need you to get the warrant going to retrieve Junior's phone records. If his phone was taken at the crime scene, there could be something incriminating on it the shooter wanted to either retrieve or hide from us."

"You believe Malone's story, then."

"Not sure. Regardless, we need his phone records no matter who has it."

"I'll get on it," she said.

He glanced at his watch. "Give me five minutes to change my shirt and freshen up, and we'll go check out Junior's condo."

"I'll get that warrant started while I wait." Londyn spun and went to her desk on the far side of the room filled with chest-high cubicles.

He headed for his own space near the window. He could see the moon hanging full and illuminating the city bustling with nightlife. He grabbed a clean shirt from his bottom drawer and headed for the restroom, where he washed up and changed into more professional attire.

He gave himself a long look in the mirror, wondering what Malone thought when she'd laid eyes on him. Interest had shone in her eyes, but she'd controlled it the moment he'd looked at her, and he didn't know if she'd gotten better at hiding it or if she just plain wasn't into him anymore. She'd never married. That he knew. But he didn't know if she was in a serious relationship.

He hadn't been kidding when he'd told her he wanted to see if she was as stunning as he'd expected. Although, truth be told, he'd barely missed running into her several times over the years when she'd been in the office to meet with detectives. She'd prosecuted all kinds of bad people, but he didn't think she'd ever represented anyone for murder, so they'd never butted heads. But now? How she looked or what she thought of him was the last of his worries. He didn't plan on letting his attraction screw up his investigation.

He grabbed his dirty shirt and took it to his desk before meeting Londyn at the door.

"I'll drive." He led the way to their secured parking garage down the street, where he'd left his PPB vehicle at end of duty. The temperatures had dropped to the upper forties, and a distinctive fall chill left the air crisp.

Londyn pulled her suit jacket closed. "Wonder if we'll get snow this year."

"You one of the nuts who likes the snow?" Ian opened the sedan, and they settled inside.

"I did before I became a police officer. Now it's a logistical nightmare." She mocked a shudder, and he laughed.

"Since we've been getting more of it, the city's doing a

better job with it." He drove the car out of the garage and onto a nearly deserted street.

He pointed them in the right direction and glanced at Londyn. "There's something you should know. I have more of a connection to Malone than I told Hoffman. One night my junior year of high school, Junior sexually assaulted Malone and would've raped her if I hadn't pulled him off her."

Londyn gaped at him. "Did you report it?"

He shook his head. "It was up to Malone to report, and she didn't want anyone to know. Especially not her brother."

"Why on earth didn't you tell Hoffman that?"

"Malone and I talked about it before the shooting. She'd forgiven Junior, and from what she said, it ended up having a positive impact on her life."

"How so?"

"She said it helped her realize what she wanted to do in life and her underserved clients benefited. And it helped her to learn to forgive."

"Sounds like she has her head on straight, if she was telling the truth. She could've been planning to do him in and wanted you to think she'd forgiven him when it could still be a strong motive for murder."

"After all these years," he said, "I doubt it."

"I hope not telling Hoffman doesn't come back to bite you and damage your career."

"Yeah, me too."

Londyn remained quiet for a few moments then shifted in her seat to look at him. "What about Malone's parents? When did they die?"

"She was six. Reed was eight."

"You think there was anything to Junior's claim that their crash wasn't an accident?"

Ian shrugged. "My biggest question right now is whether Junior's murder is related to her at all or a coincidence."

"It's clear you're not liking her for it."

"Not at all."

"Don't take this the wrong way, but is it because you know her?"

He considered the question. "I don't think so, but I have to say if I didn't know her, the evidence would have me liking her for the crime."

"Yeah," Londyn said. "The circumstances make her an obvious choice, but from what I've heard about her, she's a very smart woman and talented attorney. You gotta think, unless she lost her cool big time, that if she wanted to off this guy, she wouldn't do it in a public space after arguing with him in front of witnesses."

"True that." Ian turned into a full lot in front of the high-rise where Junior had lived on the seventh floor. Ian's phone dinged, and he glanced at the holder on the dashboard. "The warrant came in."

"Perfect timing or we would've been sitting out here until we got it." Londyn leaned forward and looked out her window. "Swanky place. Do we know what Junior did for a living?"

"Not yet." Ian shifted into park. "I checked the class reunion program, and he didn't list an employer."

"Maybe he was embarrassed about his job. Or maybe he was just too lazy to provide the information to the organizers." She slipped out her door.

Ian climbed out. "He was unmotivated in high school, and I never expected him to be a success story. Had too big of a chip on his shoulder about his size. He was barely over five feet tall. As you can imagine, he was teased all through school."

Londyn nodded. "Have you located his vehicle yet?"

"It's in the parking lot at the hotel. Criminalists are processing it, but when I searched, I didn't find anything of interest."

They crossed the lot to the front door. The sparkling clean glass automatically slid open with a whoosh and revealed a lobby furnished in contemporary furniture with clean lines. They approached the doorman and held out their credentials.

"Do you know Gilbert Flagg Jr.?" Ian asked.

"Junior. Sure." The burly man wearing a uniform of white shirt and black slacks smiled, revealing a missing tooth on the left side. "Most everyone around here knows him. He's the life of the parties."

"We need access to his condo."

"Is there a problem?"

"We just need to look around," Ian stated firmly as he wasn't ready to tell this guy that Junior had been murdered.

"I can't let you in without a warrant," the doorman said.

"Thought you might ask for that." Ian held out his phone and displayed the warrant.

"No." He shook his head. "That won't do. I need to see an official one. You know, in print."

"Fine," Ian said. "Give me access to your network, and I'll print it."

"That's not what I mean, and you know it."

Londyn leaned closer. "The judge signed the document electronically. It's valid."

The doorman crossed his arms. "But I don't have anything to show my supervisor when he asks. I've been written up twice for not following protocol. This would be my last chance, and I could lose my job."

"Like I mentioned," Ian said. "I can print this one. Just give me access."

A uniformed security guard standing in the corner crossed to them. "Is there a problem here?"

Ian flashed his badge, and Londyn turned to look at the guard.

"Oh, Ms. Steele," the guard said. "I didn't know it was you."

Ian noticed the Steele Guardians logo on the guard's chest. He worked for Londyn's family's business, which supplied security guards for large corporations.

The guard smiled at her. "Can I be of assistance?"

"We need to get into unit 706, and this nice man says he needs our warrant in print before he'll let us in."

"Well, I do," the doorman stated.

"Can't we make an exception just this one time," the guard said. "They can show me the electronic warrant too, and I can vouch for you having seen it. I can also join them in the condo to observe."

"Fine." The doorman handed a passkey to the guard and locked gazes. "You make me regret this, and I do the same for you."

The guard gave a sharp nod and led Ian and Londyn across the tiled lobby and into the elevator, where he stuck the passkey in and punched number seven. "I'm Damon, by the way. Damon Rochester."

"Thank you for your help, Damon," Londyn said. "It won't go unnoticed."

"Good to hear." He preened as the elevator whisked them up to the seventh floor and a light-filled hallway.

Damon shoved the key into unit 706's lock and stood back. "I know I told him I'd come in with you, but you'll want privacy. I'll hang right out here."

Londyn cast him a quick smile, and Ian entered while he had the chance. He heard her footsteps behind him.

"Remind me to bring you along all the time," Ian said as

he strode down a short hallway, past a kitchen, and into a wide great room with windows overlooking the city. "Million-dollar view."

Londyn mumbled something, but she was already across the room at a metal bookshelf looking through closed boxes. The room was filled with contemporary furniture and decor, and Ian figured a professional had decorated the place.

"Sure doesn't look like the kind of place I thought Junior would end up living in. It's spotless." Ian noticed a laptop on a glass-and-metal table. He made a mental note to have forensics take it into evidence right away, and he needed to pick up Junior's belongings from the medical examiner in case his pockets held anything of interest.

The reunion flyer lay on the table next to the computer, and Junior had circled the blurb mentioning Malone's service recognition along with her picture. He'd written next to it, *Tell her then. Mom too.*

Ian took a picture of the paper where it lay, then put on gloves and held out the flyer to Londyn. "Look at this."

She left the shelf behind and peered at the paper. "If he meant the accident, seems odd that he would tell his mother as well."

"Yeah, but I don't know what else to make of it." He returned the flyer to where he'd found it. "I'm going to check out the bedroom."

He went down a short hallway, passing a guest bedroom and bath, picking up a hint of a spice he couldn't pinpoint coming from the bathroom. At the end of the hallway, he found the main bedroom decorated in dark gray and black, a little too classy for the guy Ian remembered, but then not many guys were classy in high school. Ian riffled through a dresser, two nightstands, and the closet. He didn't find anything unusual, other than the fact that the clothes were organized by color, and Junior had a full wardrobe of expensive clothing.

If Junior had possessed information on how he learned about the Rices' car accident, he didn't keep it there. Hoping it was on the computer, Ian called in forensics on the way back to the great room. He told them to be sure to bring a printed warrant for the doorman. He and Londyn would be long gone by the time they arrived, hopefully sitting across the table from Malone.

He and Londyn finished searching the condo without locating anything to help the investigation, then drove back to the Justice Center building. PPB offices and the Multnomah County Detention Center were housed in the same building. Ian stepped up to the metal detector in the detention center, where he and Londyn surrendered their weapons and walked through. They were soon seated in a small interview room, Ian tapping his thumb on his knee and trying to ignore the strong smell of bleach.

The door opened, and a burly male deputy stood back for Malone to enter. She was cuffed, as was protocol for such a serious offense. Her usual meticulous hair was frizzy, and strands had fallen out of place. Gone was the dress with straps as thin as wire in a rich aqua that had hugged her curves and fueled his imagination. The blue jail prison garb was drab and worn, and he felt bad all over again. He hated the situation. Hated what he was putting her through.

She sat, her posture regal, her chin lifted while the deputy secured her wrists to the table. She looked up at the man. "Thank you, Carl."

He nodded and stepped back. "I'll be just outside. Let me know when you're done."

"Malone," Ian said. "This is Detective Londyn Steele."

"Nice to finally meet you, Londyn." Malone smiled. "I've

overheard Russ and Peggy Byrd talking about your family, and they have such good things to say about all of you."

Londyn opened her mouth then closed it as if she didn't know how to respond to a compliment from a murder suspect. Ian didn't know if Malone was sincere in her praise or was trying to disarm Londyn by using tactics she'd learned as a lawyer.

"Detective Steele will be joining me in working this investigation," Ian said.

"Great. The more detectives, the better. Hopefully, you can find the real shooter." She locked gazes with Ian. "Did you check the hallway by the ballroom? Talk to the manager? Did anyone see the shooter? Or is he on video?"

Ian held up his hands. "We're the ones who'll be doing the questioning."

Malone narrowed her eyes. "No point. I won't answer anything without Sal by my side. Told him not to bother coming until you charge me with Junior's murder. I assume you *are* planning to charge me."

"My LT presented it to the DA," Ian said, so she knew the department was prepared to proceed. "But at this time, the DA has decided not to bring charges."

"But I—" Her mouth dropped open. "I'm thrilled, of course, but it's a surprise for sure."

"I agree," Ian said. "But I don't have to tell you that you're still a person of interest and not to leave town without consulting me first. And if you've thought of something else regarding Junior's death since we last spoke, now would be the time to tell us."

"Like I said. I'll wait for Sal."

"The sooner you let us ask our questions, the sooner we'll be able to find Junior's killer and clear your name," Londyn said, her tone flat.

Malone lifted that perfectly sculpted chin. "I'll be investigating on my own. I believe in the justice system, and I know the truth will come out."

Ian wished he could be so confident for her. The system worked most of the time, but it wasn't perfect. Especially like now—if her story was true—she was being framed for murder, and even if the DA didn't bring charges now, further evidence could ensure he would have to.

4

———

Malone stripped out of the prison garb and slipped into the jeans and sweater Reed had dropped off. The police were keeping her dress as evidence for the blood and potential GSR—her favorite evening dress, but that was the least of her worries. She never imagined herself dressed like a prisoner, barely escaping a felony charge.

Or spending the night behind bars. More than once, she'd fought tears by giving herself a pep talk, reminding herself she was innocent and would clear her name. And she kept adding that it was a good experience to see what her adult clients faced when they were incarcerated. She'd always had empathy for them, but she better understood now.

Still, she'd been given special treatment. That was the only thing that made sense. Someone, somewhere had spoken up for her and gotten the DA to hold off. She would have to use the reprieve she'd been given to find the real killer, just like she'd told Ian she would.

She folded her County-issued clothing and left the cell to join Carl, where he waited to escort her to the exit. At the counter, her belongings were dumped from a large envelope onto the worn Formica, and she signed for them. She stuffed everything back into the envelope and nearly ran for the door. She prayed on the way out to never have to set foot inside that place as an arrestee again. She'd told Ian she believed in the system to get it right, but she knew justice failed more often than any of them wanted to believe.

She stepped outside, closed her eyes, and inhaled the chilly air. Sure, it was tainted with exhaust as traffic hustled by on a Sunday afternoon, but she was free, and it smelled like heaven to her.

Free for now.

She wished she could still that part of her brain and simply enjoy the moment, but the thoughts nagged at her until she opened her eyes.

Her mentor, Sal, climbed the exterior stairs toward her. His wavy brown hair was longer than most professional attorneys might wear it, and silver threads ran through the thick waves, matching his silvery close-cut beard. He was dressed casually in jeans, a black shirt, and a red fleece jacket. No matter his clothes or his hair, he always had an intensity in his gaze that told her he was assessing and weighing everything around him.

"Thank you, Sal." She hugged him. "I appreciate you coming all the way down here to give me a ride home."

He pulled back. "You sure you don't want me to take you over to Reed's condo? He's been calling and calling."

"I'm not ready to see him yet. I need to shower and clean up. I'll call him on the way to my place." Her top priority was to meet with Reed and the partners at the Veritas Center to talk about working together to clear her name, but first she needed to wash away the grime from her night in jail. She couldn't function if she didn't look her best, and she needed some high-level functioning if she hoped to find the guy who was trying to frame her for Junior's murder.

She didn't know if the killer was intentionally setting her up or if she'd just happened to be there, and the shooter had seized the opportunity.

"I promise Reed won't bug you again," she said.

"No worries." Sal's lips tipped up. "You'd do the same for me, and you know you'd be the person I would call if I was in your place. Not that I'll ever be in your place."

"Don't sound so cocky, Sal. I never thought I'd be arrested for murder either." She linked arms with him and turned to start for his double-parked car, but she came to an abrupt stop. Ian leaned against a plain looking sedan parked at the sidewalk, and he was giving her an expectant look.

"Seriously, he can't be waiting to talk to me, can he?" she muttered.

"Looks like it."

She thought to stay put and wait until he made a move, but she was ready to get home. That shower was beckoning her. She ran a hand over her hair and pressed wrinkles from her blouse before starting down the stairs, heading away from him.

"Could I have a word, Malone?" Ian called out.

She must've subtly changed course, angling a bit toward him and alerting Sal to her intentions.

"I don't recommend that," Sal said. "He's still the investigating officer and could use anything you tell him against you."

"I know what I should and shouldn't say."

"Yeah, knowing it"—Sal tapped his temple—"and remembering it in the heat of the moment are two different things."

"Then come with me." She didn't wait for him but strode toward Ian, who'd changed from last night's shirt and sweater to a blue button-down and black slacks, though he still wore the leather jacket. He'd arrived to interview her dressed that way, but she didn't take the time to enjoy how the shirt color emphasized his gorgeous eyes or the way it seemed custom fitted to his toned body.

"Oh, I see," Sal said as they got closer.

She glanced at him. "What?"

"You've got a thing for this guy." He gripped her arm. "I suggest you stop right now and back away. You're thinking with your emotions, not that fabulous brain I've always envied."

She rolled her eyes at his compliment that, under normal circumstances, might make her think twice about it. "I'll admit to having a crush on him in high school, but that was another lifetime. I got this. Trust me."

Sal shook his head. "When it comes to matters of the heart, you're such a novice that you won't know you're in trouble until after trouble strikes."

She laughed. "I'm good. Honest." She squeezed his arm and closed the rest of the distance to Ian.

"Don't tell me," she said. "You want to arrest me again."

Ian drew in a sharp breath. "I know you have some great resources at your disposal, and I was hoping you would work with me in finding Junior's killer."

"Work with you?" Malone gaped at him. "You arrest me for murder, let me spend a night in jail, try to get charges brought against me, and then you want me to help you out? You've got to be kidding me."

"I had to arrest you." He stated the words in an even tone, but his nostrils flared. "It's my job."

She looked up at the man she'd once imagined herself in love with. One-sided infatuation, yeah, but love nonetheless. Even if he *had* been doing his job, a long night in jail wouldn't let her find any reason right now why she might even like him. Sure, he was good-looking. Totally good-looking, but she wasn't shallow enough to fall for a man because of his looks alone.

And yet, he was right about her arrest. As a lawyer, she knew he had no choice. He'd said his lieutenant had brought the charges to the DA, but that didn't mean Ian agreed. Maybe he'd even been instrumental in getting the DA to hold off on charging her.

"Tell me one thing," she said, keeping her gaze pinned to him so she could evaluate the truth of his answers from his expression.

"I will if I can."

"Did you recommend that the DA file charges against me?"

He worked the muscle in his jaw. "I did."

"Now that's even richer." She rolled her eyes. "You didn't have to do that, did you? Sure, you had to arrest me. Your job demanded it, but there's no law compelling you to push for charges to be filed against me."

"Just the fact that I swore an oath to do my best for all victims. Even ones I don't particularly like. Which means, when the evidence points to someone's guilt, I arrest them and ask to have charges brought against them no matter who they are. No matter if they have friends in high places. No matter if I don't believe they're guilty."

He was looking at her through narrowed eyes. He was right. Someone went to bat for her. She was thankful for that, but right now all she could see was his judgment over her special treatment, and she didn't like it. Made her feel guilty when she was anything but.

She lifted her shoulders. "As you said, I have great resources at my disposal, and I need to get together with the Veritas and Nighthawk teams and get started looking for Junior's killer."

Ian drew a business card from his jacket pocket and held

it out. "Take this. Just in case you change your mind about helping me or if you need me."

She wasn't a fool. She would need to talk to him again before her investigation was over. That was inevitable. She settled his card into her evening bag without looking at it and started to walk away.

"Be careful, Malone," Ian called. "As you said, you're looking for a killer. I wouldn't want you to be his next victim."

Sal tucked her hand in the crook of his arm. "He's right, you know. This isn't one of your wayward teens needing their life investigated so you can try to reunite them with their parents. This is something different altogether. This is murder."

"Reed will make sure I take care." She glanced back at Ian then forced herself to look away.

"Reed will do his best," Sal said. "But, honey, you're known for ignoring him."

She couldn't argue with that.

"I know I told you to stay away from Detective Blair," Sal continued. "But there's one thing you need to remember. You and your crack team at Veritas can investigate and prod and probe, but at some point you'll need police assistance. When that happens, it could be a life-or-death situation, and you don't want to be on the outs with this detective."

Attending autopsies. One of the most difficult requirements of Ian's job, and they never got easier. He usually made it through them by thinking of other things and places. Like today. He slipped his foot into the Tyvek suit the medical examiner left for him, his mind on Malone and her rejection.

He'd made a professional request to partner with her, but her rejection felt personal. He wasn't surprised she'd said no. She was a strong, independent woman, and she had the Veritas Center professionals behind her. She could easily have them investigate Junior's murder. They wouldn't need Ian unless they required access to law enforcement databases. But his gut told him that the shooter had planned to set Malone up. She was the key to finding Junior's killer, and Ian had to find a way to persuade her to work with him.

He zipped up the suit, put on a face mask and shield, and entered the autopsy suite. Three stainless steel tables sat in the center of the room that had large stainless steel sinks, refrigerators, and freezers along the walls.

Junior lay on the closest table, face up, eyes wide and wearing a blank stare. His chest had been sliced open. Dr. Albertson stood over him. She was slender, medium height, with a short bob of gray hair and plenty of wrinkles, which were covered by a clear face shield.

She looked at him. "I got an early start on the day and began without you. Nothing to report here regarding the cause of death. Just what we expected. Two gunshot wounds to the chest, one piercing the aorta. He would've dropped immediately. I didn't find any signs of defensive wounds or skin cells under his nails, which we didn't expect to find."

"Gunshot wounds were inflicted from a distance?" he asked.

"Definitely not up close. There's no stippling around the wounds or gunpowder on the shirt."

Exactly like Malone reported.

"This is pretty cut and dried as far as a homicide goes."

"I guess I didn't need to take the time to be here."

"Not so fast," she said, a glint in her eyes. "You should

know, if the victim hadn't been shot, he probably wouldn't have lived much longer."

Ian's interest perked up. "Why's that?"

She pointed to an odd shaped organ that looked like a narrow cornucopia you'd see on a Thanksgiving table. It was located near his ribs, and a large discolored area took up two-thirds of the organ.

"An advanced tumor of the pancreas," she said.

"He had pancreatic cancer?"

She pointed at a small mass. "It's spread to his lymph nodes and blood vessels. Stage three."

"Do you think he knew?"

"No signs of radiation or chemo, so maybe not."

"Wouldn't he have symptoms?"

"Most assuredly at this stage, but men, and young men in particular, often ignore symptoms, which is why pancreatic cancer is called the silent killer."

Ian didn't know if her news was important at all. Especially if Junior didn't know about the cancer. If he did, and if he knew he didn't have long to live, would it have made him want to make things right? Was that why he needed to tell Malone about her parents' car accident? But how would he even know about the accident, and how was it related to Junior?

Ian needed to get moving on answering those questions. "Anything else?"

"No," Dr. Albertson said. "His bag of belongings are by the sink, and you can expect my official report later in the week."

"Thank you." Ian hurried to grab Junior's belongings and leave the autopsy suite.

In the outer room, he stripped out of his protective gear but left his latex gloves on. He looked through the plastic bag at car keys, a wallet, small pocket knife, and breath spray. He took out the wallet and found a thick wad of twenty-dollar bills, a driver's license, one credit card, an insurance card, and a worn photo of his parents, who Ian met at Junior's death notification visit. No receipts, notes, pictures, or anything that could lead Ian to find the killer.

Frustrated, Ian closed the bag and discarded his gloves. He dug out his phone to type a message for Londyn.

Junior had stage 3 pancreatic cancer. Request his medical records. We'll see if he knew about it and if it motivated any of his actions.

Malone thought about Sal's comment for the entire drive home and during her shower, where she stayed until her fingers resembled wrinkled prunes. By the time she was dressed in her favorite jeans paired with a warm fleece top and had watched the online church service for the day, she changed her mind about Ian. She had to set aside her emotions and do what was best to find Junior's killer. His parents deserved that. Which meant she needed to call Ian to see what he had in mind when he'd asked her to partner with him.

She dumped out her evening bag on the kitchen counter to reveal his card and settled on a barstool to make the call. She expected to get voicemail and mentally prepared her message.

He answered on the second ring, and she stumbled to think of what to say. "It's Malone. I...I want to hear what you meant by us working together."

He didn't respond, and the silence stretched. Uncomfortable, she opened her mouth to say something else, but what? How could she be so wishy-washy around him when she was usually a take-charge person?

"Would it be okay if we talked in person?" he finally asked.

She let out a silent breath. "When?"

"The sooner, the better."

Did she want that? Want to see him? She had to, she supposed, if she was to work with him. "I guess you could come by my place."

Now, why did she suggest a private place instead of a public spot? She couldn't take it back now.

"Great." His enthusiasm surprised her. "I can get your address from your arrest record."

"I just bought my childhood home. The place where we lived before our parents died." Another thing she hadn't needed to tell him, so she quickly gave him the address.

"I can be there in thirty minutes."

"See you then." She hung up and ran her fingers through her wet hair. She might be fine with letting it dry on its own if she weren't going anywhere or wasn't seeing anyone, but she would dry and style it for a visit from Ian.

In the bathroom with the eighties' glass block shower, she picked up the dryer and brush and went to work. With each pull of the bristles, she wished she wasn't so concerned with appearances—a product of losing her parents. She'd lived in three foster homes. The first two for fewer than six months. Neither were the best of situations, but the third home was wonderful. She and Reed had had two loving, caring, Christian parents to guide them.

Still, every moment of every day, she'd known her living situation was temporary. Things could change in a heartbeat. She could come home from school one day to be told she and Reed were being placed elsewhere. She had to be prepared at all times to make a good impression for that new family. Plus, if she took care of her hygiene and appearance, did well in school, followed the rules, and did everything she was asked, she wouldn't give her foster family any reason to split her up from Reed. That would've been just as hard to handle as losing their parents.

Years later, she couldn't seem to shed the need to appear put together. A shrink would likely have a field day with her insecurity.

She applied her makeup and took a last look in the mirror. Satisfied, she went to the bedroom and grabbed a professional blouse and a clean pair of jeans before going to the family room to pace and wait. She took long steps through the living room in the large craftsman house.

She'd only moved in a month before, but immediately she'd started to try to return the home to what she remembered. She'd stripped the paint from the woodwork on the banister, all the trim, and the built-ins. At the rate she was working, it would take her years to complete the house, but she didn't care. She felt close to her parents here, and that was all that mattered.

A car pulled up outside, and she stopped at the large picture window on the way to the front door. The same drab blue sedan Ian had been leaning on outside the Justice Center parked in the drive. No way Ian would be caught dead driving such a sedan in his personal life. She figured him for a motorcycle or pickup kind of guy. This must be his police-issued vehicle.

The doorbell rang, but she waited a few seconds before answering. She didn't want him to think she was standing around waiting for him, when that was exactly what she'd been doing.

She opened the door, and he held up two bags of takeout from a local restaurant that she loved. "I figured we could have lunch while we talk."

"Bribery?"

His eyes narrowed. "No bribe. Just thought I could help."

"I appreciate your kindness." She stepped back. "Excuse the mess. I started remodeling the place to return it to what I remember from when I was little."

"I'm surprised you can remember much."

"I vividly remember walking through the house the day we left, memorizing each little detail down to my dad's slippers sitting by the door over there." A night without sleep meant tears she could often control threatened to break free, and she took a breath to extinguish them. "This way to the kitchen."

She led him through a small dining room with garish flower wallpaper to an equally brash kitchen with cranberry countertops and black cabinets.

"Oh, wow." He looked around and set the bags on the counter and started removing containers of Mexican food. "This looks recently remodeled."

"Is that your diplomatic way of asking if I'm responsible for this?"

"You caught me." An easy smile that drew her closer spread across his mouth.

Their gazes connected, but the lighthearted moment quickly changed, the air charged, and she had to take a deep breath to keep from moving closer. She whipped her attention to a cupboard and got down plates to set them next to the bags. "There's enough food here for a family for a week."

"I didn't know what you'd like, so I got an assortment of tacos and wraps. I figure that will give both of us leftovers." He handed her the receipt. "Take a look at what I got and choose what you want."

She read down the long receipt and searched the bag for a street corn chicken taco, adding it along with spicy rice and avocados to her plate. She cut a fiesta wrap in half and slid it beside the rest of her food. The tangy scent had her stomach rumbling. "Don't judge me for the quantity of food.

I haven't gotten food from here since I moved back to this side of town, and I can't wait."

"No judgment as long as you return the favor." He piled his plate with two wraps and two steak-and-queso tacos.

"Let's head to the dining room." Sitting next to him on counter stools would be too close. She grabbed a bottle of water from a bag and led the way. She sat at the head of the table so he would sit at the side so she could face him as they talked.

She offered a prayer for the food then dug in. The minute the spicy flavor hit her taste buds, she forgot all about the night in jail and Ian's reason for being there.

"So good." She took another huge bite of the taco, and an explosion of flavor burst in her mouth.

"You look like you were hungry." He polished off half a taco in one bite.

She wiped her mouth with a napkin. "I didn't realize how much. Thank you for thinking of it."

He took a long pull of his water bottle. "My pleasure."

She could almost pretend they were on the date she'd always imagined they would take in high school. She'd imagined dating him back in the day, when she'd thought he'd have taken her to a dive with great food and maybe people who were different than she was, people who went with his bad-boy vibe.

He set down his bottle and turned it in circles. "I couldn't help but notice your Mustang out front."

She smiled. "A '64, just like the one my dad owned. I loved riding in that car as a kid and always told him I would own one just like it. I bought it a year ago."

"Is it your everyday car?"

She nodded. "Why?"

"Not the safest vehicle to be driving on a regular basis.

No shoulder belt. No airbags. And it wasn't made to withstand a crash like today's cars are."

Crash. Right. Like her parents' accident. "I hadn't thought about it that way."

"I saw a lot of crashes when I was a patrol officer. Makes me think about the vehicles people drive." He shook his head. "But I'm not here to lecture you on car safety. Tell me more about the guy who shot Junior."

She flashed her gaze to him. "You sound like you believe me."

"I do."

"But you—"

"I couldn't share my opinion in front of uniforms. I had to act impartial in front of them."

She shook her head. "And here I thought you didn't believe me."

"I don't know you that well, Malone, but I do know that I am drawn to you. Have been since we were in high school. I'd like to think I couldn't be attracted to a murderer, but my experience as a detective says it's possible."

"I...well, I guess that's an interesting way to look at it." She didn't know what else to say. Not when something she'd always longed for had happened. He'd admitted he was attracted to her.

She took a bite of spicy rice mixed with cool avocado to keep her mind off thoughts that didn't help move the investigation forward. "I can't tell you anything more about the guy than I've already told you."

"What about smell? Did he have a scent at all?"

She closed her eyes and ignored the food to think. "No. Nothing."

"His clothing? Expensive or bargain quality."

She kept her eyes closed and brought the man to mind, seeing his clothing vividly. She opened her eyes. "Expensive.

The shirt had a label at the hem. It was an expensive brand Reed likes to wear. And his boots were leather. Worn but stylish."

"Okay, so we have a man who has money to blow on clothes."

"Yes." Excitement had her reaching out for his hand. "This is a start, right?"

He nodded, gaze flicking to her hand resting on his.

Suddenly self-conscious, she let go, picked up her taco, and took a bite, the sweet corn melting on her tongue.

"And your level of detail helps reinforce that he does exist. You can't just pull such detail out of the air unless you're a practiced liar. A vibe I don't get from you."

She swallowed. "I feel like there's something else I saw, but it's not registering. I'll keep thinking."

He nodded as he chewed.

"I kept wondering last night if the guy came to the hotel to shoot Junior or if it was a spur-of-the-moment thing," she said. "Like maybe he went to the reunion, and Junior said something to him like he did to me. I concluded he most likely came to shoot him, or he wouldn't have a ski mask with him, unless he had gear for skiing in his car."

Ian set down his taco. "Would you be willing to look at footage from the hotel video? To see if you can ID him by his clothing when he arrives?"

"Sure."

"I have my laptop in the car, and we could review the files when we finish here if it's okay with you."

"Reed's likely getting mad at me for not showing up. Any minute now, he'll send a search party. He's asked the Veritas and Nighthawk Security team to meet with me to develop a plan to find this guy."

Ian leaned back. "What if we went over to Veritas and then came back to review the files over leftovers?"

"Smooth way to insert yourself into our meeting."

"I didn't think you'd notice." The right side of his full mouth quirked up.

You keep smiling like that at me, and I won't notice anything else ever again.

Still, she couldn't think of a reason to keep Ian away. After all, she'd often heard it said to keep your friends close and your enemies closer. Right now, she didn't know where Ian fit in the picture, but she did know she liked having him close.

5

If Ian were prone to nerves, the Veritas conference room filled with the five muscled Byrd brothers and the Veritas partners would make him flex his confidence muscles. But being in law enforcement, Ian was used to testosterone-filled rooms, and he relaxed in his chair while Malone updated the team, who didn't at all seem upset to be there on a weekend.

As she described Junior lying on the carpet, Ian's mind wandered to the autopsy and his pastor's message that he'd caught after leaving the morgue. He'd spoken on Hebrews 6:10. *God is not unjust; He will not forget your work and the love you have shown Him as you have helped His people and continue to help them.*

It was one of Ian's favorite verses, one he used as his work mantra. He was helping people. Sure, he worked for murder victims, but his job was to be their advocate and to aid the grieving people they left behind. Thinking of his job as being God's hands on earth helped Ian stay optimistic in a job that could easily make a person jaded. He'd really needed to hear the message after the autopsy.

And in moments when he was the recipient of angry

glares from people surrounding him because he'd arrested their friend, remembering why he did his job was important. Those stares were nothing compared to the ones he sometimes got from mourning families when they didn't think he was working fast enough to find justice for their loved one.

Sierra Rice, Reed's wife and the Veritas Center's trace evidence expert, eyed him as she flicked straight blond hair over her shoulder. "Is the ballroom still sealed, or can I get in there to nose around?"

All eyes landed on Ian, and he sat forward. "Our forensic team has one last thing they want to do. When they finish, we'll turn it over to the hotel manager. Should happen today."

"Can you let me know before you release it?" Sierra asked. "I'd like to work the scene, but I want to get in there before it's contaminated."

He nodded. "Though you should know the manager is jonesing to get it cleaned for an event he has booked tonight."

"Good to know. Thanks." She slid her business card across the table to him then looked at the others. "Which means we'll have to make it worth his while to let me have a few hours with the space."

"We can handle that." Maya Lane, the business founder, turned to Malone. "Don't worry about costs. You're family, and we take care of family."

Ian liked the strength of the woman's convictions. He'd heard plenty of stories about how gifted these scientists were, but he hadn't known how much the team was a tight-knit community. What he wouldn't give to have grown up with a family like that instead of his shallow one, where it was all about the next greatest and popular thing.

He'd once thought getting married and having his own

kids would give him the family he craved, believing he could create whatever he wanted, but what made him think he knew anything about being a parent? The only example was the dysfunctional pair who'd raised him. More like nannies who raised him. He'd rarely seen a solid marriage firsthand other than a few times when he'd been invited—along with other coworkers—to barbecues that Londyn's parents held for their business. Her mom and dad and her aunt and uncle, who'd founded Steele Guardians, at least acted like great parents on the surface.

The team investigator, Blake Jenkins, strode to the white-board and grabbed a marker. "So all we have is a shooter wearing pricey black attire and boots." He jotted the information on the board before spinning to look at Ian. "What can you tell us about the gun?"

"Springfield Armory XDS."

"Kind of a small carry for such a big guy," Grady Houston, the team weapon's expert said.

"Not the sort of weapon I'd choose if I planned to take someone out," Ian said. "But it's heavier than many small guns, and most shooters almost always shoot heavier guns better and more comfortably."

Grady gave Ian a look of respect. "You know your weapons. Or at least this one."

"I'm a fan and like to carry the best weapon for the job." Ian didn't add that he was more than a fan of weapons, that he qualified in his department with weapons and scopes most detectives wouldn't likely use, including a night-vision scope. Not the sort of thing needed often in a city setting, but one day he knew it could come in handy. Besides, it was crazy cool.

He continued to look at Grady. "I have to admit I had to do a bit of research on this one." Ian gave a tight smile. "It fits well in pants pockets and wouldn't be noticeable at the reunion if he'd been a guest. That, along with the weight, is why I think the guy chose it."

"Makes sense to me." Grady leaned back.

"He only had two bullets in the magazine," Ian added.

"That explains how he knew Malone wouldn't shoot him, and he wasn't expecting return fire," Grady said. "Or he had another piece with him."

Reed aimed a narrowed gaze at his sister. "I wonder if handing that gun to you and walking away was his plan all along or if he just took advantage of the situation."

Malone's shoulder stiffened. "But how could he know I'd be with Junior?"

"How many people who lost their parents would ignore the bait Junior put out there for you?" Reed pinned Malone with the intense stare all law enforcement officers perfected. Ian was proud of her for not wilting under it. "Not likely any."

"And do you think the bait was true?" Ian asked. "Do you think your parents' accident wasn't an accident?"

Malone shifted her focus to Ian. "I doubt it."

"I agree," Reed said. "The collision was investigated by the county sheriff's office, and they concluded our dad had been driving too fast for the conditions and ran off the road into a ravine."

"True or not, I'm sure going to look at Junior's claim." Malone's tone held the iron will he'd heard she'd become known for in her job as a prosecutor.

"Starting where?" Aiden Byrd asked, not at all put off by her intensity.

"I'm not sure." Malone frowned.

"I can try to hunt down the accident report," Ian said. "But it'll likely be a paper record, and we'll need to get an agency to go into their archives to dig it out. Could take time."

"Too bad we don't have their vehicle to look at. But it's been twenty-seven years. I'm guessing the car was scrapped."

"Maybe not." Reed leaned forward. "It was a vintage '64 Mustang convertible, just like yours. Someone might've bought it."

"Parts for vintage cars are always in demand," Blake said. "We can easily research the VIN number and see if it's still on the road. Though you should know, VIN numbers weren't standardized until the eighties. Means we might encounter an issue."

"Even if it *is* in service," Grady said, "whatever caused the crash would've been fixed."

He had a good point, but... "If we find the guy who bought it, he might be able to tell us what he found wrong with it when he took possession of it."

"What we need is the VIN or plate number," Blake said.

Malone perked up. "The executor for our parents' estate was a friend of our dad's. He was very thorough, and he kept records and belongings that he thought we might want. I recently moved it all from storage to my garage, and I know there are photo albums in the boxes. Our dad loved to take pictures of his car. I'm sure we could find the plate number there."

"I wouldn't be surprised if the paperwork doesn't have the VIN number in it too," Reed added.

Ian looked at Malone. "We can search the boxes when we leave here."

"I'd love the help." She smiled, but it was forced.

Why? Was it the topic of their parents' death? The thought of spending more time with him? The thought of going through those records?

Reed cleared his throat. "If I didn't have an investigation that was threatening to break wide open, I'd be there to help. As it is, I need you to keep me updated on every detail."

Malone smiled at her brother, a smile filled with love. "I'll keep you in the loop."

Blake peered at Ian. "Once you have that VIN number, I know you can search NCIC for the information and don't need our help. I'd still like the information once you locate it."

The National Crime Information Center was a database only for law enforcement use, and Blake wouldn't have access to it. He did have access to consumer sites, but they didn't provide as much information as Ian could obtain.

"Give me your email address, and I'll send it to you," Ian said.

Blake flicked a business card down the table and changed his focus to Reed. "Let's suppose that Junior was right and your parents' death wasn't an accident. Any idea who might've wanted to kill them?"

Reed shoved his chair back and came to his feet. "We were just kids. We had no idea our parents might be targeted." He ran a hand over his head. "Our dad was a corporate attorney. Our mom was a kindergarten teacher. Just your basic, happy family. Until the accident. So, no, I have no idea."

Blake swung his gaze to Malone.

She twisted her hands on the table. "I have no idea either."

"It looks like we need to do a deep dive into their lives to see what we can find." Nick Thorn, the team's cyber expert, looked eager to get started. "I'll get moving on that right away."

Malone nodded.

"I can work with him," Erik Byrd, the only Byrd brother

who didn't have dark hair, peered at Malone. "I handle computer work for our agency."

She gave him a tight smile. "Thank you. Both of you. I'm a little uncomfortable digging into our parents' past, but I know they were good people. We won't find anything bad."

Ian wanted to have the same belief that she had, but she was just a child when her parents died and could be way off-key here.

"We could also review Junior's computer to see if he left any details on the accident." Nick faced Ian. "You'll have to release it to us, though."

Ian knew they'd do a great job, but he couldn't accommodate them. "That will have to stay in-house with the regional computer lab."

Erik nodded. "They're top-notch. They'll do a good job." Erik was a former PPB officer, so he would know about the lab that most agencies used in the area and their skills. "If there's something incriminating on the hard drive, they'll find it."

Grady leaned forward. "I don't suppose I could get a look at the murder weapon."

Ian shook his head. "That would break the evidence chain. I probably shouldn't even be here. Conflict of interest and all."

Reed planted his hands on his hips and eyed Ian. "Then why are you?"

Reed was still mad that Ian had arrested Malone. Ian got that. If Ian were Malone's brother, he'd be upset too, but he wouldn't question help when it was offered. At least he didn't think he would.

"I asked Malone to partner with me on the investigation." Ian held up his hands before Reed could speak. "And before you say anything, I know it's unorthodox for law enforcement to partner with a civilian, especially one who's been arrested for the crime you're investigating. But in this instance, I think Malone is central to the investigation, and the partnership will produce faster results, which will help find out if this murder is related to your parents so you can both move on from the incident."

"Or did you just want access to the Veritas partners' expertise?" Reed kept his gaze pinned to Ian and waved his hands to encompass the room.

Ian wanted to tell Reed about Junior assaulting Malone, allowing her brother to see her connection to Junior and to Ian, but on the drive over, Malone had asked him to keep the assault to himself. She believed Reed would feel guilty for not protecting her, and she didn't want him to have any angst over something he couldn't change. "I won't lie and say it's not appealing to work with all of you, but I honestly think Malone is the key to closing this investigation, and if we're working together, we'll resolve it faster."

"It doesn't matter, Reed," Malone said, a pinched expression on her face. "I agreed to work with Ian. End of story. So let's move on. In addition to looking into our parents' backgrounds, we should be researching Junior."

"Erik and I can do an online search," Nick offered.

"I notified Junior's parents of his death," Ian said, "but they were in too much shock to question. I'll go back to see if they have any idea on who might want him dead."

Blake jotted the information on the board. "I'll be glad to look into any friends."

"I also learned at the autopsy that Junior had stage-three pancreatic cancer," Ian said. "I have no idea if this is a factor or not, but if he really knew that the Rices' accident wasn't one, he might've wanted to update Malone before it was too late. Detective Steele, Londyn, is looking for Junior's doctor, and we'll see if Junior knew he had cancer."

Reed dropped back into a chair, and Sierra took his

hand. "I don't get how this guy knew anything about them. He was a kid when they were killed. Makes no sense."

"Our deep dive might provide that answer," Nick said.

Ian could only hope and pray that was true.

Blake added the word *cancer* to the board and tapped it with his marker. "We have a good start. I suggest we reconvene tomorrow morning to review the results."

"In the interim"—Reed met and held Malone's gaze —"You'll stay with us. You'll be safe here. When you leave the building, Nighthawk will provide a security detail."

"Now, come on." She snapped her chair forward. "There's no indication that I'm in danger. If the killer wanted to take me out, he could have done so when he killed Junior."

"I'll be with her most of the time," Ian said. "I could bunk on her couch."

Malone recoiled, and Ian's heart took a direct hit.

"No offense." Aiden Byrd eyed Ian, but his gaze lacked criticism. "Your specialty is finding and bringing in the bad guys. We're experts at protection, and we'll do more than bunk on her couch. We'll do threat assessments for every trip and provide transport in an armored vehicle."

Malone blinked a few times. "I don't think—"

"Humor me on this one. Please." Reed ran a jerky hand through his hair and took a deep breath as he stared at his sister.

"Fine." She lifted her chin. "But I'm still in charge of where I go and who I see."

Aiden gave an easy nod. "We wouldn't have it any other way."

"Unless it's too dangerous," Drake Byrd said. "Then we'll talk, and by talk, I mean veto it."

Drake laughed and so did the others, even Malone, though Ian knew that when it came down to deciding where she might go, she would still be in charge, no matter what the Byrd brothers decided. And that thought put fear in Ian's already bruised heart.

~

Malone rode in the back of a Nighthawk Security vehicle as Aiden drove toward her house. Brendan rode shotgun, and Clay sat in the back seat with her. Ian followed in his own vehicle. Overkill for sure.

She thought the past thirty minutes in the Nighthawk office had been a waste of time as the brothers had done a threat assessment about taking her home, where she would review records and videos with Ian. She doubted anyone was lying in wait to kill her. She'd meant it when she'd told Reed that the shooter could easily have taken her out at the ballroom. But at the pain in her brother's eyes, she'd known she had to agree to whatever he wanted.

She hadn't seen that level of anguish from Reed since their parents died, and she'd flashed back to the days when they'd been too frightened to do anything but huddle together. If only they had a living relative. Just one. They could've gone to live with them and not faced the uncertainty of foster care. But both their parents had been only children in long lines of onlys and were born to older parents who'd died.

She'd never noticed the lack of cousins or aunts and uncles until she and Reed had nowhere to go. She'd never forget the look on the social worker's face when she realized the pair of them had no one to take them in. A mixture of pity and sadness.

Malone shook off the memories and breathed deeply until Aiden pulled into her driveway and parked next to her Mustang. She thought briefly of Ian's comments about safety. When this was all over, she might need to consider his warning.

Clay held out his hand. "If you'll give me your key, Brendan and I'll clear the place."

Another waste of time, she was sure, but she reached into her purse and handed her ring to him. Ian pulled up on the street. Clay and Brendan hopped out and took the steps to the front door two at a time. They looked so similar that it wasn't hard to tell they were brothers. Except Erik. He looked like his sister, Sierra.

Ian set his laptop on the roof of his vehicle and leaned against the side of the car to make a phone call, giving her time to study him without him noticing her. She'd wondered if he might be intimidated by the Byrd brothers and Reed, but Ian had held his own in the meeting without a hint of nervousness.

The Nighthawk guys were all former law enforcement officers. Maybe there was some unwritten brotherhood that they felt with Ian. She might've been thrown for a loop if she hadn't known everyone in the room, but honestly, there was only one person throwing her for a loop. The guy who had his ankles casually crossed, his hand clamped on the back of his neck, and his attention pointed at the ground.

He suddenly stood straight, his hand going for the gun holstered at his hip. The garage door started to rise, and he focused on it. He might've appeared casual on his call, but he was hyper-aware of what was going on around him.

"Looks like we're cleared to move." Aiden looked over the seat at her. "We'll head straight into the garage and close the door behind us. No stopping for anything."

They'd shared the arrival procedure at least three times now, but she guessed their protectees often failed to follow directions.

Brendan remained at the garage, and Clay came out to

open her door. Aiden met Clay, and they each stepped into place at her sides. They moved at a quick clip, and she kept up with them on the way to the garage. She heard Ian moving behind them. Computer under his arm, he had to duck to get inside the dimly lit garage before the door closed on him. He didn't look too happy about that.

"Okay, we'll take up our positions outside," Aiden said. "You need us for anything, you have our number. If the threat level changes, we'll let you know."

"She'll be fine with me," Ian said, pulling his shoulders back, the first sign that the Byrds bothered him.

"You going to start in the garage with the boxes?" Aiden asked.

Ian shook his head. "We have video from the hotel to review. I'm hoping we'll see our shooter and can run him through facial recognition to get an ID."

"Then let's get to it." Malone jogged up the three stairs to the house, and the others followed.

Aiden took up the rear and locked the door.

"Your keys." Clay handed the ring to her.

"Thanks." She took the keys, and the brothers stepped out the front door.

"Lock up," Aiden warned as he pulled it closed.

She let out a long breath and turned the deadbolt with a solid click. "They're a little bit intense."

"Little bit." Ian rolled his eyes. "But in their line of work, they have to be."

She remained standing by the door. "I just wish they didn't think I needed their services. It seems like such a waste of their time and resources."

"Then why did you agree?"

"For Reed's sake."

"The two of you seem close."

"Very," she said. "We weren't before our parents died, but things changed when we were the only family we had left."

He met her gaze. "I'm always shocked by how life can change in the blink of an eye. Just like the rug is pulled out from under you, and you're helpless to stop it."

They were getting off track, but she couldn't help her curiosity. "Sounds like you speak from experience."

"Not from my own experience. More from seeing it happen on the job."

Nicely deflected. "Are you close to your family?"

He lifted his computer. "We should get started on the video."

He didn't want to talk about himself. Message received. She led the way to the kitchen.

He set his computer on the island. "I feel bad that my parents are alive, and I don't see them when you would likely give anything to have yours back."

"Yeah. Yeah, I would." She took a seat at the counter.

He settled on the stool next to her, and she caught a whiff of his scent. The leather in his jacket mixed with some spicy cologne or shampoo. It was a manly smell that she liked, and she had to fight a strong urge to inch closer while he slid the laptop between them.

"FYI, I got a call from the computer lab when I got here," he said, his focus on his computer as he opened it. "They started on Junior's laptop, but it's encrypted, so it will take longer. If they can even crack it."

"Only one reason to encrypt a computer. You have highly confidential information you don't want others to see."

"And in my experience, it's often illegal information." He opened a file on his computer, his long fingers flying over the keyboard. "I had a tech review the files overnight, and he isolated the video to all males arriving and exiting the building. Take a good look at each guy and let me know if any of them fit the shooter's description." He started a video playing.

She studied each man as they moved, and mentally dressed them in the shooter's clothing, but none of them moved right. The video came to an end.

She leaned away from him. "The shooter had kind of a swagger. None of these guys did. I suppose it was too good to be true to think the shooter waltzed in the front door big and bold for us to see."

"We have video on the other entrances and the front desk too. And he could've come early and hid out, so if he's not in any of these clips, I'll have Tech go through the earlier ones."

He started the new file playing, and the screen filled with the side entrance by the ballroom, the entrance she'd used when she'd arrived. Oh, how naïve it had been to worry about seeing old classmates. If she'd only known. Never in a million years would she have thought the night would come to an abrupt end due to a murder, one she was being framed for.

Not if she could help it.

She counted the men this time as they passed before her eyes. By the end of the recording, they'd looked at twenty-seven guys, none remotely right for the man who'd terrified her.

"Next," she said, not taking her focus from the screen.

"This is the last door that was open that night. The others were accessible only with a keycard. He could have booked a room to change clothes and leave much later."

"I didn't think of that," Malone said.

"I'm working on that premise with Londyn," he said. "She's working on comparing the registered guests to the reunion list and arranging interviews with all the males.

She's asking them to voluntarily allow her to take their photos. Anyone who says no will automatically be placed on a prime suspect list. We hope you'll look at the photos when they're available."

"Of course."

He started the video, and she watched to the end. "Sorry. No."

They reviewed the front desk files too, but none of the men were right.

Ian got out his phone. "Let me text our tech staff to keep compiling the earlier videos."

She watched him tap the keys, his concentration pinned fully on the phone. They were done in the house and would head out to her garage and open up boxes. Somehow, she felt as if they would be opening Pandora's box and more trouble would come tumbling out. If not trouble, old memories to stir her emotions and deepen her pain.

Joy too, though, from flipping through old photo albums of her parents. She'd taken one special family photo into foster care with her and had clutched that frame to her heart whenever her parents came to mind. She burned the photo into her mind in case she lost it. And as she got older, memories of how her parents looked had faded, and the photo gave her a way to remember what they looked like.

Just thinking about it brought tears that clouded her vision. She hid her eyes from Ian and rubbed them away.

Ian stood. "Ready to go to the garage?"

She slid off the stool and led the way. She could do this. She hadn't felt up to it before. Why, she didn't know, but she'd put it off for years. Now she had a purpose, and whatever she found, even if it hurt her heart, could bring her and Ian closer to discovering the truth about her parents' deaths.

She pulled her shoulders back and went straight to the first stack of boxes.

Ian pulled a Leatherman from his pocket and sliced open the top one. She glanced in to see games and toys. She lifted out the game called *Peanut Panic.* The board held a motorized cart that went around tracks and scooped up peanuts.

Her heart melted. "This was one of my favorite games."

Ian took out the box. "I've never heard of it."

"The executor couldn't store everything I wanted to keep, but I couldn't part with this game." She frowned. "I wanted to take it with me to foster care, but they told us that possessions often got lost or stolen. I didn't want to lose it. As it turns out, I'm glad I left it behind. Very little of what I took with me remains." Except that picture. That she made sure of.

"Were your things lost or stolen?" he asked.

"Both. When we were moving from one home to the next, we were allowed to store our items with social services. One time they lost most of it. Some of the things were stolen in our second house."

He locked gazes with her. "You had a bad experience in care?"

"Just part of the time," she replied, trying to remember only the good. "Our third home was great, and we stayed with those parents until we went off to college on full scholarships."

He set the game aside and took out other items that belonged to Reed. "You said your dad was an attorney. Is that why you became one?"

She shook her head. "I wanted to help put people behind bars who hurt kids. And people like Junior. Even though I've gotten over what he did to me, it left me feeling vulnerable. And I didn't have anyone to turn to. That's why I became a prosecutor."

"But you left the DA's office."

"You know how often offenders get away with their crimes. That wore on me. Big time. So I thought I would approach it from the other side and help the victims."

"Is that better for you?"

She sighed. "So much better. I finally feel like I'm making a difference."

He closed the box and shifted it to the floor. "I feel the same way in my job, but unfortunately, I only help people after they're gone."

She rested her hand on his arm. "These victims and their families need someone to stand up for them too."

"I know. It's just...it gets... Sometimes, it's hard to take. Other times, like with Junior, I know I'm doing the right thing, but part of me thinks he must've brought this on himself." Ian ripped the tape off the next box with force. "Still, even people like Junior often have a history growing up that explains their actions. They're still responsible for their actions, but they didn't have the right guidance growing up."

"You think that's Junior's reason for being the way he was?"

Ian cocked his head. "Only time will tell, but honestly, once I saw his true colors the day he tried to assault you, I didn't bother trying to figure him out. Just did my best to intervene if I ever saw him try to hurt anyone else. Of course, I kept an eye out for you too."

And there it was. The reason she shouldn't be alone with Ian. They had a history. A thing. A connection. One that went back to days of loving from afar, but she'd always felt it was deeper, and yet, not fully formed. She wanted to finish forming it. Because being with him felt easy. Right. And he seemed to feel the same thing.

6

Despite the reason, Ian liked the time he was spending with Malone. He felt like he was having a conversation that was long overdue. One where they got to know each other better. He'd always thought he would like what he learned about her, and he was right. He only hoped she was thinking the same thing about him. Not that it mattered. They were not only being drawn together, but they were both pushing away too. Still avoiding.

She lifted a box flap, revealing photo albums. "Not sure your theory holds weight all the time."

"What do you mean?"

"Your parents liked to have wild parties. Did you have the right guidance?"

"Not exactly," he said.

"And look how you turned out."

Right. He thought her earlier silence had meant she wanted to drop the conversation, but she wanted to continue, and he'd go with it.

"Thanks to my youth pastor." Memories of the leader Ian still kept in touch with made him smile. "I didn't even believe in God. Andrew didn't care. I was twelve, and he was doing a service project at school. Somehow, he roped me into helping. I discovered how good it felt to help others, to not take and take and take like my parents taught me to do. So I kept going back. Learning more and more. Filling up a hole in myself that I think my parents were—are—futilely searching to fill. God became a big part of my life back then. Still is."

She looked up. "I don't remember you going to church when we were in high school."

"I did. Just not around here." He paused to decide if he wanted to share the reason. After all, he'd never told anyone, but a burning desire to tell her took over his wish for privacy. "I had this thing about not letting anyone see the real me at school. Not sure why. Maybe it was because we moved a lot when I was a kid. Guess it was easier to let people believe I was like my parents than to get close to someone only to have my family move again. So I attended church in McMinnville."

She shook her head, a tight smile on her face.

"What?" he asked, even more curious now about what she was thinking.

"The games we play growing up. It's crazy."

"And what games did you play?"

She picked at the corner of the box flap, and he thought for a moment she might not share.

"I worked hard to be invisible," she finally said. "To follow the rules and not get in trouble. I'd witnessed bad foster homes, and I knew Reed and I were very blessed to be in the last home. I couldn't give my foster parents a reason to not want me. Or a reason to separate me and Reed."

He looked at her long and hard and saw beneath the hard shell she wore to the little girl who was still afraid to be rejected and removed from her brother. It took everything Ian had in him not to circle the box and take her into his arms. To promise to be by her side and protect her for the rest of her life.

The thought scared him to his depths. He'd never, not once, had that desire. Sure, he served and protected on the job, but the deep emotion flooding his brain and heart was different. It was almost visceral. And he was the wrong guy to be having such feelings. If he'd learned anything about himself over the years, he'd learned that he wasn't cut out to have a deep *I do forever* kind of relationship.

He nodded at the box. "I'll carry this into the house. That way we can sit down and go through the pictures once we're done reviewing all the other boxes."

"Great." But the pain of his abrupt change of subject cloaked her tone with a heaviness that hurt his heart even more.

She'd shared her greatest fear, and he pretty much ignored it, preparing to run out of the room. He wanted to ask for a do-over, but no good would come of that. None. He snatched up the heavy box and climbed the stairs. He put the albums in the living room and headed for the kitchen to get a couple bottles of water.

Back in the garage, he handed one to her. "Thought you might be thirsty."

"Ever the gentleman."

"Hey, now." He worked hard to conjure up a smile and take on a light tone. "Don't go ruining the tough-guy rep I worked hard to develop."

She laughed, but it was halfhearted.

He set down his bottle and turned to another box, telling her he was done talking in a not-so-subtle way. He only had to step away for a minute to put aside the discussion he'd always wanted to have with her and focus on the work.

He dug into the box, finding a large jewelry box, a few scarves, women's sweaters, and a handful of books. He heard her searching another box, and he picked through the jewelry box, then flipped through the books to be sure they didn't contain anything unusual. All he located was a torn bookmark with Malone's school picture on it. He could easily imagine her as a child, sitting on her mother's lap and listening to a story. Wasn't hard to then picture Malone as a mother, lavishing on her child all the love she'd missed out on from her birth parents. But he didn't even know if she wanted children. Or wanted to get married. No way he would ask and take them back to the personal realm.

Her phone rang, and she looked at it. "It's Sierra." Malone tapped her speaker button. "I'm with Ian, so I put you on speaker."

"It's about the ballroom," Sierra said. "I found the GSR that you mentioned. The only other evidence I located were boot prints. They contained bark mulch and dust that carried in on the treads of your shooter's shoe. Or, at least, I'm assuming it's your shooter. Find his boots and we can compare with the prints I lifted."

"Great work," Malone said.

Ian had to agree. The criminalists didn't have boot prints on the evidence list.

"Mulches are unique," Sierra added. "We can compare to any mulch if we locate his home."

"Couldn't he have just cut across a mulched area at the hotel?" Ian asked.

"He could have," Sierra said, and Ian heard a baby crying in the background. "But I've already done a comparison to the hotel's mulch, and it's not a match. Let me know if you locate a suspect's boots, and I'll do the comparison."

"Thanks, Sierra," Malone said.

"As you can hear, someone's hungry." Sierra chuckled. "I gotta go. Call me if you need my help with anything else."

The call ended.

"It would be nice if our department could afford to use Veritas's services on a regular basis," he said. "Not that I'm dissing our criminalists, but the Veritas team members take things up a notch and work faster."

"I am very fortunate to have a connection," Malone said sincerely. "They often help my clients for no charge, and I know they do a lot of other pro bono work too."

"Reed's lucky to be married to someone who works there. Wish I could marry into a connection." He chuckled.

Their gazes met, and her expression changed from interest in the boxes to interest in him. He hoped she wasn't thinking he was serious. He wouldn't entertain the idea of marriage even as a joke. Getting married was the last thing on his life's to-do list.

He jerked his gaze free and went back to searching his box. They silently worked their way through stacks of boxed memories while the air sizzled with tension. Finally, he happened upon what looked like office records. He dug through the files to find records compiled by the executor for the Rices' will. A white binder held the accident report and a photocopy of a bill of sale for the Mustang.

He held up the accident report and she stepped closer to view it.

"Says here that the roads were wet," Ian said. "Your dad lost control on a curve, and the car plunged over an embankment then hit several trees—just like Reed said."

"Yeah, it's what we were told, but seeing it in print..." Malone choked up and shuddered.

Oh, man. Ian wanted to comfort her. Badly. She'd suffered so much, in many ways like the families he helped on a daily basis. Better to think of her like one of his victim's family members and move on.

He took out the bill of sale for the Mustang and handed

it to her. "The car was totaled, but the executor sold it instead of taking the insurance money."

"To a Freddie Peck." She looked up at Ian. "And the receipt has the VIN number. Can we look it up right now?"

"Sure," he said. "I can access the information on my laptop."

He escorted her into the house. Malone sat on the velvet couch, dropped the bill of sale on the table in front of her, and clutched her fingers in her lap. She nibbled on her lower lip, and he had to look away before he imagined kissing that very lip.

He grabbed his laptop, dropped onto the far end of the couch, and picked up the bill of sale. He logged into the department's restricted system and entered the VIN number. Individuals could look up VIN numbers online, but no matter the money paid for such a service, the report would never reveal the owner's name and address.

He clicked enter and sat back while the icon churned on the screen. When it opened to reveal the record for the Mustang, he caught Freddie Peck's name.

He read down the record.

"Looks like we've got good news and bad news," he said to Malone. "Which do you want first?"

"Bad news."

"The records show the vehicle still belongs to Peck," Ian said. "He was issued a salvage title at purchase. Means the vehicle wasn't roadworthy at the time. A regular Oregon title has never been issued beyond the one your parents held, so he must not have rebuilt it."

"What did he do with it then?"

"My guess, and it's just that, a guess." Ian kept hold of her gaze. "He scrapped it and never did the paperwork."

"Like we thought." She ran a hand through her thick hair. "You said there was good news."

Ian nodded. "He still lives at the same address in Gaston, and we can ask him in person what he did with the car."

Ian opened Malone's front door two hours later, Clay spun, his hand on his sidearm.

"Stand down," Ian said. "We're just coming out to go to Gaston."

"Roger that." Clay informed his brothers over their comms unit that Ian and Malone were exiting the house.

Ian took a long look around before he led Malone down the walkway. He didn't care if the super protection team was on her detail. He felt personally responsible for her, just like he had back in high school, and he would do his due diligence. Besides, all good law enforcement officers would do the same thing. Trust was something that went out the window not long after joining a law enforcement agency, and every moment of a workday was devoted to finding the truth and staying alive while doing it.

Brendan waited in front of the garage, his hair blowing in the crisp late afternoon wind, his eyes alert. Aiden had taken a stance at the vehicle by the open back door. If possible, his intensity beat Brendan's.

Ian nodded at both men as he waited for Malone to slide into the back seat. He climbed in after her and quickly closed the door. Ian didn't like leaving his vehicle behind, but it was easier to ride with the Byrds for the nearly hour drive to Peck's place in the small country town of Gaston.

Aiden set off, and Malone's leg kept touching Ian's as she seemed more willing to sit closer to him than Clay. He should probably take it as a compliment, but her touch was bringing to mind all kinds of things not related to their upcoming visit.

Visit. Right. Focus on that. They hadn't called ahead to see if Peck was home. Ian didn't want the man to know they were coming. The element of surprise more often than not brought out the truth. When people didn't have time to concoct a story, any attempt at lying was easily spotted. Not that Ian expected Peck to cover anything up.

A quick search by Nick confirmed there was no connection between Peck and the Rice family except for the car purchase. Peck had been a mechanic at the time and had been on social security disability since about that time and hadn't worked at all.

Aiden pulled out onto the highway, and Ian relaxed a notch. With the armored vehicle, he didn't have to be worried, but he wouldn't let his guard totally when he was with Malone until the killer was behind bars.

He grabbed his phone to catch up on emails and texts. First email was from Londyn. "Londyn located Junior's doctor. She'll interview him and request the records."

He got a murmur of *good job* from Aiden, but Malone didn't speak. She started chewing on that lip again. Ian wanted to ask what had her spooked, but he didn't want to open that topic with the Byrd brothers in the vehicle.

Ian put his phone away when they approached Peck's three-acre plot predominantly covered with stately pines and maple trees. A winding dirt driveway led them toward a large clearing that held a small house needing a new roof and a fresh coat of paint. Peck had the drive posted with no-trespassing signs, which could spell trouble, though it was just as likely that the guy simply didn't like company.

Aiden parked in front of the small house, where a long wheelchair ramp ran to the door. A white metal garage with two tall doors stood further back in the lot.

Aiden looked over the seat at them. "We'll go ahead and make sure things are safe."

Ian might want Malone to hang back, but he wouldn't take the chance that the sheer presence of the brothers might scare Peck off.

"That's a negative," Ian said. "You all stay with Malone. I'm talking to the guy first."

Ian didn't wait for agreement but got out and marched through thick piles of colorful maple leaves that crunched under his feet. At the door, he knocked on the worn wood that had once been painted white.

Seated in a motorized scooter, a man with a long silvery beard and equally long hair opened the door and glared up at Ian. "Didn't you see the signs? This is private property, and I don't appreciate trespassers."

Ian held out his credentials and introduced himself.

"And you need an entire posse to talk to me?" He ran a hand down his beard and looked at Aiden and Brendan, who hadn't listened to Ian and had come to stand at the end of the ramp. "I ain't got no beef with the law. I'll answer your questions."

"You alone here?" Ian asked.

"Wife's gone into town for groceries, so yeah."

"Mind if I look inside and confirm that?"

Peck narrowed his eyes. "Mind, yeah, but if it'll get you to leave sooner, I'll let you."

He rolled back, the cart's motor humming and the wheels squeaking. Ian entered the large room that served as kitchen, dining, and living area and smelled of cooked cabbage. There were two open doors on the back wall. The furniture was worn mauve and blue fabrics popular in the early nineties. Ian crossed the room to the doors and peeked inside to find a small bathroom and bedroom with a patchwork quilt on the bed.

Peck was telling the truth. He was alone. At least inside the house.

Ian poked his head back outside and looked at the brothers. "He's alone. Malone can come in."

"Malone?" Peck asked. "Who's that?"

"Someone who wants to talk to you."

"Don't know a Malone," Peck grumbled. "Don't even know if it's a man or a woman."

Aiden escorted Malone through the door and signaled to Ian that they would be watching the exterior.

Peck ran his gaze over Malone. "Woman, I see."

Malone gave him a quizzical look.

"Didn't know if a name like Malone belonged to a man or woman," Peck said.

"It can be either, and people get confused all the time." Malone smiled at the older man. "Thank you for talking to us, Mr. Peck."

He squinted up at her. "Am I supposed to know you?"

She shook her head. "In the mid-nineties you bought a vintage Mustang that belonged to my parents."

"Yeah, right. I bought a Mustang. So?"

"So records say you still have it," Ian said.

"I do." Peck fired Ian a testy look. "Not that it's any of your business."

Malone's eyebrow arched. "But you never applied for a regular registration."

"That's because it's sitting in my workshop in the same condition as the day I bought it." He grimaced. "Planned to restore it, but not a month after I bought it, a motorcycle crash left me paralyzed. Try fixing up a car without the use of your legs. Doesn't work so well."

"I'm so sorry," Malone said.

"You got nothing to be sorry for," he muttered.

"How did you hear about the car?" Ian asked, thinking it was best for them to move on.

"It was towed to the shop where I was a mechanic." He looked at Malone again, his bushy eyebrows knitted together. "So it was your parents who died in the crash?"

She nodded.

He took a deep breath. "I'm real sorry about that."

"Thank you."

"Did you look the vehicle over before you bought it?" Ian asked.

"I saw enough to know that if I couldn't get it road-worthy I could recoup my money in parts." His gaze turned skeptical. "Sounds like you're looking for something in particular."

"We've recently learned that the car accident might not have been an accident," Malone said. "We hoped you still had the car so we could have a look and determine if it was tampered with."

Those heavy silver brows dipped then rose. "You mean like someone sabotaged it to cause an accident?"

"It's possible," Malone said, her focus riveted to the old man.

Peck shook his head. "Man, that's cold."

"Can you tell by looking at a car if it's been tampered with?" Ian asked.

Peck shook his head. "Not me, but I can walk you through checking a few things."

"Could we do it now?" Malone asked, sounding hopeful. "I would really like to know what happened to them."

"Follow me." Peck motored to the door. "And bring your monkeys along too. Might need their help."

He whirred outside and down the ramp, then mowed down leaves and tall grass heading toward the garage. Ian motioned for Aiden, Brendan, and Clay to follow, and they all tromped through the brittle leaves and thick scrub to arrive at the building.

"One of you bruisers lift the door," Peck said. "Hasn't been opened in some time. Could be a challenge."

Brendan grabbed the handle and tugged. Took a few attempts and two hands, but he finally got the corroded door to grind up and along the tracks, the squeal putting Ian on edge. The candy-apple red Mustang sat just inside, facing forward. The front end was smashed into the passenger compartment, the passenger side wheel bent at an odd angle.

Malone gasped, and her hand flew to her mouth.

"I shoulda warned you it was bad to look at," Peck said. "These old cars aren't designed for impact like today's models are."

"I knew it was totaled, but I didn't imagine it was this bad." She shook her head. "Looks like they had to pry the doors open."

Peck gave a solemn nod. "Honestly, looking at it now, I don't know why I was thinking I could restore it. Young and naïve, I guess."

"So how do we see if the car was tampered with?" Ian asked.

"There are two simple but very effective ways to mess with a car and cause an accident," Peck said. "First is to cut the brake line. Second, to loosen the tie rods." Peck wheeled closer to the car. "I would think the police would've checked the brakes, but probably not the tie rod."

"Can you explain what that is?" Malone asked, moving next to him.

"Metal bars that connect the tires to the body of the vehicle. We'll need to jack up the frame to get a good look." He pointed at the workbench. "There're a few jacks over there. Grab 'em, and I'll tell you where to put 'em."

Ian was closest to the bench, so he picked up two rusty looking bottle jacks and started to hand one to Peck.

Peck held up his hands. "Not me. One of you guys will have to do it. Start with the front tire."

Ian dropped to the dirt floor by the car.

"Jack up under the body of the car to let the suspension hang down," Peck said.

Ian placed the jack and glanced back at Peck. "Here good?"

Peck nodded.

Ian cranked the jack until the tire hung free.

"Now grab the tire at three and nine o'clock position." Peck leaned forward. "Push and pull on it. You shouldn't feel any movement."

He took hold of the tire as directed and shook it. The wheel rattled and wobbled.

"You definitely have a malfunctioning tie rod," Peck said. "We call that a death wobble."

Malone took a sharp breath. "What happens exactly?"

"Worst case scenario?" He rubbed a hand over his whiskered jaw. "If a tie rod completely fails, the wheel will break free of the steering assembly. That causes the driver to lose the ability to steer the vehicle."

"And someone could crash," Ian added.

"Would most likely crash." Peck sat upright. "I need you to look at the nuts holding all of the tie-rods. It's like a long metal arm going from the body to the tire. Don't have a cell phone but know you can make a video call to one of these other guys or Malone as you look. They can show me what you see, and I can tell you if you're in the right place."

"I have Malone's number." Ian got out his phone and placed the call, then crawled under the car and aimed the camera at what he thought he should be looking at.

"Yeah, yeah, that's it." Peck sounded excited. "You're looking at the ball joint. Check that nut. It looks like it's about to fall off."

Ian snapped on a latex glove, thankful he always carried them in his jacket pocket, and grasped the nut. It came off in his hands.

"Just like I thought," Peck said. "Been loosened. That could happen on its own. Not likely that loose, but it could. We find more than one of them like that, and you have a legitimate case of tampering."

Feeling sick to his stomach, Ian moved to the other side of the car, where the wheel was already dangling. How had Malone's dad felt when he couldn't steer the car, his wife depending on him? It was the stuff of Ian's nightmares. Someone counting on him and him not being there for them.

"No need for you to look at this one," he said.

"Show it to me," Malone called out.

Ian was glad she was holding the phone for Peck so she didn't see this in person. It was going to be bad enough on video. He aimed the camera at the spot where the nut should have been located, but the ball joint was no longer connected to the tire. "The tie rod doesn't appear to be damaged, but the nut is missing."

"How could the deputies have missed this?" Malone cried. "It's so obvious."

"We're looking for tampering," Ian said. "They probably weren't."

"And crash investigations in rural counties weren't as thorough back in the day," Peck added. "They must've thought the crash caused the tire issue."

Ian took a few pictures of the ball joint, crawled out from beneath the car, and came around the vehicle to look at Peck. "In your opinion, then, this definitely wasn't an accident."

Peck shook his head hard, his hair flying in the breeze. "Not an accident at all. Someone wanted this car to crash."

Ian looked at Malone. "And now the question is, who murdered your parents?"

The silence in the Nighthawk SUV was nearly deafening, and Malone couldn't think with the tension pressing in on her. Why wasn't anyone talking? Throwing out questions or scenarios? She couldn't stand it any longer.

"Why is everyone so quiet?" she asked.

"Guess we're waiting on a cue from you." Ian faced her. "You just learned your parents were most likely murdered. That's got to be hard to hear."

She swiveled to face him. "It is, but you know me. I'm a doer. And I want to do something about it. Find the person responsible."

He frowned.

She didn't like that response. Not at all. Her gut cramped. "What's wrong?"

He lifted a hand as if he was going to take hers then let it drop. "I want you to have realistic expectations for what we just found."

"What do you mean?"

"I'll get forensics to process the car. We might get a break and find evidence, but can we use any of it to convict the killer? The car hasn't been under control of law enforcement, and a defense attorney could easily say the tie rod nuts were loosened after Peck bought the car. The evidence we located today might not help."

"The chain of custody," she said, not liking what she heard. Not liking it at all. As a former prosecutor, she knew that could invalidate anything found on the car.

"Not that I'll let that deter me," Ian said. "I'll start by opening a formal investigation. That'll allow me to get forensics out to Peck's place. I'll have to work with County, as the accident happened out of my jurisdiction, and Peck's place isn't in our control either. But I'm sure the detectives at

County will be glad to let us handle it. Maybe we can find DNA or a print on that nut."

"Would it even last that long?" Malone asked, allowing just a bit of hope to surface and ease the knot in her stomach.

She got murmurs of *don't know* and *good question* from the guys. She took out her phone and called Sierra. When her sister-in-law answered, Malone tapped the speaker button. "You're on speaker again with Ian and the Byrd brothers."

"Go ahead," Sierra said.

"How long does touch DNA last?" Malone asked.

"Depends on the scenario," Sierra said. "Exposure to heat, water, and sunlight are the biggest factors that degrade DNA."

"We just saw my parents' car. It's still in the same condition as the day it crashed. It's been kept in a windowless garage. It's dry, but the building is metal. Probably got pretty hot in the summer. The nuts on the tie rod are rusted."

"That could be a problem," Sierra said. "The only thing to do is try to collect it, if it exists. You'll want someone who's very experienced in DNA to do the work. Someone like Emory."

"Thanks, Sierra." Malone hung up and looked at Ian. "I know we have a conflict of interest here, but Sierra's right. Emory is the best person to handle it. What if you got permission for her to do the work?"

"This could be related to Junior's murder and we still have a potential conflict of interest," he said.

She clutched his arm. "You could have one of the state DNA scientists observe and document her every move to try to eliminate any suspicion."

"That might work. When I go in to open the investigation, I'll propose it to my lieutenant."

She tightened her grip. "Can you talk to him the minute we get back?"

"Sure. You could even come with me to review pictures that Londyn has likely taken of the suspects she's interviewed."

Malone released Ian's arm and swiveled to look at Clay. "Is it okay for me to go to the precinct with Ian?"

"Should be fine," Clay said. "We're very familiar with the location, and the three of us can move you quickly and safely inside."

"Agreed," Aiden said.

"I'm in," Brendan said.

"Thank you," she said, already thinking about capturing the killer, then entering a courtroom and watching him or her stand trial to pay for the heinous crime that permanently altered her and Reed's lives.

7
———————

Ian and Malone left the Nighthawk team in PPB's lobby for the return trip to her house, and Ian led Malone down the hallway and into the busy bullpen. The area smelled like bitter burned coffee, not an unusual aroma, as the near empty pot was often left on the burner by a tired detective.

Londyn sat behind her desk, running a finger down a column of names on the reunion attendance list. Her large eyes were narrowed, and her hair was pulled back today, revealing her long neck. She looked up at them and smiled, but it was tight.

"You remember, Malone," Ian said, resting against the corner of her desk.

"Of course." If Londyn was put off by seeing their suspect in the detective's bullpen, her impartial mask didn't reflect it, but she had to be wondering why he'd brought her there instead of just having Londyn email the photos to him.

Londyn picked up a stack of files from the chair by her desk. "Have a seat."

Malone dropped gracefully onto the chair. Her designer clothing and boots made her stand out in the department, even sitting next to Londyn, who dressed fashionably and was more put-together than most of the detectives, who often looked rumpled after long hours of work.

Ian focused on Londyn. "I hoped you'd have photos from your interviews for Malone to look at. Assuming that you were able to do some interviews."

Londyn leaned back in her chair and took a long swig from a can of diet cola. "I went through the first half of the list and got right over to the hotel before people checked out. Everyone agreed to let me take their photos, and I have a few guys who could fit the build. None of them admitted to knowing Junior, though."

"You think they were blowing smoke?" he asked.

"The truth. Unfortunately." She ran her hand over her hair that needed no smoothing. "I'm just about done reviewing the second half of the list from the hotel manager, and I'll be heading back to the hotel in a few minutes. But I can make time to show the pics."

"Thank you," Malone said.

"Don't thank me. If you identify the guy in my photos, my next interviews aren't as urgent." Londyn chuckled, then looked at Ian. "But seriously, if I didn't have to go back to the hotel, it would give me more time to lean on Junior's phone company. They're taking their sweet time in getting the files to me."

"Not unusual," Ian said. "But frustrating."

Londyn mimicked pulling her hair out and chuckled. "I did talk to Junior's doctor. He knew about Junior's cancer and had referred him to a specialist, but he had no records from the specialist saying Junior had gone to see him."

"So the cancer might've been a factor in what he planned to tell Malone." Ian pondered the news. "And his mother," he added, remembering the notation on Junior's copy of the reunion flier.

Malone looked up at him. "You plan to tell his parents about the cancer?"

Ian shrugged. "It might make them feel better, knowing he was spared the suffering of death from cancer. And perhaps knowing they were going to lose him anyway might help with the grief."

"I think it would," Malone said. "Now that I know my parents' accident wasn't one, it helps to know the crash wasn't my dad's fault."

"Maybe I *will* tell them then." Ian stared over Londyn's head and thought about when he'd met with Junior's parents. Ian still wasn't sure what he would do, but he would take Malone's comment into consideration.

"How did the visit to Peck's place go?" Londyn leaned back. "Did he know if the car was tampered with?"

"He didn't, but he still has the car in the same condition." Ian explained what they'd learned.

Londyn's eyes widened. "Seriously. Wow. Who'd have thought that car would still be around."

"It was a lucky break. I'm going to talk to the LT and open an investigation. It's a long shot that there'll be DNA or prints on the vehicle after all these years. Having an expert work the scene might be essential to recovering it. So I'll ask his permission to use the Veritas DNA expert to handle the car. I'd appreciate your support on this."

"Of course." Londyn looked at Malone. "Any thoughts on why your parents were murdered?"

"None."

"The Veritas team is doing a deep dive on their background," Ian said. "Hopefully it will produce a strong lead."

Londyn pinned her focus on Malone. "You and your brother must be unsettled by the news."

"Yeah." Malone clutched her hands tightly in her lap.

Ian ignored the continuing need to comfort her and stood. "Okay if I leave you here to look at the pictures?"

"Not a problem."

"I'll come back after I meet with the LT and finish opening the new investigation." He crossed the room to Hoffman's office and knocked on the open door.

"Good, take a seat," Hoffman said. "I was hoping for an update on the reunion murder."

Ian sat in a side chair and brought his supervisor up to speed. He followed by explaining about how Malone's parents died and that this could be why Junior was killed. He ended with a request to let Veritas handle the DNA. "They'll eat the costs."

"I don't know." Hoffman leaned back in his chair. "I know they're top-notch professionals. Even used them before. And I like the idea of having a state DNA expert working as a witness to the process."

"If there's any DNA to be had, Emory Jenkins is the one to find it," Ian added, hoping to seal the deal.

"You're probably right." Hoffman tapped his finger on the arm of his chair. "Go ahead, but keep me in the loop. And what about other forensics on the vehicle?"

"I'll ask the state lab to provide someone for that too."

"Good. Good. Now what about forensics from the hotel? Anything?"

"Nothing we didn't know about. GSR and the weapon, analyzed for prints and sent off to the state crime lab." Ian knew it would be handled a lot faster if Grady could process the gun, but Ian would take his win on the DNA and not push his luck. "Also, Sierra Rice did her own analysis after we released the scene, and she found mulch she believes was carried in on the suspect's boots. She can match it to other mulch if we locate his home."

"I want play-by-play updates on the DNA and any forensics located on the car." Hoffman snapped his chair forward. "And don't make me look like a fool for agreeing to this."

"I won't." Ian left the office before Hoffman could change his mind.

Ian glanced across the bullpen to Malone and found her still looking at photos on Londyn's computer, Londyn leaning over her. A lead from those pictures would be great, considering they didn't have a lot to go on.

At his desk, he found the phone number for the state forensic lab and asked to speak to the DNA supervisor. Thankfully, she said working with Emory was an honor that anyone in her department would relish, and she immediately agreed to monitor the tests whenever Ian needed her. As a bonus, she also agreed to bring criminalists to process the car.

Stunned at the easy cooperation after he'd prepared for a battle, he dialed Blake Jenkins from the card he'd handed to him at the earlier meeting. Ian would call Emory directly but it was after Veritas's closing hours and he didn't have her number. He shared his need with Blake.

"She's right here," Blake said. "I'll give her the phone."

Ian heard a child babbling in the background, and Blake quickly explained Ian's request.

"Name the time, and I'm there," Emory said.

"How about tomorrow at noon?" he asked, thinking that would give him time in the morning to follow up on other items, attend an update meeting with the Veritas team, and meet with Londyn too.

"Text me the address, and I'll be there." She shared her phone number. "Will I see you there?"

"Yes and also the DNA supervisor from the state lab will be observing."

"I love Deborah, so that'll work."

Ian thanked Emory again and disconnected the call,

then dialed Peck and arranged for the team to work on the car. The man grumbled at first about having so many people on his property again but finally agreed.

Everything arranged, Ian took a long breath as he opened PPB's investigation program on his computer and started an active case for the death of Joanna and Lewis Rice. It took nearly an hour to record the basics. By the time he finished, Malone was turned away from Londyn's screen, and the two were talking. Had she finished all the pictures or had she found their suspect?

Eager to know, he started for Londyn's desk, his mind switching to Malone—and not in a professional capacity. He liked seeing her. Maybe not in a detectives' bullpen. It would be better elsewhere, but he just plain liked having her around. He needed to change his focus. To pin it to the case. To find her parents' killer and Junior's too. That was his job. Not falling for Malone Rice.

When he reached them, she smiled up at him, and his heart responded with a leap. He managed to curtail the size of the smile he sent back her way. Not only because he didn't want to encourage her, but Londyn was appraising them too, and he didn't want her to see his interest in Malone.

"Any luck with the pictures?" he asked.

"No." Malone got up and rolled her head.

"Which means I'm heading out to the hotel again." Londyn stood. "And then I'll be calling to arrange interviews with the people who attended the reunion but didn't stay at the hotel."

"We'll review additional videos. If you email the photos you take, Malone can look at those too."

"Will do." Londyn pocketed her phone and notepad. "I'll walk out with you."

Ian gestured for the women to go first, and in the lobby,

they found Clay, who caught sight of Malone and used his comm device to ask his brothers to join him.

Clay nodded at Londyn. "Long time no see."

"Not since your wedding. I'm assuming you're still blissfully happy."

Clay's broad smile said it all. "Best four months of my life."

"You're like the poster child for marriage," Londyn said, her tone more serious than the comment deserved.

"You should try it."

Londyn frowned. Ian, remembering she'd just gone through a breakup, stepped forward. "We should get moving. Lots to do."

Londyn flashed him a thankful look. "I'll call you later."

She exited and paused only long enough to say hello to Brendan, who stood on the sidewalk out front.

Clay turned to Malone. "Straight into the vehicle."

Malone nodded, and Clay took lead, Malone in the middle, Ian last. He didn't expect any trouble, but he kept his head on a swivel until he was seated in the back seat with Malone and the door was closed tight. Clay climbed in on her other side.

Brendan hopped into the front, and Aiden wasted no time getting them moving. On the short drive, Ian updated the guys on their progress on the investigation. While he spoke, he couldn't miss Malone twisting her hands together. She was nervous, but she'd done a great job at hiding it with only moments, like now, when she revealed her inner turmoil.

Aiden pulled into her driveway and parked next to her Mustang. Ian really didn't like her driving an unsafe vehicle. She wanted to be close to her parents. He understood that. But he didn't want to lose her in a crash the way she'd lost them.

She leaned forward and rested her palms on her knees, her fingers relaxed for the first time since she'd gotten into the SUV. Maybe arriving home brought her comfort. Being there could calm residual issues from her childhood, he supposed. His parents were still alive, and he would like some solace from growing up with them. Losing parents as a child would do an irreversible number on the child, especially when they were fabulous parents, as hers apparently had been.

Finding her parents' killer could help her find peace. And in the time they had together, Ian could also do his best to help her get over any residual loss she might be feeling. For some reason, that was as important to him as bringing in a killer who'd been free for far too long, and that was a new experience for him. One he didn't altogether hate.

Malone locked her front door, wanting to get straight to work looking at the other videos with Ian, but she couldn't ignore her business. Her clients often had emergencies so she didn't like to stay out of touch. She looked at Ian and found him watching her with an odd collection of interest and pity. She liked the interest, but why the pity? She would ask, but she needed to stay on a professional footing with him.

Especially after seeing him in his own environment at work. She'd thought it could help her peg him, but it didn't. One minute, she'd thought she knew what he was like, and the next he changed things up. He'd come across as vulnerable and dangerous at the same time, a combination that seemed impossible. A combination that was very intriguing. And beguiling. Something she needed to guard against.

She took a breath. "I need to check my emails and return any messages I might have gotten today."

"I could stand to review mine too," he said. "I'm juggling several investigations."

"Let's use the kitchen counter again."

He held up his computer. "Lead the way."

She did and had to admit, even if she wanted to remain professional, she liked having Ian at her side while she worked. They were comfortable with each other, the silence not strained at all.

It took nearly an hour to handle the most urgent things, but when she finished, she closed her laptop. Ian was focused on his computer screen but must have felt her eyes on him because he looked at her.

A slow smile spread across his mouth, and his happiness sparked a warm, languid feeling inside. One she could easily get used to.

Despite digging deep for her usual willpower, she could barely resist tracing his full bottom lip with her finger. She swallowed and pushed off her stool. "I'll get the leftovers out."

"I thought we could look at the videos while we eat. That would still give us some time to finish reviewing the boxes in the garage for any other information that might give us a lead on their crash."

"Sounds like a plan," she said, though she didn't know if her appetite would hold up while watching videos, looking for a potential killer.

She got the food out and heated it in the microwave, the tangy spices soon filling the air. They plated their food, moving comfortably around each other in the kitchen. The time together felt easy, as if they were on a date rather than trying to clear her name as a murder suspect.

She set her plate on the counter. "I didn't ask what time you'll be going out to Peck's place tomorrow."

"Noon."

She climbed onto a stool. "Can I come with you?"

He sat beside her and placed his loaded plate next to his computer. "Why would you want to? It'll just be Emory and a criminologist processing the vehicle with the state lab expert overseeing it all."

"I don't know," she said honestly. "I just have this deep need to go. Like it brings me closer to my parents or something. I know it doesn't make sense, but that's how I feel."

"I don't want to give any defense lawyer something to call into question."

"Which a good one would do."

"A good attorney like you." He chuckled.

"I don't represent murderers, but yeah, I'm good at my job."

"And modest."

She laughed and took a bite of the burrito she'd chosen, the tender chicken and gooey cheese melting in her mouth.

"Seriously, though, if you really want to be there, I guess it would be okay. As long as you don't step foot in the garage before the place is processed."

Her heart soared at his kindness, and she grabbed him in a hug. She expected him to push away or at least remain still, but he scooped her closer, and she clung to him.

"Thank you," she whispered, smelling his unique musky smell mixed with another scent she couldn't pinpoint.

He pushed back. "I'm glad to help when I can."

She thought there was a but coming. Instead, he opened his computer and got the video playing, then picked up one of his tacos.

Just like that. Like she hadn't hugged him at all. Like he hadn't returned the hug with gusto. Which he had, and he certainly hadn't been complaining. But he clearly didn't want to acknowledge his feelings, and she would follow his lead. She tucked into her meal while keeping her eyes on the video.

They ate in silence, and she was about to lose hope of seeing a suspect when a guy walking toward the exit caught her attention.

"Stop," she said, her mouth full of burrito.

He paused the recording.

She swallowed and leaned closer. "It might be him. The build is right, and his walk is right. Keep playing it."

Ian started the video again, and the man exited the hotel, but before he did, he glanced back. Half his face was visible.

Ian hit pause. "Know him?"

"Can you make his image bigger?"

Ian enlarged the picture, but all it did was make the picture grainy.

"Can you back it up and play it again?"

"Sure." He reversed and let it run.

"I really do think it's him, but I don't know him. At least not from seeing this video. My ID wouldn't likely hold up in court, though. After all, I didn't see his face, only his body and movement." She looked at Ian. "You know how that can be distinct, right? And I had such a long time to watch him walk when he came toward me with the gun." She tried to keep the image of the shooter in the ballroom from popping into her brain, but it played in brilliant technicolor, and she shuddered.

"Hey." Ian rested a hand on her shoulder.

The urge to turn her face and seek even more comfort had her almost swaying his way. She wanted to seek the touch of his skin on hers, but she sat like a statue and tried not to encourage him with cries of distress or anguish. After all, she wanted his touch as a woman wanted a man's touch, not as a detective might comfort someone helping on his investigation. She wondered if his earlier hug had been motivated by a desire to comfort and nothing more.

How many times was she going to feel those strong emotions with him? Wanting things to be different? But she had to face facts. They weren't, and if she'd learned anything from losing her parents at such a young age, she'd learned that wishing for something did no good. Doing was what made things happen. Or not doing, as in this case, or not getting in trouble growing up and inviting a chance for their foster family to want to send her packing.

"We'll find this guy." Ian squeezed her shoulder and let go.

"Is this image clear enough for facial recognition?" she asked.

"I don't think so, but we can give it a try."

"Can we send it to Nick at Veritas? He might be able to enhance it, and if not, know someone who could."

"Sure, and we can also ask Reed. The FBI manages the national facial recognition software, and they might have the necessary tools to do it."

She nodded. "I'll text them both if you'll prepare to send the photo."

"Why don't we finish looking at these videos first? Our guy might come back in the door, and we'll have a better look at him."

"That sounds good." She tried not to pin her hopes on that fact but demolished the rest of her burrito as she watched. She didn't even taste the food, but she had to eat to keep up her strength to help nab the killer.

They didn't see the suspect again, so they emailed the video to Nick and Reed and moved on to the garage. Three stacks of boxes remained, one of them all paperwork and books that her parents had loved. She remembered seeing a picture of the built-in bookshelf in the living room loaded with these books, and she couldn't wait to put them back on the shelf in the same order. Hopefully, the other decorative items were in the remaining boxes.

"Would you look at that." Ian lifted something from the bottom of a box and held up a zipped nylon case. "You know what this is, don't you?"

She shook her head.

He slid open the zipper and set the case on the box to reveal a full-sized telephone handset with a cord. "It's a bag phone."

He lifted the end of another cord. "This plug goes into a car cigarette lighter to get power and allow the owner to make calls. It was used before cell phones were common. Not a lot of people had them because they were expensive, and the calls were really costly too. I wonder if your mom and dad had it in the car at the time of their crash."

Hope built in Malone's stomach. "If they did, do you think we could get phone records to see who they called?"

"We'll need to go through the boxes of paperwork to see if the executor kept phone bills. And while we're at it, we can look for bills for the landline at this place too."

Pumped by a potential lead, they switched their attention to the other boxes and flipped through folder after folder until Malone located a utilities folder. She paged through the papers and held the file up. "Phone bills for the house."

"Perfect," he said. "Set it aside, and we'll keep looking for the bag phone records. I'll get the information to Londyn so she can work on compiling a list of names to go with numbers we find."

Still looking through the boxes, Ian paused to study a

folder. "This is interesting. Not related to the phone but to your dad's work."

He turned the file, allowing her to look at it. She read articles about how Chinese drywall containing formaldehyde had been imported into the United States. The drywall off-gassed volatile chemicals and fumes. It worsened when temperature and humidity rose and gave off a sulfuric odor. Smelled like rotten eggs and caused copper surfaces to turn black and powdery. People in homes with the drywall installed had breathing issues.

She looked up. "What if my dad's company imported this drywall and tried to cover it up? Could he have been planning to blow the whistle?"

Ian's lips pressed together. "If so, it's certainly something that would cost the company a lot of money to repair."

"I'm assuming there would be class action lawsuits too. That would add even more to their costs."

Ian met her gaze and held it. "If the people in charge at the company wanted to keep it quiet, it certainly could be something worth killing to cover up."

8

Early the next morning, Malone shifted on the stool at her kitchen island, Ian sitting next to her. She tapped her foot and couldn't wait to go to Peck's place. Like she'd told Ian, she didn't know why, but just knowing that Emory and the criminalist would process the car gave her hope that she would find the person who killed her parents. Even after hearing the news the night before, she was still shocked to learn they'd been murdered. She needed answers. Desperately. Not only who killed her parents, but who killed Junior and how his murder was related to her, if it even was.

Hopefully, the video call from Nick and Erik would provide some of those answers. They'd canceled the morning meeting with the Veritas partners, as Nick and Erik were the only ones on the team with an update. Malone and Ian were waiting for them to join the call.

She shifted on her stool again and resumed thumping her foot on the rung as she waited for the guys to appear on her computer screen.

"You look antsy," Ian said.

"Sorry. I think things are settling in. It's starting to hit me." She took a breath. "I never imagined Junior's claim at the reunion would turn out to be true."

"I get that." He held her gaze. "But it's good to know the truth, right?"

"Yeah, sure," she said.

"I hear a *but* in your tone."

"But now I know it wasn't a fluke accident. Someone intentionally ended their lives."

"I see the families of victims all the time. Witness their suffering at such a sudden loss of life. But I've never felt it as deeply as I do with you." Conviction rang through his tone.

His words touched her heart, but she didn't know how to respond.

"This is personal for me now," he continued. "It's never been personal in the past. Sure, the families suffering is hard to take, but I made sure I remained impartial so I could continue to do my job well and not burn out. But today..." His voice cracked, and he looked away.

She couldn't hold back and took his hand. She held it tight, but she still didn't know what else she should do. Best course was to keep quiet rather than risk saying the wrong thing.

His computer sounded a chime for their video, and she jerked her hand free as if caught disobeying by the teacher in school. He glanced at her, then accepted the incoming call.

Nick and Erik sat next to each other and shared a screen. They both had dark circles under their eyes.

Malone swallowed away guilt at being the cause of their lack of sleep. "You guys look tired."

Erik scrubbed a hand over his face. "All-nighter, but it was worth it. We have some interesting info."

"You want us to start with your parents or Junior?" Nick asked.

"My parents," Malone said, as she wanted information on them more than anything.

"They checked out as expected," Erik said. "Like Reed mentioned, your dad was a corporate attorney and your mom a kindergarten teacher. Your dad worked for a huge local construction company, Ground Floor Builders. They're big in commercial building. I didn't find anything negative about the company, but the building trade can often take shortcuts or use substandard materials that come back to bite them. So I think it would be worth talking to someone at the company who might have more information."

"We found a file that said the company was importing Chinese drywall containing formaldehyde," Ian said.

"That would be worth covering up if they installed it and had to remediate it," Nick said. "Nothing came up in my searches, but this might suggest how your dad got wind of it, and they found a way to hush it up."

Malone didn't know what to think at this point. "Or the company just fixed the buildings where they'd installed the faulty product and my parents' crash just occurred at that time."

"Could be." Nick tapped his chin. "But your dad must've had a reason for having those papers at home, and the executor had a reason to keep them."

"Is he still alive?" Ian asked. "Can we talk to him?"

Malone shook her head. "He died from a heart attack a little over a year ago."

"Then I'll start an algorithm to search specifically for the drywall as it relates to this company," Nick said. "I'll let you know if I find anything."

Ian looked at Malone. "I wonder if there's anyone at the company who might remember your dad."

"Way ahead of you there," Erik said. "I'll email you a list of executives who still work there."

"Perfect," Malone said. "Thank you, Erik."

"That's it for your parents." Nick stifled a yawn. "I've been working on Junior's background. He had a falling out with his dad about five years ago. He once worked for his dad's company, Flagg Contracting, but then his dad disowned him."

Ian's expression brightened. "Do you know what their falling out was about?"

Nick shook his head. "Junior posted on social media that they'd parted ways, and he seemed bitter about it, but he didn't share why."

"I'm already planning to interview his parents again," Ian said. "I'll ask about it. But when I did the death notification, they didn't mention the estrangement. They didn't seem to know much about Junior's current life, though, so that tracks with a separation. They had no idea who or why someone might want to kill him."

"Then they're in denial or they really don't know anything about their son or they're lying," Nick said. "It also looks like Junior was a middleman in a local drug syndicate run by Tirone Olivo."

"Olivo?" Ian's mouth dropped open. "He's known to nearly every police officer in the city. But he keeps his hands clean, and the drug squad can never get anything on him. They've tried to tie him to the mafia but never made any connection there. On the surface, it seems like he's on his own and above board."

"Exactly," Nick said. "He looks like an ideal citizen on paper. Heads up an import company, bringing in Italian furniture. The business appears to be legit and originated when his family emigrated from Italy."

Ian shook his head. "I know the drug squad has searched his furniture shipments in the past, but they've never produced anything illegal."

"Which is why he's been a major drug player in the area for so many years," Nick said. "No one can break into his organization."

"How did you make the connection with Junior?" Malone asked.

A smile slid across Nick's face. "I wrote an algorithm to scrape the internet for any mention of Junior. Found a couple of pictures with him attending street parties thrown by Olivo's import company. Then a couple of photos with him and several low-level dealers on social media." Nick rolled his eyes and shook his head. "When are these creeps going to learn that you don't brag about criminal activities on Facebook?"

"I hope never," Ian said. "Helps us catch them. I ran Junior's name through our system, and he doesn't have a record. But now that I know about the Olivo connection, I'll get with our drug squad to see what they have on him."

"I'm guessing he's known to them too," Erik said.

Malone could hardly believe what she was hearing. "But what does any of this have to do with my parents' accident? Did they have something to do with this Olivo guy? Was he even in the drug business back then?"

"Yes to being in the drug business at the time of their accident," Nick said. "As to a relationship to your parents, I didn't find any connection. Doesn't mean there isn't one. I just haven't located it. Maybe they're connected through work. I've got a search running for any link between Ground Floor Builders and Flagg Contracting. Not that they are even in the same realm. Flagg does home remodels and Ground Floor is all about commercial buildings. I'll keep after it for you."

Malone smiled at him. "I don't know how to thank you for putting all of your time into this."

"You and Reed are family," Nick said forcefully. "We take care of our own. You need anything else, just let me know."

Malone's heart bloomed under his kindness, and she had to look away before sobbing like a baby over something that most people wouldn't even react to. But she had no family other than Reed. Zero. So it meant the world to her that the Veritas partners had adopted them.

"Did you have any luck enhancing the picture I sent?" Ian asked.

"I have a buddy who's much better at improving video quality," Nick said. "He's working on it, but you should know that we really can't do a whole lot to improve the image. That could be a problem with facial recognition software since it identifies facial landmarks and maps the geometry of the face. Certain items need to be present for it to work well, like the distance between a person's eyes and the distance from forehead to chin. I think we have what we need, but we won't know until we run it against the database."

"Reed's also got someone at the FBI working on it," Malone said.

"Good move. Not that I'd usually respond that way if a client brought in the FBI for something I can handle with the help of a buddy. Not so with facial recognition. The feds are still the pros in this arena, and we need all the help we can get. Let me know if he gets a match before I do."

"Will do," Malone said. "And please let us know the minute you have anything."

Nick nodded. "Keep me updated on your interviews with Junior's parents. If it turns anything up, we can add the details to our search."

"Thanks," Ian said. "If only we had guys as skilled as you working for our agency."

"Yeah," Nick said. "We all flock to the private sector."

"We can't compete with the money you make there," Ian said.

"Hey, it's not the money." Nick grinned. "It's the equipment, baby."

Erik and Nick looked at each other and laughed, but Malone knew they were serious. Not only couldn't public agencies provide anywhere near the salary IT professionals made in the private sector, but budgets didn't stretch to include the state-of-the-art and frequently updated equipment that Malone had seen in Nick's lab.

Nick and Erik said goodbye, and their pictures disappeared from the screen.

"I really am blessed to have such support," she said, closing her laptop. "I don't suppose I could come with you on that interview."

She expected a quick no, but he tilted his head and honestly seemed to be considering it.

"Never mind," she said. "I know you could get in a lot of trouble for bringing me along."

"It's not that," he said. "You came within inches of a killer the other night. If Junior was one of Olivo's men, he could have someone watching Junior's parents, and the fewer people who know you're connected to this investigation, the better."

Ian straddled a chair at Detective Jason Nix's desk. As lead detective in the drug squad, Nix was the person on the squad most likely to know about Junior's involvement in any drug dealings. Ian wasn't surprised at the detective's wrinkled denim shirt with the cuffs rolled up, or the gray-and-silver hair, worn a little too long and scruffy. Both fit with being a member of a squad who at times had to go under-cover and fly incognito as they interacted with suspects on the street.

Nix leaned back in his squeaky chair and linked his hands over the beginning of a middle-age paunch. "So you want to know about Junior Flagg."

Ian nodded. "He was murdered at his class reunion."

"You don't say." Nix's eyebrows rose. "He's been on our radar for a while but the guy managed to stay just the right side of the law at all times, and we were never able to nab him."

"He works for Olivo?"

Nix nodded. "Pretty high up in the organization. We've been watching him for some time, but Olivo taught him well, and he'd kept under the radar. We don't have a single thing that we were able to charge him with."

"Any chance his murder was Olivo's doing?"

"There's no word on the street about them having a falling out, so doesn't seem likely." Nix scratched the silvery five-o'clock shadow on his chin. "There is something going down with Olivo right now, though. He's off his normal pattern. Hasn't been to work for a few days, and his kids aren't at school. He has an eighteen-year-old boy and a sixteen-year-old girl. We can see shadows through the blinds so there's movement in the house, but none of them have been seen outside the house for four days."

Interesting. "Stay-at-home vacation, maybe?"

Nix shook his head. "We called his office, and his assistant said she had to reschedule his calendar, so it wasn't planned."

"I guess this is unusual for him."

"Very. He's quite gregarious and outgoing. He entertains

a lot and attends all of his kids' school functions. And the kids have company most days. The mom is like this super mom who's made her house the place to hang out."

Ian figured if the parents of these kids knew what Olivo really did for a living, they wouldn't be letting their son or daughter hang at the Olivo house. "What do you make of the change?"

Nix shrugged. "Never can predict these guys. But the thing with Olivo is that he's structured his organization so he can live a normal life most of the time, and his guys do all his dirty work for him. It could just be a normal life thing. Could be sick. Someone in the family could be sick. Grandparents died out of state. Something like that."

"What about a threat to him and his family?"

"Would have to be someone with a death wish of their own to threaten him, or worse, threaten his kids. Olivo would have him for breakfast."

"Or gun him down, if it was Junior."

Nix leaned forward. "Yeah, sure, but like I said, nothing on the street about that. I've got feelers out all the time regarding him. We'll see if they produce anything."

Ian thanked Nix and headed out of the office to interview Junior's parents. They lived in a posh area of Forest Park on the west side of the river. Ian had rarely spent any time in that part of the city, so he enjoyed winding up the steep hills with large homes on each side of the road and tried to imagine how the residents left home on the few days when the metro area saw freezing rain or snow. He would want to stay home, but people didn't quit killing each other because of bad weather, so that wasn't an option for him like these residents likely had.

Ian pulled up to the Flaggs's two-story home painted a deep gray. It had multiple roof peaks with shake shingle siding highlighting the front peaks. He parked in the driveway by the garage with carriage style doors and noticed two vehicles inside. Hopefully that meant both parents were home.

He knocked on the front door and stood back to wait. He hated leaving Malone behind, but he'd meant it when he'd said that the fewer people who knew about her connection to Junior's murder the better. A man was dead. Gunned down. Ian didn't want that to happen to her. Thankfully, she had the Nighthawk team with her. Protecting her. Otherwise, Ian wouldn't have been able to leave her house.

The door opened, and Junior's father stared at Ian as he ran a hand through his thick brown hair that had a tint of gray at the temples. Junior had resembled his father, except Junior's hair was blond, and he was a good foot shorter. Ian put Gilbert Sr. in his early to mid-fifties, and he was in great shape for his age. A big man, he had muscles that seemed built in a gym and wore a confidence about him that Junior had lacked.

"Detective." Flagg smiled, not seeming at all worried about the visit. "What brings you here?"

"I have a few questions for you." Ian tried to sound light-hearted. "Would it be okay if I came in?"

"Of course. Whatever you need." Flagg stepped back and led the way through a massive two-story foyer with wrought iron railings and gleaming tile floors to a family room with equally tall ceilings. Muted gray paint covered the walls, and various shades of blue accented the room in the furnishings. The place looked more like a magazine picture than a room where people lived every day.

Flagg gestured at a sofa that faced another matching sofa. "Can I get you anything to drink?"

"Thank you, but I'm fine." Ian smiled. "If your wife is home, it would be great if she could join us."

"Let me get her." He stepped out of the room and called, "Karen. The detective is back and wants you to join us."

Silence filled the cavernous space until the *clip-clip-clip* of high-heeled shoes came toward them. Karen wore jeans and a black sweater, both designer. Her blond chin-length hair was immaculately combed, but her mascara was smudged.

She perched on the edge of the sofa across from Ian. It was easy to see that Junior got his diminutive stature from her. "How can I help you?"

"First, let me say again how sorry I am for your loss," Ian said.

She gave a firm nod, but her chin quivered.

"We appreciate that," Flagg said, sounding sincere as he leaned against the fireplace mantle.

Ian decided if he could help ease their grief he would. "Before we get started, I wanted to tell you that the autopsy has been completed. The cause of death didn't change, of course, but the medical examiner learned that Junior had stage three pancreatic cancer."

"Cancer!" Karen grabbed hold of her blouse.

"But he didn't say anything." Flagg frowned.

"Could this be what he was trying to tell me about?" Karen worried her lower lip. "Would it have been terminal?"

Ian nodded. "The ME seemed to think so."

"Then he would've died anyway," Flagg said, his tone flat and unreadable.

Karen flashed her gaze to her husband. "But we would've had more time with him."

"He didn't suffer this way," Ian said.

Karen nodded. "A positive, I guess."

"I was hoping, now that you've had some time to process Junior's death, that you might've thought of someone who might have wanted to kill him."

Karen shook her head hard.

"I have no idea." Flagg sat next to his wife and took her hand.

She looked at his hand in horror, as if she wanted to whip it free. But she remained frozen and stiff in her seat.

"I've been looking for employment records for Junior but can't find any," Ian said. "Can you tell me where he worked?"

Karen opened her mouth to speak, but Flagg jumped in. "He did odd jobs for cash. Didn't make much. He was a disappointment, for sure. But I figured he would sort himself out and come back to work for the company."

"Sort out?" Ian asked.

Flagg clenched his teeth for a moment. "He started working for me right out of high school, and I wanted him to take over for me. He did all right for many years, but then he got a wild hair and decided that he didn't want to take over. He wanted to be a beekeeper, if you can believe it." Flagg rolled his eyes. "Who does that? Who? You can't make any money at that. He decided he was going to sell the business after I retired and take his inheritance. I couldn't have that, so I told him to go take care of the bees and see if he could live on that, figuring he'd be back in a month or two."

"But he never did come back," Karen said, her tone sad. "And he didn't raise the bees."

Flagg shook his head. "I must've spoiled the kid too much."

At that, Karen jerked her hand away. "Spoiled. Is that what you think?" Her voice rose, and her breathing came hard and fast. "Because that's not how I saw it. Not at all."

Flagg faced his wife, his eyes wide and intense. "I gave him everything. Clothes. Electronics. Cars. His condo that I'd paid a fortune to remodel. Whatever his *little* heart desired."

"See, there you go." Karen fisted her hands on her knees. "He's dead, and you're still mocking his size. It wasn't his fault he was small, and you never let him live it down. Never."

"I didn't—"

She flashed up a hand. "You can't deny it, Gilbert, so don't even try. Your belittling and constant criticism killed him."

"Now, wait a minute." Flagg's voice shifted from kind to angry in a heartbeat.

"It's true. He cut ties with us because of you," she said. "And he had to find some way to live. You forced him to turn to the drugs." She clapped a hand over her mouth.

They both swung their gazes to Ian and looked at him with surprise, as if they'd forgotten he was in the room.

"Drugs?" Ian asked, when he knew full well that Junior worked with Olivo.

"It's nothing." Gilbert's words carried vehemence, but then he relaxed his posture and forced a smile.

Karen didn't say a word.

"Karen?" Ian asked.

"Junior started selling drugs," she blurted out.

"Karen," her husband warned.

"I won't be silenced anymore." She lifted her hand again but let it fall as her face creased with guilt. "Maybe it's my fault he's dead. If I had stood up to you, maybe he'd still be alive."

"Nonsense," Flagg said, his tone patronizing. "You couldn't do anything for him. He was destined for this path."

"You're wrong, as usual, and it's time the truth came out." Karen shifted her gaze to Ian. "Apparently, Junior was good at selling drugs. He moved up the chain and was a right-hand man to the boss." She swung her face to Flagg. "Which he could've been for you, if you'd only given him a chance and time and encouraged him to do the beekeeping thing on the side instead of mocking him."

"Do you know who he worked for?" Ian asked.

"A man named Tirone Olivo."

"Are you sure?"

Karen nodded. "I tried to ignore Junior's lifestyle. Flashy car. Nice clothes. Lots of dining out. Luxury vacations. I knew he had to be doing something illegal to have all of that. I confronted him about a year ago. It took me that long to work up the courage. When I did, he told me everything. He was proud of what he'd accomplished and was glad to finally be able to tell someone about it."

"Proud?" Flagg scoffed. "If either of you had told me, I would've turned him in. We don't break the law, Karen. Ever."

"Which is why he didn't say a word to you, and I didn't tell you until yesterday." Karen gritted her teeth. "But you knew something was up. You had to."

"Did you ever meet Olivo?" Ian asked Karen to keep her talking.

"Once." Karen shuddered. "He was quite charming and seemed normal, but there was a dangerous vibe underneath it all. Junior told me he was a ruthless, terrible man, and he wouldn't let Junior go when he wanted to take a break."

"Was this recent?" Ian asked.

She nodded. "Something spooked Junior, and he said he had to fix it. Could've been the cancer, too, that set him on the path he was on when he died."

Now, Ian thought they were getting somewhere. "This thing. He said it had to do with Olivo?"

She shook her head. "He just said he discovered something that he had to fix, and that he was sorry, but it had to come out. That it wouldn't be good for the family. So I figured he did something with Olivo, and he planned to go to the cops, and it would all make the news."

"Did he come to you people?" Flagg looked hopeful.

"There's no report of him filing a complaint or communicating with our department in any way," Ian said, wondering. Did the thing Junior had mentioned cause his death? Did it have something to do with why Olivo had hunkered down in his home with his family?

"Then I don't know what he was up to," Karen said.

Ian turned his attention to Flagg. "Before Junior died, he spoke with one of our classmates whose parents had died in a car crash in the nineties. He told her that the crash wasn't an accident, and if she wanted to know about it, to meet him in the room. She did, but before he told her anything, he was shot."

"Do you think these parents were involved with this Olivo thug too, and he killed them?" Karen asked.

"Perhaps," Ian said, but he doubted they had any involvement with drugs. Still, he couldn't rule that out. "The classmate has just moved back into her parents' old home, and I'm wondering if that somehow triggered Junior's comment. Her parents were Lewis and Joanna Rice. Do those names ring a bell?"

"No." Flagg paused, eyes narrowed. "No. I don't believe I've ever heard of them."

"Me either," Karen said. "And I have no idea how Junior knew about them."

"You should know," Flagg said, sounding solemn. "Our son had very low self-esteem and had a habit of embellishing things to make himself seem more important. He had trouble getting girlfriends too. I wouldn't be surprised if he was just making up the story to find a way to connect with this woman."

It sounded like Flagg contributed to Junior's low self-esteem, as his wife had claimed.

Karen fired a testy look at her husband. "You're so quick to say he was wrong, but maybe he wasn't." She shifted to lock gazes with Ian. "Whatever you need to find this killer that I can provide, it's yours. Anything. I will see that my son's death is avenged."

9

_____

Ian was once again ensconced in the back seat of the Nighthawk Security vehicle next to Malone, heading out to Peck's house. He updated the others on his interview with Gilbert Flagg. As he finished, his phone chimed, and he looked at the text. "Blake found a friend of Junior's. Name's Timothy Richardson. He wasn't in our class. Sound familiar?"

Malone shook her head. "Did Blake talk to him?"

Ian nodded and read the rest of the text. "He claims not to know about Junior's job. Thought he was an importer. They met in a bar a couple of years ago. Basically, just hung out to watch sports and drink beer."

"Not a real lead then."

"Blake will have Nick do a deep dive, so we'll see." Ian moved on to his emails and read one from the firearms examiner. "Interesting. The gun used to kill Junior only had your prints on it."

"How's that interesting?" Malone asked. "It's what you'd expect with the shooter wearing gloves."

"That's not the interesting part. The gun was used in a gangland slaying a few years ago."

"I don't believe it," Malone said, eyeing Ian. "Could Junior be the killer from back then? I mean, you tell me Junior's not only a drug dealer, but high up in his organization. Now this? Junior never struck me as the kind of guy to have the courage to sell drugs much less be brutal enough to move up the chain or kill anyone."

"I didn't think so either," Ian said. "But his mother was certain about the drugs, and in an odd sort of way, even proud of his advancement."

Aiden glanced in the rearview mirror. "Are you thinking his murder is related to Olivo?"

"I was leaning that way, and now that we know the gun was used in a drug slaying, it seems more likely that Olivo or a rival is behind killing Junior than it being connected to Malone."

"You'd think if the intent was to set Malone up, that the gun wouldn't have a history," Aiden said.

"Maybe it was a spur-of-the-moment decision." Brendan looked between the seats at them. "The shooter saw an opportunity to deflect suspicion from his organization for a while by handing the gun to Malone."

"That's what I was thinking," Ian said. "But even if it's not connected to Malone, we need to solve the murder of her parents too."

"That's important," Clay said. "No doubt about that, but we need to find this shooter first. If finding Malone in the room was a surprise to him, he could be rethinking things in the light of day and be worried she might ID him."

"I'll text the latest info to Nick," Ian said. "Could help in the facial recognition search. Then I'll call Nix at the drug squad to see if he remembers the earlier shootout where the gun was used."

Ian turned his attention to his phone and sent the text to Nick but had to leave a message with Nix. Ian wished he were closer to the precinct so he could meet with the guy in person again, but Peck's property was coming up, and Ian needed to focus on that right now.

The Veritas van was already parked near the house, but no sign of the people from the state lab. Ian glanced at his watch. Only eleven forty-five. With fifteen minutes to kill as he waited, Ian would use that time to look the car over again.

Aiden parked behind Emory's vehicle, and she slid out from the passenger's seat. Blake got out from the driver's side.

Emory slid her hand into the crook of Blake's arm. "I brought Blake along in case we need him for something."

"Translated, she wanted company on the drive out here." Blake laughed.

Emory grinned at her husband. "I have never been able to fool this guy. Not from the moment I met him."

"Actually, you did." Blake looked at the others. "She has a twin sister who was missing a few years ago. I was a sheriff back then and tasked with finding Cait. I showed up at Veritas and almost fell over when I saw Emory."

"I didn't know I had a twin," Emory said. "We were separated at birth. So I almost fell over, too, once we figured things out by looking at Cait's DNA that Blake brought to have analyzed."

"That's some story," Ian said.

"You don't know the half of it." Blake chuckled.

Ian heard a vehicle turning into the drive, and he spun to see the state van pull in.

"Looks like we're all here," Ian said. "I'll go tell Peck and get his permission to head to the barn."

Malone stepped over to him. "I'll come with you in case he needs convincing."

Emory's eyebrows rose above her black glasses. "I thought he already agreed."

"He did," Ian said. "But he seems like the kind of guy who might change his mind on a whim."

"Then by all means, go." Emory made a shooing motion with her hands. "I don't want our trip out here to be a waste."

"It's not a waste to spend quality time in the middle of a workday with your spouse," Blake said. "And I even bought you a burger on the way."

Ian smiled at their bantering as he and Malone walked to the house.

"They're a cute couple," Malone said.

Ian nodded but didn't want to get into a discussion about couples. It could lead to the growing feelings between him and Malone when he had a job to do. He knocked on the door and stood back, enjoying the soft breeze playing over his skin and the warm sun on his face.

Peck answered the door in his mobility scooter. "I see you got quite the group here."

"Are we good to go out to the garage, or do you want to take us out there?" Ian asked.

Peck tilted his head. "Don't mind you going out there, but I'd like to watch those CSI people at work."

"Okay, sure," Ian said, surprised at the older man's interest. "As long as you stay on the sidelines."

He frowned.

"Don't worry, Mr. Peck," Malone said. "I'm sidelined too. We can keep each other company."

He smiled up at Malone. "Then lead the way, missy."

They started for the garage, and Ian waved the team on. They would want to move their vans closer to the building to keep from hauling equipment. He got the garage door open and waited for the two vans to back in and park.

Ian introduced his team to Peck, and then Deborah from the state lab introduced herself and Vance, the criminalist. He nodded but didn't seem very interested in the group.

Ian liked that about Vance. He was there to do a job, and he was focused on his mission. Didn't mean Ian wouldn't take a look at the car again while he was here. He trusted the techs, but he trusted his own eye better for finding things that could relate to a homicide.

"Let me get photos before anyone enters the garage." Vance had already slipped into the Tyvek suit, booties, and gloves, and he slung a camera strap over his head before moving toward the garage.

Ian went to the box of gloves and booties on the back of the van, then stood next to Malone and Peck off to the side of the open door. He watched Vance snap his photos.

"Be sure to get close-ups of the tie rods when you're done with the wide-angle shots," Emory called out.

"Not my first rodeo," Vance yelled back. After he'd taken his wide-angle pictures of the car, he looked back. "You can begin now, but don't touch anything before I shoot it."

Ian looked at Emory and Deborah. "I'll do a quick search of the vehicle again in case I missed anything the other day. Let me know if I'm in your way."

The DNA scientists nodded, and he slipped on the booties and gloves.

Ian stayed well away from Vance, who squatted by one of the questionable tires. He angled his camera but frowned, then lay down on his back to scoot under the car.

The convertible top had been retracted, allowing Ian to lean over the crushed driver's side door, where it was obvious that no one could have survived the mangled wreckage. He felt around the leather seat that had been pushed into the back. He slid his hands in the crease but didn't find anything. He moved on to the back seat. Same thing.

Ian quickly slipped around the vehicle before Deborah or Emory swooped in. He checked the creases in the back seat, then on the passenger side and found nothing. The seat and floor mat had been shifted back, so he lifted the mat and felt under the seat. His fingers touched something, and he pulled out a torn off slice of paper. The edge looked as if it had been ripped from a thread-bound book, not a notepad. Before he did anything more with the paper, even turn it over to look for any writing, he called out to Vance to take a photo.

He stomped over there. "What do you have?"

Ian explained.

Vance sighed. "I would've found that in due time."

"I know," Ian said but didn't apologize for looking.

Vance snapped pictures. He grabbed a plastic tent number and scale from his bag and set them next to the paper and took additional pictures. "I'll get an evidence bag."

Ian flipped the paper over. In neat writing someone had printed the words *Detective Wisniewski 12:30*. Ian took his own picture, then left the garage to talk to Malone.

He motioned for her to join him out of Peck's earshot. "I remember the accident report said your parents crashed around eleven-thirty a.m., but do you know where they were headed?"

"No one knew where they were going. Just that they were heading west."

"Any chance they could've been on their way to see a detective?" Ian held out his phone to display the photo he'd taken.

Her eyes flashed wide. "If they were, it might make more sense that someone ended their lives to stop them."

As it neared the dinner hour, Malone climbed into the Nighthawk SUV with Ian and the Byrd brothers for the drive home. Her stomach was tied in knots. It had been a good news, bad news kind of day, and she was letting the bad news win. On the positive side, Emory had located DNA on the tie rods. On the negative side, her parents might've been on the way to see a detective when they died, and her mind was racing with reasons why they needed to see one.

Had someone been threatening them? Harassing them? Had they been afraid for their lives? Terrified even?

She knew how that felt. Sort of, anyway. Through her clients. Battered women who wanted to protect themselves and their children from monstrous men who loved to pummel others. As the miles rolled past, the memories of the fear in those women's eyes just kept battering Malone, and her gut was on fire with acid.

Please, please don't let my parents have been fearing for their lives. I can't bear the thought of the people I loved most in the world being in such a situation.

But the note was written in her mother's handwriting, and Detective Wisniewski did exist. While they'd waited for the forensics to be processed on the vehicle, Ian had made some calls to ask about the detective. He finally learned that the guy had worked at the Washington County Sheriff's Department, the agency that patrolled the area where her parents' home was located. The detective was retired now, and the sheriff's office didn't have a current address for him, so Ian was trying to get the detective's details.

His phone chimed, and he looked at the screen. "It's Nick."

Ian answered. "I'm with Malone and a few of the Byrd brothers. Mind if I put you on speaker?"

"Go for it. They'll want to hear this." His adrenaline-packed voice came over the phone even before Ian tapped his speaker button.

"Okay, go ahead," Ian said.

"My search to connect Ground Floor Builders with Flagg Contracting was a bust. I didn't find any projects they worked on together or any connection between the company executives and Flagg. And both companies have solid reputations."

"I didn't think you'd find a connection, even a legit one," Ian said. "Two different construction worlds. Plus, I might not like Flagg's personality, but he seems like he's on the up and up."

"That's my take," Nick said. "I can keep the search running indefinitely, but I wouldn't pin my focus on this connection."

"Okay," Ian said. "What else do you have?"

"Your shooter's name."

"Way to bury the lead," Ian grumbled.

"Who is it?" Malone leaned closer to the phone.

"Mickey Snipes. He's Olivo's other lieutenant."

"How did you find him?" Ian asked.

"We got a few responses to the partial facial recognition photo, so when you texted me the info about Junior's connection to Olivo, I added those details to my algorithms. Snipes came up and looks like he's our guy." Nick sounded so proud of himself, and he should be. "I'll text photos for you to look at as soon as I hang up."

"We still don't have a way to place him at the murder scene," Ian said, sounding discouraged. "At least not a way that will get us an arrest warrant. Our best hope is connecting him to the other murder where the gun was first used."

"I thought about that, too, so I cross-referenced the

information on the gun," Nick said. "Snipes knew the guy who was taken out, but I didn't find a strong connection."

"I've got a call in to the drug squad for them to locate the old murder file for me," Ian said.

"Get back to me if there's anything you learn that might help my searches," Nick said. "And after you look at the pictures of Snipes, let me know if you don't think he's your guy, and I'll keep searching."

"Thanks, man." Ian ended the call. His phone dinged. "Pictures of Snipes from Nick."

He held his phone out to Malone.

Her stomach clenched as a mug shot of a white male with dark hair cut short, a broad nose, and a long narrow face filled the screen. "The shape of his face is right. I need to see a full body picture."

Ian swiped through a few more closeup photos to a shot where Snipes stood outside a local bar, his thumb hooked into his jeans.

"Oh my gosh." She pointed at his hand. "That's what I've been forgetting. He has a birthmark in the shape of a heart. It's so small you can almost miss it. But I saw it when he put the gun in my hand. Zoom in so we can see if I'm right."

Ian pinched his fingers over the photo, revealing the birthmark.

She grabbed onto Ian's arm. "It's him. Nick's right. He's the shooter."

"Yeah, we got him all right." Ian smiled. "And you can testify to seeing the birthmark."

She nodded. "Which means once you arrest Snipes, I could be out of danger."

Ian's smile fell. "Unless Olivo wants to help out his lieutenant and stop you from testifying. That could escalate the danger."

Malone's heart sank.

"Sorry," Ian said. "I had to tell you the truth no matter how it hurts."

"I know, but you could've maybe given me a few minutes of peace." She attempted to laugh but couldn't really force one out.

Ian took her hand. Shocked, she looked at his face, then glanced at Clay to see if he noticed. He had a knowing look on his face, so yeah, he'd noticed all right. But Ian didn't seem to care. Which touched her heart. He was thinking of her, not the investigation. Not the Byrd brothers. Just her.

She looked back at him and smiled in earnest this time. He clasped her hand tighter. They didn't say anything, just sat linked together for the remainder of the drive. Even when Aiden pulled into the driveway, Ian kept holding on.

He leaned closer to her. "I'll be taking off to get an arrest warrant for Snipes. If we can find him, we'll bring him in."

She nodded, wishing he didn't have to go. She wanted him to come inside and see where this handholding led. Which was precisely why it was a good reason for him to leave.

But she couldn't let him go on such a dangerous mission without letting him know she cared.

"Be careful," she whispered and clung to his hand. "I don't want to lose you."

10

Near the SERT tactical van, Ian pinned his focus to the front door of Snipes's small bungalow in an older area of the city where homes were in need of repair, Londyn doing the same thing next to him. The Special Emergency Reaction Team commander knocked on the worn wood with flaking white paint. He was dressed in all black gear with tactical vest, helmet, and face shield, just like the rest of his team. They held assault rifles and stood at the ready, should they get a negative response from Snipes.

Ian wanted to make the arrest himself, Londyn too, but department policy required SERT be called in for high-risk warrants where the suspect was probably armed or was believed to be involved in a criminal act like murder.

"Police!" the commander shouted. "We need to speak with you, Mr. Snipes."

As Ian and Londyn waited for him to answer, Ian glanced at the SERT members positioned in strategic locations on the property, though he couldn't see the ones stationed at the back door.

"He's running," the commander called out.

No. He wasn't getting away. Ian bolted from his location.

The bulky vest got in his way, and he tugged it down as he ran. Gun drawn, he charged across the lawn and down the side yard.

The side door banged open, taking out the SERT officer positioned there. Unarmed, Snipes bolted toward the back fence. Ian kicked into gear.

Pounding over brown grass. Snipes moving fast. Faster! The worn wooden fence loomed ahead. If Snipes made it over the top, they could lose him.

Ian couldn't let that happen.

Snipes clasped the top of the boards. Ian had no choice. No choice at all.

He launched himself into the air. Grabbed Snipes by the shoulders. Jerked him down to the ground, dirt pillowing around them.

Dragging in air, Ian quickly got to his feet and put a knee in Snipes's back. "Mickey Snipes, I'm arresting you for resisting arrest and the murder of Gilbert Flagg Jr."

"Didn't kill no one," Snipes grumbled. "And no one said anything about arrest to me. I was just going for a walk in my backyard."

Ian didn't respond to the guy's comment. Whatever Ian said could be used in court by Snipes's attorney. Being part of Olivo's tribe, Ian could bet the attorney would be highly paid and very talented. Ian slapped cuffs on Snipes's wrists, spotting the heart-shaped birthmark.

He was their guy. Ian couldn't wait to tell Malone.

He swept his hands over the guy's body, surprised when he didn't find a gun or knife. No weapon at all. Ian didn't know why the guy had run, but he at least didn't carry a weapon and make things worse for himself.

Ian drew Snipes to his feet and turned him around to read him his rights.

"We have a warrant for your arrest and one to search

your house and vehicles." Ian took the documents from his pocket and put them in Snipes's shirt pocket "If there's anything you'd like to tell us, now would be a good time."

"Yeah, don't leave the toilet seat up." He laughed hard, but it sounded forced.

Ian gestured at the SERT officer who'd been knocked down and was now standing nearby with the commander. "My friends here will be taking you down to county lockup."

The officer stepped forward and put his hand on Snipes's shoulder, the other on his cuffed hands, then started him moving forward as Londyn joined them.

"This's no skin off my nose," Snipes called over his shoulder. "I'll be out in a blink of an eye. You'll see. Back out in a flash."

"He could be right," Ian said to Londyn. "Olivo will likely send an attorney to at least try to bail the guy out."

"I don't appreciate you going cowboy on me." The commander marched up to Ian. "We're here for a reason."

"He would've scaled the fence," Ian said.

"Then we would've scaled it after him." The commander lifted his face shield. "Know that this will go in my report."

"You do what you have to do." Ian made a mental note to tell his LT to expect blowback from this arrest. "Did your men clear the house?"

The commander nodded. "It's all yours."

He stormed away.

"You're going to get a hand slap," Londyn said.

"As long as that's all it is, I'm good." Ian changed his focus to the house. "Let's see what we can find inside that will make everyone forget about me failing to follow procedure."

Londyn headed for the door that Snipes had bolted out of, and Ian followed her.

They entered through a tiny kitchen with old cabinets

and stained countertops. The room smelled like garlic and onions, and the scent carried through a small dining room and into a hallway.

"I'll take his bedroom." Ian pointed down the hallway. "You take the family room."

They split, and Ian passed a small bedroom and reached another one set up as an office. He paused to step inside and look at the papers on the desk. The usual bills and junk mail were stacked on one end. He put on gloves and flipped through the envelopes but didn't find anything of interest. He wanted to look at the laptop, but he wouldn't wake it up and change the state of the machine, which might interfere with evidence. He needed to get the computer techs out there as soon as possible.

The closet was empty, so he moved on, walking past a bathroom straight out of the forties with turquoise wall tile and black and white floor tiles. Next up was a larger, but still small, bedroom at the end of the hall. The king-sized bed took up most of the room, and the covers were rumpled in a bunch at the foot of the mattress.

The room held a tall dresser and an old wooden chair. Clothes were piled on the chair. Ian photographed the pile of clothes, then lifted the top purple shirt and a pair of worn blue jeans to reveal a black shirt and pants. On the floor by the chair, were a pair of leather boots, worn but polished, just as Malone had described.

Ian took pictures again, lifted the pants, and searched the pockets. He found a folded piece of paper. He opened it, and his heart leapt.

"You'll want to see this, Londyn," he yelled.

When she arrived in the room, he held out the paper, and she smiled.

"The reunion flyer." She pointed at the clothing. "Looks like we've got the connection to Junior that we need."

"I'll call forensics in, and we'll get these items logged as evidence," Ian said. "They can process it all for GSR. We really could have enough to put this guy away."

~

Ian hadn't expected Snipes to talk in their interview, but before Ian had even said a word, Snipes asked for an attorney. Snipes had the attorney's number memorized, forcing Londyn and Ian to step away without even asking a question.

"We need to get an in-person lineup going for Malone to take a look at this guy," Ian said to Londyn as they approached her desk. "She can't ID their faces, but we can have them walk for her and say what the shooter said to Junior before he plugged him. Plus, she can look for the birthmark."

"I'll talk to the lawyer when he arrives and try to interview Snipes again." Londyn frowned. "He probably won't say a word. No use in you wasting your time here. And I'm sure the attorney will drag out scheduling the lineup and make us wait until tomorrow so he can confer with Olivo first."

A suspect's attorney needed to be present for in-person lineups to prevent bias or improper procedures by the officer in charge.

"Seems likely. Let's plan to do it first thing tomorrow. After all that's happened today, Malone could use a break."

"You've got a thing for her." Londyn cast an appraising look at him, one that he'd seen in the interview room.

He honestly felt like a suspect who was guilty of some crime, but his only crime was caring about one of his witnesses. "I'm not saying I do, but if I did? What then?"

The depth of convictions that Londyn was known for in

the department rang loud and clear in her expression. "Then I'd have to keep a better watch on you to make sure you don't do or say something you might regret."

He'd wondered if she'd report him or support him, and now he knew what Londyn Steele was made of. He'd be glad to work with her again. "Thanks for having my back."

"Anytime." She smiled. "I've got the last of my interview photos ready to send to you. I'll do that now."

Ian thought about the interviews and how they fit in the investigation at this point. "Since Snipes wasn't in our class, you wouldn't have interviewed him at the hotel."

"Correct."

"We've got a lot on Snipes but not irrefutable proof that he's our guy. Was there anyone you talked to who you like for the murder?"

"There are people who I haven't talked to yet, but there was no one in the list of men I interviewed." Londyn's phone dinged, and she dug it from her jacket pocket. "Well lookie here. Junior's phone records."

"That's good news." Ian worked hard to let it erase his disappointment with Snipes clamming up.

"You want me to work on these records or interview the final male guests?"

"Phone records." They seemed more likely to lead them to a direct connection between Snipes and Junior.

"I'll get started." Her eyes sparkled with excitement. "And if you want, I'll request Snipes's records too."

"Excellent." Her enthusiasm was contagious, lifting his spirits. "Let me know what you find."

"Of course." She dropped into her chair.

He crossed the room to his desk and took a seat to call forensics. First, he got the criminalist on the phone who'd handled Snipes's clothing.

"Like you thought, we found GSR on the shirt, pants, and boots," the criminalist said.

"Any touch DNA?" Ian asked.

"We have samples, and I'll personally deliver them to the state lab today."

Ian hated that they didn't do DNA in-house, but the state lab was the only agency that ran DNA for law enforcement in the area. Thankfully, they had multiple locations including one on the east side of the Portland metro area.

"Let me know once you drop it off, and I'll try to get it bumped up the priority list."

"That would be great."

Ian didn't know if he would be able to cut the DNA processing line that always existed, but murder trumped most everything, so he was hopeful. "What about the boots? Find anything there."

"A trace of mulch."

Ian explained that Sierra had found a boot print and cedar mulch at the hotel.

The criminalist didn't speak for some time, and when he did, his tone, had deepened and turned terse. "Have her call me."

He obviously didn't like that Ian was using Veritas, but too bad. "Anything else I should know about?"

"We located several weapons and ammo. Not the murder weapon, of course, as you already have that, but the lab will run them to see if they connect to any unsolved murders."

"Let me know what you find."

The criminalist promised to do so and ended the call.

Ian looked up to see Detective Nix crossing the bullpen toward him, and Ian sat back to wait for the guy to reach his desk.

"You called me." Nix took a seat and leaned the chair back on two legs.

Ian updated the detective on Snipes and that they'd learned that the gun had been used in a prior shooting. "I know homicide would've investigated, but I was hoping you remembered that investigation, and I could get the drug squad's take on it."

"Snipes, huh?" Nix cocked an eyebrow. "We've had our eye on him a long time, but he's part of Olivo's team, and he's just as careful."

"Do you remember the shooting?"

"Like it was yesterday." Nix frowned. "Took place in a residential area, and a six-year-old child was killed. But none of Olivo's guys were on the radar for this shooting. That includes Snipes."

"Ballistics don't lie," Ian said. "Could be Snipes got the gun from someone else who did the shooting back then."

"Very possible. We didn't have any suspects. It was a drive by, and no one saw the car. Or if they did, they were too afraid to say so. The bullets and slugs didn't carry any fingerprints or DNA." Nix shook his head. "We're dealing with much smarter criminals these days. TV shows and movies have taught them how to avoid arrest. Guys like Snipes and Olivo wear gloves when loading and handling guns. They know how to not get caught and have been doing it for years. It's actually surprising Snipes used a dirty gun."

"He could've gotten it from someone he trusted who told him it was clean."

"That's the only thing that makes sense." Nix gritted his teeth. "And if that's the case, once Snipes and Olivo learn that it was used in the earlier shooting, the guy who provided the gun is going to wind up dead, too, and you'll have another murder investigation on your hands."

~

Malone had been waiting for hours for Ian to return and update her on the investigation, but all she'd gotten was a text saying he was delayed. She couldn't sit around and do nothing, so she changed into her old jeans and a T-shirt and grabbed a hammer to swing away at the half wall by the front door. She needed to get her frustrations from the day out of her system.

She understood why the wall was there. It created an entryway instead of leaving an open room to walk straight into. The wall had existed when her family had moved in, but her dad hadn't liked it, and he'd started to take it out.

He'd ripped off chucks of drywall, but he immediately attached a fresh sheet of drywall over the hole. Apparently, there wasn't flooring under the wall, and he had to find matching flooring before he went any further. He knew it could take some time, and he didn't want to leave the wall open during that time.

He died before he found the wood, and contractors had come in to seam and tape the drywall her dad had installed. She wouldn't have the same problem. She'd already found a floor refinisher who could piece in matching wood and refinish it all. She would take the wall out now in her father's honor.

She slammed the hammer into the sheetrock, the crunch satisfying. She jerked the hammer out and swung a few more times. Her doorbell rang, stopping her mid-swing. She ran a hand through her hair and went to the peephole.

Ian stood waiting on the stoop. Of course he would arrive just after she changed into clothing not fit for public. He was talking to Drake, who'd relieved Clay.

She unlocked and opened the door, the cold night air rushing in and sending a shiver over her body. She stepped back for Ian to enter.

"Taking your frustrations out on the wall, I see." He grinned.

She laughed and turned her attention to Drake. "You warm enough out there?"

"Been colder," he said.

"Let me know if you want something warm to drink." She smiled at him and closed the door.

"I really appreciate them being here for you when I can't be," Ian said.

"Me too, but there haven't been any signs that I'm in danger, and I hate to keep putting them out."

"I assure you, they don't mind."

"How do you know?"

"Because they think like me. If losing a bit of sleep or being cold keeps a person safe, then we're glad to do it." He smiled at her again. "And I know you understand that too because I've heard you're the same way with your clients."

"Sure, if a client needed me to step up, I would. But honestly, I hire people like Nighthawk to do security for me." She chuckled.

He laughed with her, and she loved the sound of it bouncing off the walls of her home. She almost took a step over to him to rest a hand on his arm but came to her senses. "How about you? Want something warm to drink?"

"What do you have?"

"Coffee, tea, hot chocolate, cider."

"Hot chocolate sounds good."

She spun and went to the kitchen to take out a cherished recipe from the box on the counter. "This is my mom's recipe. She kept all of our favorites in this box, and I grabbed it before we left. I'm so thankful it was never misplaced or stolen."

Ian sat on a barstool. "Not likely something that would bring big bucks on the black market."

She thought about it.

"You look puzzled," Ian said. "Did I say something wrong?"

"It wasn't only things of value that disappeared in foster care." The memories assaulted her, and she hurried to the cabinet by the island. "Other kids were often mean and destroyed things out of spite. As an adult, I understand they were just lashing out. Maybe they'd lost something important, and it helped them cope by destroying something someone else loved."

He reached out to take her hand. "I'm so sorry you had to go through that."

She didn't move. The connection felt good. "Don't feel bad for me. It was the path God had for me, and my struggles made me who I am today. So much good is coming from my understanding of being orphaned. I can relate to the homeless teens I work with in a way I couldn't have if I hadn't experienced the loss."

"But I don't want to see you hurting. Not ever. I..." He tightened his fingers around hers and looked at her hand. "I've come to care for you. Deeply. Beyond my high school crush."

"You." She jerked her hand back. "You had a crush on *me* in high school?"

"Is that so hard to believe?" He leaned back against the counter, looking at home in her house.

"You didn't let on at all."

"But I was there, right? Where you were? Events, clubs. Ever since Junior assaulted you, I thought it was my job to be your defender." He reached for her waist and drew her to stand between his knees. "Corny, I know. But I still feel that way."

She didn't know what to say, so she just looked at him.

"You're probably way too independent to need a defender." He reached up and tucked a strand of hair behind her ear.

She wasn't too independent to love his touch. She wanted to place her hands on his shoulders, move closer. She swallowed and remained where she was standing. "I like the thought of a defender. Of you having been there watching over me in case I needed you again." She held his gaze. "But you had to know I was mooning over you. Why didn't you tell me how you felt?"

He leaned back but kept his hands on her waist. "I don't think I'd be any good at a serious relationship, and you always struck me as a serious relationship kind of girl."

"Okay, that's a lot to unpack, but I'll start with the relationship. Have you had a bad experience?"

"Nothing serious, but I also haven't had good role models. My parents have been married for thirty-seven years, which, for Hollywood, is noteworthy, but for them it's all about how they can band together to make the most money. Then spend it as fast as they make it. It's more like a business partnership than anything."

"But no love?"

He shook his head in sad resignation. "They lead separate lives most of the time. They've both been having affairs for as long as I can remember. They don't come right out and talk about them, but they don't bother to hide them either."

Her heart broke for him. She'd at least had six years of being raised by parents who loved each other. "You're right. Not good role models, but you recognize that and know you want the real deal."

"But can I do it, or will I fall into the kind of relationship my parents had because that's what I've known?"

"I don't know you all that well, but I do know you have a sense of commitment and know right from wrong. You're a believer who seems to live your faith, and God provides good instruction in the Bible on love." She gave in and rested her hands on his shoulders. "I know you would be a great husband, and any woman would be lucky to have you."

"I'd like to think you're right, but old habits die hard, as do old beliefs."

She didn't know what else to say to help him, but she would think about it later and try to find a way to help him. "So tell me why you think I'm a serious kind of woman?"

"You have a depth to you, a depth I don't think I could ever fully unearth. You don't seem frivolous and easily swayed. And you're serious in your approach to life. So, why wouldn't you be in your love life too?"

She shook her head. "My love life? I don't have one. Never have."

"You?" His eyebrows rose, tempting her to run a finger over them. "I can't believe that. You're so gorgeous, guys have to be hitting on you all the time."

"Thank you for the compliment." She resisted fanning herself from the warmth building from his kind words and closeness. "I get hit on at times, but when I've kissed guys, the thing with Junior always comes to mind. Maybe I'm not as over it as I claim to be."

"I could try it," he said.

"Try what?"

"Kissing you." A mischievous look glinted in his eyes. "Like an experiment. You know, for your mental health."

"I don't know."

"If you want me to stop, you just have to tell me."

"I'm not really..."

He stood and drew her closer. "I've dreamed of this. Many, many times."

The passion in his eyes was her undoing, and she didn't

resist as his lips came down to lock on hers. The revulsion she usually felt didn't come. Instead, pure joy flooded her body. She snaked her arms around his neck and deepened the kiss. She could do this forever and not come up for air.

His phone rang, breaking the moment. He drew back and glared at his phone on the counter.

"It's Londyn." He blew out a breath. "I should take it."

He picked it up. "Hold on for a second, Londyn."

He muted his phone and focused on her. "Well? Revolting?"

"No." She smiled. "Kissing you, Ian Blair, was everything I ever imagined. Everything."

11

———

Nerves peppered Malone as she waited in the homicide bullpen the next morning for the suspect lineup to begin. Sure, she didn't want to see the man who'd ruthlessly gunned Junior down in front of her, but more than that, she was nervous about seeing Ian for the first time since last night. She touched her lips. Remembered the kiss. She'd slept very little. Maybe she'd feared that if she went to sleep the kiss would somehow become a dream and not be real.

But it *had* been real, very real, and her reaction was just as authentic. For years she'd kissed the wrong guys. Frogs. And here was her prince. Ready to make things right and good for her. Except he wasn't ready. He was beaten down under years of having dysfunctional parents. Malone may have lost her parents early in life, but she'd at least witnessed great self-sacrificing love. Even her final set of foster parents, if not as in love as she remembered her parents having been—and honestly, her memories might be embellishing their connection—were good role models for her. Loving God and loving each other. Loving all the kids.

She started to sigh.

No. Stop. Detectives surrounded her, and she didn't want

to draw their attention any more than she'd already done. She looked at Ian's desk for a distraction and wasn't surprised to find it neat and tidy. She was the same way. Something they had in common. But what else did they share?

Nothing that she could think of. Maybe she should watch for things in common while they were together to see how compatible they might be.

Wait. Was she thinking about getting together with him?

Her usual obstacle seemed to have been removed. The kiss had been everything she'd dreamed, just as she'd said. But was she willing to risk starting a relationship with him only to discover he wasn't cut out for it? She thought she knew him well enough to know he could commit to someone and be happy, but she could be wrong. And more importantly, he didn't know for sure. Maybe he didn't want to. Maybe he was just using his parents' marriage as an excuse not to get involved.

Oh, man, she was a mess.

Thankfully, Ian strode across the room, taking her full attention. He wore dark jeans and a pressed button-down shirt. His expression was tight, his eyes narrowed.

Uh-oh. Not good. "Something wrong?"

"No. The lineup is ready. Since you've witnessed lineups before, you know the procedure."

"I do, and I know you can't be there so you can't potentially transmit which man is the suspect." She stood. "Let's get to it."

He spun and led her across the room. She felt the inquisitive gazes of detectives following her. As an attorney, she'd interacted with many of them, and maybe they were making up stories in their heads about why she was there. She'd be doing that, anyway, and detectives were naturally curious and observant.

Ian took her down a long hallway to the end and opened the door. Inside stood attorney Renaldo Peoples, who was known for representing career criminals. He was high priced and Snipes likely couldn't afford Peoples. Olivo was probably footing the bill to get his guy out.

A black opaque window filled one wall. She knew after Ian left the room, the officer would turn out the lights on her side of the window, and another officer would turn on lights in the room where the suspects would appear. Though she knew that Snipes might not be in this lineup, in her gut she knew she would likely come face-to-face with the man who'd shot Junior.

"Ms. Rice." Peoples held out his hand. "Good to see you again."

She shook his hand that was warm and plump, and for some reason, she thought it fit the man who did things in excess in court, often receiving the judge's censure.

Ian read her the rules of the lineup, and she signed the statement, as did Ian, the officer, and Peoples.

"I'll see you after the lineup is complete." Ian stepped to the door and closed it behind him.

The officer looked at her. "This will be a visual and voice lineup. Each person will enter one at a time and be wearing a black ski mask. Each one will also say, 'You messed with the wrong person.' Each person will also be holding a number." His gaze slid to Peoples, and he asked them both, "Any questions?"

He got shakes of heads in response, and he flicked off the light.

The room on the other side lit up on the far side of the glass, and she heard another officer say, "Number one, step into the room. Turn and face the glass and say, 'You messed with the wrong person.'"

He did so, and she watched for the swagger as he walked

148

in. Listened for the tone of voice. Looked for a birthmark. Not him. She was sure. The officer had the next two guys do the same, and neither of them were right either. Number four was called into the room, and he strutted over to the mirror. Yes! That was the swagger she'd seen. A cocky self-importance in his walk. He uttered the words.

She gasped and clamped a hand over her mouth as she stepped back. She didn't mean to react, but with his voice and walk, she was instantly transported back to that ballroom. The gunshots going off. Junior collapsing. Death. Sudden death beside her. The man held up his number, and she caught a glimpse of a heart-shaped birthmark on his hand.

"All right, number four, you're all set," the officer in the suspect room said. The man walked out.

Number four. Snipes. She knew it was him. Malone wanted to look at the officer and share her assessment, but she shouldn't. Not with Peoples watching her every move. He would interpret her look all wrong. He'd think the officer somehow led her to know that number four was Snipes. She wouldn't botch the line-up.

Numbers five and six went through the same drill. She watched, but they weren't the shooter.

After all the men had filed through the room, Malone turned to the officer. "It's number four."

His expression was blank. He had no idea which guy was the actual suspect. "Without using a numerical scale, how certain are you?"

"One hundred percent."

"Do you need to see any of the men again?" he asked.

"I'm absolutely positive it's number four," she said firmly.

The officer flicked on the light switch, and the window went black.

Peoples's only reaction was a twitch of his jaw. "I'd like to speak with my client now."

"I'll see you out," the officer said to Peoples, who muttered something under his breath.

Peoples flashed Malone an irritated glare. Looks like she'd been right.

When Peoples was gone, Ian stepped into the room. "Ready to go?"

"I know you can't tell me if I was right, but I know I was." She smiled at him.

He held her gaze, transmitting the same deep emotions that had filled his eyes the night before when he'd kissed her. She wanted to rush over to him and repeat the kiss—never let it end. But this wasn't the time.

"If that's all, the guys are waiting to take me home," she said.

"I got the files from the gangland shooting and Junior's phone records from Londyn. I thought we could go through them together."

"Sure, but not here, okay? I feel like all your fellow detectives are staring at me."

"I would be if I were them." He grinned.

"It's not that." She chuckled, the laugh out of place, all things considered. "Honestly, I think they're mentally measuring me for prison garb."

He laughed.

"I'm serious. I feel like they're trying to figure out if I committed murder."

"Detectives can imagine all kinds of things." He rested a hand on the doorknob. "We can work at your place or mine, if that's better."

"Mine. That way the Byrds don't have to do another risk assessment."

Ian opened the door and stepped back so she could exit. "I am most impressed with their thoroughness."

She passed him and had to force her feet to keep going. "I've always recommended the Nighthawk agency, but now that I've experienced their services, I can really personally attest to their abilities."

"As an observer, I can too," he said as he caught up to her from behind. "By the way, if your jail appearance says anything, you could pull off that prison garb quite well. The pale blue looks striking with your coloring."

He grinned, and the smile warmed the cold places in her heart left after seeing Snipes in person.

Ian picked up the files on his desk and directed her to the exit. He stayed close to her side, much closer than he needed to while in the secure building.

The elevator doors opened, and Londyn stepped out.

Ian held up his stack of folders. "We'll be reviewing the phone logs you highlighted. I'll get back to you."

"You got it," she said. "And I'll keep working on finding contact info for Detective Wisniewski. His driver's license address isn't valid anymore. Looks like he dropped off the radar."

Ian's forehead wrinkled. "Let me know what you find the minute you do."

"Will do." Londyn headed back to the bullpen.

"I sure hope she can find him," Malone said as she boarded the elevator.

"She will." Two words, but they held certainty.

The doors closed, and she faced Ian. "Sounds like you really respect her."

"This's the first time I've worked with her, but she has a great reputation in the department. The way you can now vouch for the Nighthawk guys, I can vouch for her."

They rode the rest of the way in silence. Malone really

wanted to ask what he was thinking about, but if his mind traveled in the same direction as hers, he was thinking about how private this space was and wondering if they could experience a quick kiss before hitting the ground floor. She couldn't keep thinking this way. Her best bet was to not be alone with him in confined spaces.

The moment the doors opened, she bolted out and almost raced past Clay at the front door.

"Hold up." Clay stepped in front of her. "I need to notify my brothers that you're ready to go."

He leaned into his mic and shared the information, then listened for a moment. "Okay. We're clear. Straight—"

"Into the SUV," she interrupted. "No stopping or distractions."

"You got it." Clay took her elbow and walked her out.

Brendan waited midway to the vehicle, and Aiden sat in the driver's seat. Exactly like she expected, and she slid into the back seat with no issues.

Ian leaned into the vehicle. "I'll see you there."

She'd been looking forward to the drive to sit near him. Inhale his unique scent. Sneak glances at his strong profile. Maybe press her leg against his, making it seem accidental, of course.

Ah, no. No. She'd gone and fallen for him. Or was she still remembering the guy she'd had a crush on? Was she focusing on the past with him like she was doing with her parents? If so, how could she know?

She leaned back and pondered their time together. She was much more mature now. Not experienced with guys, though. Could she know her feelings? She'd gone beyond his physical appearance to get to know the man inside. The kind and companionate man. The man who put others first and worked tirelessly for the weak. A man who knew himself well, even if she didn't like the conclusion he'd come to about his potential for a relationship.

When they reached her house, she was surprised that Ian was parked on the street already. He slipped out of his vehicle and came around the back of the SUV to open her door.

"Please keep the door closed while the guys check the house out," Aiden said.

Ian slid in and closed the door behind him. He could've stayed outside, but she was thrilled that he chose to sit next to her. She felt like a giddy schoolgirl all over again.

Clay and Brendan got out of the vehicle. Brendan stood by the SUV and continuously scanned the area while Clay headed up the sidewalk. Near the front door, he came to a sudden stop and halted his approach to the door. He dug his phone from his pocket, and it looked like he took a picture of something then raced back to the SUV, signaling for Brendan to join him inside the vehicle.

"Package on the doorstep." Clay's expression, when he looked her way, kicked her pulse into high gear. "Your first name only, written in marker, and the word *urgent* scrawled below it."

He held out his phone and let everyone look at his photo of the package.

"Only one thing to do," Ian said, his eyes narrowing. "Evacuate the area and call the bomb squad."

Malone was stunned into silence and could only stare out her window at the house.

"We're going to fall back." Aiden revved the engine. "This vehicle might be reinforced, but it can't withstand a bomb."

"Make it, at least, a hundred feet," Ian said, moving closer to her. "I'll call it in while you guys go door to door and warn the neighbors."

Aiden floored the gas, and the SUV catapulted out of the drive and onto the street. He kicked it into drive, and they roared up the road.

Malone's heart rate ratcheted up even more, and she clenched her hands, wishing she could do something besides just stay put and remain calm. And if she couldn't maintain her calm, fake it so she didn't distract the guys from doing what they'd obviously been trained to do.

"We'll evacuate your neighbors." Aiden and Brendan bolted from the vehicle.

Ian spoke into his phone. "This is Detective Ian Blair." He gave his badge number. "A suspicious package was left at the home of a person we're protecting in a murder investigation. I need MEDU to check it out."

Metro Explosives Disposal Unit. She'd worked with them when she'd had to report a husband who'd sent a suspicious package to his estranged wife.

Ian listened, his gaze focused outside, glancing around to take in the neighborhood. He suddenly launched into recounting the situation to dispatch and sharing Malone's name and address.

Her address. Really? Being said in conjunction with a potential bomb. Unbelievable.

"Thank you," Ian said. "I won't be holding while you make the arrangements. I need to notify my department."

He glanced at Malone. "Squad will be on the way as soon as they can muster."

"Good," she said, the one word holding all of her stress. She didn't want to give Ian more to worry about, so she blew out a breath. "Thank you for remaining so calm and managing the situation."

Ian gave a sharp nod and looked over the neighborhood with the eyes of a professional law enforcement officer. She was seeing people she was just getting to know exit their homes. On one side of her home, the Toulanes's Jeep sat in their driveway. On the other side, Sandy and Mike's minivan was parked on the street, as usual, so their preschoolers could ride their trikes in the driveway. Across the street, it looked like Beatrice and Hank weren't home.

Brendan and Aiden were approaching the front doors while Ian phoned his lieutenant. She watched the brothers talk to the people she was causing to fear and panic. Maybe needlessly.

When Ian ended his call, she looked at him.

"What if this is nothing?" she asked. "We'll have scared everyone for no reason."

"Not no reason." He shoved his phone into his pocket. "The package has to be checked out."

"Do you really think someone sent me a bomb?"

He lifted one shoulder and let it drop. "We always have to look at worst-case scenarios."

"So the squad will come out for nothing."

"They all understand that's a possibility, and even if they don't find anything, it'll be a good training exercise for them."

"I suppose." She watched her neighbors get in their cars and drive off. She wished she could talk to them. Reassure them. But the Byrds and Ian would never let her out of the vehicle. And even if they did, what could she say to calm their fears when there might be a bomb sitting on her stoop.

She sat quietly, Ian at her side, watching the commotion until Aiden and Brendan slid back into the SUV, their expressions guarded. No one spoke.

She couldn't stand the silence. "What happens now?"

Ian met her gaze and held it. "Now we wait."

Which they did. For nearly thirty minutes. During that time, patrol cars arrived and cordoned off the street. Ian got out to meet the patrol officers, and he remained with them until the bomb squad arrived in a van. Soon, two MEDU officers scrambled around to the back of their vehicle and flung open the doors.

They stepped into huge ugly green suits that reminded her of Teletubbies. "They have such a dangerous job."

Brendan turned from his spot in the passenger seat. "The suits have rigid ballistic panels covered in flame-resistant Nomex. Plus body-protecting Kevlar. They're well-protected."

"How do you know the details?" she asked.

"I planned to try out for the squad," he said, longing in his voice.

Aiden looked at his brother. "But I botched that for you."

"Nah. It was Dad's transplant that changed my career path, but I get to do far more in my current position than I ever would've on patrol."

"And you get to work with your brothers." From beside her, Clay cast a wry smile at his brother.

"I thought we were talking about positives." Brendan laughed, and his brothers joined in.

Malone loved how they could joke with each other, even in such a situation. Could she work with Reed and be this fun-loving? They were both pretty serious type-A people. Wouldn't likely work. Better to remain brother and sister only.

A guy dressed in black tactical pants and a black polo shirt with the squad logo on the chest jumped out of the driver's seat of MEDU's van and started shouting so loudly that she could hear his commands through the SUV's thick glass.

"That's the team leader, Sergeant Charlie Zamsky,

yelling out orders," Brendan said. "He served on an explosive ordnance disposal team in the army, and of course he graduated from the FBI's Hazardous Devices School."

"Of course?" Malone asked.

"All certified bomb techs are required to graduate from the school."

She hadn't known. When she'd seen the squad in action the last time, she didn't have Brendan or anyone else to give her play-by-play information.

Ian joined Zamsky, and they had a quick conversation before Zamsky took out what looked like a nearly indestructible laptop and placed it on the hood of his vehicle. A large silver robot came rolling down a ramp from the back of the van and rolled toward her front door. Two arms protruded out front with long pincers acting as hands ready to seek out the package.

"Zamsky uses that computer to maneuver the robot," Brendan said. "He'll start by taking an initial X-ray of the suspicious package. If the X-ray proves the item isn't explosive, he'll give us an all clear."

The robot slowly approached the brown box.

"He's taking that X-ray now," Brendan said.

Zamsky looked at his computer screen then looked up to Ian and said something. Ian's shoulders relaxed.

"Looks like it's not a bomb," Aiden said. "Hope Ian can get the X-ray forwarded to his phone so we can see what the box *does* contain."

Zamsky brought the package back with the robot and took if from the arms. He put it in a large plastic bag and tapped the corner of the package on the hood of his vehicle.

"What's he doing?" Malone asked.

"By tapping the box, he's gathering any suspicious powder inside into a quantity that will show up on an X-ray."

"Suspicious powder, like anthrax," Clay added.

"Glad they're checking," she said. "I once got a letter from an irate husband that we worried was something bad, but it turned out to be baking soda."

Zamsky took the package, set it on the ground, and adjusted the robot.

"He's taking another X-ray," Brendan said. "The machine they use can give amazing detail on the box's contents."

Zamsky said something to Ian, then handed the box to him. Ian shook Zamsky's hand. While the squad packed up, Ian marched in their direction.

"I wish I could tell from his expression what's in that box."

"Must not be dangerous or contain a hazardous substance if he's bringing it with him," Clay said.

"But his expression says it's not good," Aiden added.

Ian slid into the back seat. "Feel free to open this, but if it was delivered this way, I doubt you're going to like what you see."

He took the box from the bag and sliced the box open with his Leatherman.

She held her breath and lifted the lid. A large picture of Sierra, Reed, and baby Asher at the park lay in the bottom of the box. Written in sloppy red marker it said, "Testify and the baby dies."

12

Malone's hand shook, and she could barely keep her phone to her ear. "C'mon. C'mon, Reed. Answer. Please answer."

She paced her living room, moving past Ian, who stood watching her. She pivoted and reached for him. He grasped her free hand, and she came to a stop and looked at him as she waited for Reed to answer his phone. The warmth of Ian's hand helped still some of her panic, but she still couldn't settle down until she talked to her brother and knew he and his family were safe.

"Malone," Reed finally answered. "Everything okay?"

She blurted out the information about the package and started walking again. "I need to know all three of you are safe."

"Sierra and Asher are at Veritas. They're fine. I'm in the office."

"You should go home. Now! I know the Center is safe, but you should be with them. Protect them."

"Yeah. I will." He sounded too calm for having heard about a threat to his child, but that was Reed. Strong and unflappable on the surface, even if he was cringing inside.

But he'd always put up a good front for her. And he didn't like to accept help.

She had to make sure he did today. "Please let me send the other Byrd brothers to your office to escort you home."

He didn't reply.

"Please, Reed," she begged. "I agreed to do it for you when there wasn't a threat against me. Your family has a direct threat now. An escort is a good idea."

"Fine," he said, sounding irritated, and she could easily see him shoving a hand in his hair. "But whoever sent the picture threatened the family of a federal agent, and I'm going to report this to my supervisor. We'll open our own investigation."

"Do that, but be quick. I want all three of you together."

"I'll call Sierra and warn her, and the center's guard too. And put her partners on alert. Maybe have Blake stand watch outside our condo door until I get home." He let out a shuddering breath. "And what about you?"

"I wasn't threatened."

"But the person who sent the package knows where you live. You can't stay there, even with the Nighthawk team on duty."

"I'll come stay with you."

"Man," Reed said. "I don't like that."

"I thought that was what you were going to suggest."

"I was, but you offering it up and not arguing tells me how rattled you are."

"Yeah." She didn't elaborate because Ian was watching her every move, and she didn't want him to know that she was more frightened than she'd ever been in her life. "I'll pack my things, and we'll be on the way to the center."

"Call when you leave. I should be there before you." He paused, and the silence hung in the air like the bomb they'd believed the box could've contained. "Be careful, sis. Be very careful."

"I will. I promise." And she meant it. She believed Olivo was behind the threat. He didn't want her to testify against Snipes, and he was playing dirty to stop her. Problem was, she couldn't prove it.

She shoved her phone in her pocket and looked at Ian. "I'm going to pack a bag and stay with Reed until this is all over."

"I heard." He moved closer and took her hands.

She wished they weren't still trembling, but they shook like a terrified puppy facing a giant bear.

"I wish you could stay at my place." His gaze was dark with concern. "I want to be the one to make sure you're safe, not fob it off on someone else."

"The Veritas Center is secure, and Reed will be there."

"I know it's the right place for you. I just want to be there too."

"You could be, I suppose. Or at least we could mention it to Reed. He might appreciate an extra person. But honestly, they have guys on the Veritas team who have the skills to do the job too. Not to mention the Byrds might want to remain on duty."

"Yeah, there's no need for my help." He released her hands and, without a word, drew her into his arms. "I hope I'm the only one who can provide this kind of comfort when you're worried."

She rested her head on his shoulder and slid her arms around his trim waist. Reed could give her a hug. As could Sierra. But *this* hug? This cocooning of Ian's arms around her body? *This* hug erased her fear and replaced it with yearning for a relationship with this wonderful man.

The warmth of his body seeped into hers, and she wasn't

sure where she started and he ended. They seemed melded in unity and purpose. And more. So much more.

She shouldn't do this, but she needed something good in her life. And her feelings for Ian and his for her were good. And pure. She needed pure when evil in the name of Tirone Olivo, who would be willing to kill a baby to get what he wanted, surrounded them and made everything scary and ugly.

She leaned back and traced a finger along Ian's cheek, enjoying touching the contour of his rugged face. She stroked his wide jaw with a peppering of whiskers and ran her finger over his full bottom lip.

His eyes darkened and filled with passion. "You'd better stop that unless you plan to kiss me again."

"I plan to kiss you again." She rested her hands on his broad shoulders and rose up on her tiptoes, but before she could lift her lips to his, he lowered his head and pressed his against hers.

The earlier kiss had been soft and gentle, but this one spoke to the depth of his feelings. She'd thought since Junior's attack that such a kiss might scare her, but it didn't. Not at all. The exact opposite. She slid her hand up to clutch the thickness of his hair and draw him even closer.

Yes. Yes. Yes. She wanted this wonderful, extraordinary man in her life. Not just today. Not just for this kiss. But forever.

Problem was, she didn't know what she was going to do about it.

~

While Malone packed, Ian knocked on the robin's egg blue door of the house across the street. Malone didn't have a security camera outside her place, but Ian had spotted one on the garage of the neighbor across the street, and he hoped it caught the person who'd delivered the package.

He got out his ID, noting how his hand shook. Not enough that another person could tell. But he could. He didn't know if it was from the package and warning that told them that a vile man like Olivo had inserted himself in the mix, or if it was leftover emotion after Malone's kiss.

There was something new. Fresh, in her kiss. Almost like a promise. He was thinking about a future with her, but should he be? He still didn't have his head on straight. And kissing her like he had instead of walking away was tantamount to leading her on. She didn't deserve that from him. He would need to have a talk with her later.

But when? Once she was behind the iron fortress of the Veritas Center, how much would he see her? When would he be alone with her again? They would always require an escort while in the building due to security, but would Reed let her outside? Would she want to leave?

Because if Ian knew anything right then, he knew she was freaked out big time. Otherwise, she would never have suggested she stay with Reed. He suspected the woman he was coming to know would try to maintain her independence and argue about leaving her home until she won.

The door opened, and a middle-aged woman with curly hair, round glasses, and a frumpy look stared at him. "If you're selling something, I'm not buying. No matter what it is."

He held up his ID. "Detective Ian Blair, Portland Police Bureau."

"Oh." She raised her hand to clutch her cardigan sweater in the same color as the door. "Is something wrong? My husband. This isn't about him, it is? He's not hurt, is he?" Her words rushed out faster than he could get a breath to answer.

163

"No, ma'am."

Her shoulders sagged at the news. "I'm Beatrice Paulson. I watch a lot of detective shows, and I know how you detectives like to get those details."

"You're right about that, ma'am. This's about your neighbor across the street."

"Sweet Malone?" She glanced around him at Malone's house. "What happened?"

"She had a suspicious package delivered."

"Oh my." Beatrice's fingers tightened on the sweater. "Must've been while I was out, or I probably would've seen the driver who dropped it off. How can I help?"

"You have a security camera on your garage. I was hoping it might've caught whoever delivered the package."

She frowned. "I know the camera can see her house, but I don't remember ever getting any alerts when something happens over there." She narrowed her eyes. "Honestly, my hubby put the camera in. He gets the alerts and tells me what he thinks I need to know. I'd much rather go out and talk to my neighbors than watch them through a camera."

"Could we look at your files to see?"

"The app is on his iPad. I can try to find it. Come in." She stepped back, and he entered the dark house that smelled like pine cleaner.

She led him to her kitchen, where a bucket of water sat with a mop inside. "Sorry, I was mopping, but looks like the floor's dry. Can I offer you something to drink?"

He smiled at her when all he really wanted to do was get a look at that iPad, but she was being kind and helpful, and he needed to be patient. "I'm good, but thank you."

She gestured off-handedly at the stools and sat. An iPad clasped in a case with a camouflage pattern stood open on the counter.

"My husband is a hunting fanatic." She tapped the

screen a few times. "Interesting. Looks like there're a few files that recorded while I was out."

"It probably picked up the police and bomb squad arriving."

"Bomb squad?" Her gaze flew to him. "I really missed something, didn't I?"

"No bomb. Just a precaution."

Her expression troubled, she returned her focus to the tablet.

"Start with the most recent video first," he said. "That'll likely be the delivery, and the others, recordings of the police and squad."

She tapped the screen and swiveled the case, allowing them both to see the screen.

An orange drone with the drone manufacturer's name printed in black on the side swooped down over the road and dropped the package on Malone's doorstep.

"A drone." She clutched her blouse. "Oh my. Wait until I tell my husband."

Ian didn't want word getting out about the drone. If Olivo was behind delivering the package, Ian didn't want Olivo to learn that they had footage of the delivery.

Ian looked at her. "Telling your husband is fine, but promise me you two won't tell anyone else."

She frowned. "If you want."

"I insist." He made sure his tone was firm and unyielding.

"Okay."

"Let's look at the other videos."

She opened the next ones, and it did indeed show police cars and the bomb squad arriving, and all the commotion that came along with them.

He got out a business card. "Can you please send all of the files to this email address?"

"Hmm." Her frown deepened. "I don't know how to do that."

"I can show you how." He pointed at the menu. "You have to download the files before sending them."

She selected the download button, and the files arrived in a flash. "Where did they go?"

He helped her find and send the videos to his email.

"That was easy enough." She smiled at him.

He stood to thank her. "We've already canvassed your neighbors, but you have my card in case anyone remembers seeing anything. Or if you noticed anything unusual in the area."

"Of course. I'll call right away." She walked him to the door but stopped shy of opening it all the way. "Can you tell me what was in the package?"

"I'm afraid not, but it was personal, so you shouldn't have any problems."

She opened the door the rest of the way and nodded across the street. "Looks like Malone's leaving."

"Thanks again for your help." He jogged across the street in time to catch her before the brothers took off. "I'll meet you at the Center. I have something I want you to look at."

"I'll wait for you in the lobby." She twisted her hands in her lap.

He shook his head. "Not safe with all the windows out front."

"We'll take you in through the secured parking ramp," Clay said, then looked at Ian. "I'll wait and open the gate for you, and you can follow us up."

"Great. Thanks."

He followed them to Veritas, his gaze searching for anyone tailing them. Clay fulfilled his promise of opening the gate. Once beyond it, Ian idled his vehicle to allow Clay to climb in.

"Drive all the way to the top," Clay said. "That level has the best access to the skybridge. Then you can go to the condos or the lab from there. But your first stop will be the lobby to get a visitor pass. You have to wear it at all times when you're outside the condo. And you need one of us to escort you while you're in the building."

Ian shook his head. "I knew you had tight security for the lab, but not the condos."

"The lab needs to protect evidence and samples," he said. "Sure, the doors all lock and require fingerprint readers to get in, but the Veritas partners stake their reputations on being able to maintain chain-of-custody. We all aim to help them keep it."

"Sounds reasonable." Ian reached the top level.

"Park close to the door."

Ian found a spot and swung his car into it. Ian followed Clay as he made quick work of getting Ian's pass from the security guard in the lobby. Ian had hoped to catch up with Malone, but she either didn't come down for a pass or she'd already gone to Reed's condo.

Ian hung the lanyard around his neck, and Clay took him to the fifth floor condo. Ian knocked.

Reed opened the door, his expression stony. "I've handed off my current investigation, and before anything else happens, I want a full update on finding whoever threatened my wife and child. They won't get away with it. Not while I'm still alive and breathing."

Malone stood beneath the pounding spray of the shower in Reed and Sierra's guest room, letting the water refresh her. She'd felt bad leaving Ian to fend for himself with Reed and Sierra the moment he arrived, but Malone needed a shower.

She had to remove an internal coating of slime left from the box, and a shower symbolized that for her.

Reed, Sierra, and Asher were all the family she had, and she couldn't abide them being in danger because of her. If she had to back down and not testify to make it go away, she might just do that. And what would that make her? A coward or a wise woman?

She finally understood to a degree why many of the battered women she worked with wouldn't bring charges and testify against their spouses. They were setting priorities, and they prioritized their children or their own lives. She was prioritizing her family.

Malone turned off the shower, towel dried, and swiped her hand across the steamy mirror to look at herself. "Those women weren't letting a killer go. You would be."

Argh. What do I do? Will Olivo ever leave us alone even if he's arrested for his crimes and imprisoned?

Her days as a federal prosecutor told her that many drug kingpins continued to run their organizations from prison and called the shots. If Olivo wanted her family dead, he would find a way from prison to have them murdered. They could all go into witness protection, but she didn't want that. She couldn't be responsible for her brother and sister-in-law having to give up jobs they loved, because once you entered the program, you were forbidden to do anything remotely connected to your prior profession. It made you too easy to trace.

Help us. Please. Please. Please. Help us.

Still frustrated, she stomped to the bedroom and dressed in comfy yoga pants and a warm baby blue fleece top that surrounded her in coziness.

She ran a comb through her hair and fired a confident look at herself in the mirror. She was already putting her family in danger, and no way would she add showing them her angst. She would have to fake how she felt. Same with Ian. Still, they were all perceptive and might pick up on her worry. She would have to double her effort to hide it.

She left the bedroom and came to a stop. She hadn't expected to see the scene in front of her. Sierra was in the kitchen doing dishes. Reed was sitting at the dining room table flipping through the file Ian had brought with him. That was all normal, but Ian? He sat on the plush couch holding baby Asher, who was a little over five months old. Ian made funny faces at the baby. Asher grinned and giggled, drool running from his mouth.

Ian grinned, too, his eyes alight with joy and affection.

He looked up and caught her watching him. He smiled broadly, one side of his mouth quirking up higher than the other. Her heart melted, just like that, into a big old blob of honey. He seemed like a natural with the baby, and yet this was the man who thought he couldn't get married. If he changed his mind, did he even want children? Did she?

She had no idea. She'd always thought she would be alone and dote on Reed's kids, but now? Now she was as confused about that as she was about whether she should testify.

She gathered herself together and crossed the room. "How did you end up babysitting?"

"My fault," Reed called out but didn't look up. "He gave me a breakdown on the investigation, and I wanted to read this file."

"I took this little fellow because I didn't think he should be looking at a h-o-m-i-c-i-d-e file."

"You don't have to spell yet." Malone laughed. "He doesn't understand."

"I don't know." Ian grinned. "He seems pretty advanced to me."

"Do you want me to take him?"

Ian looked down at Asher. "You're good here, right buddy?"

Asher babbled joyfully.

Ian looked at her. "We're good."

Surprised, she started for Reed to look at the file and talk to him about the threat, but someone knocked on the door.

Reed and Ian both came to their feet, their hands going for their guns.

"Relax." Sierra came from the kitchen and started for the door. "It has to be someone we know if they're inside the building."

"I'll get it." Reed stepped in front of her. "Security, even the best, can be compromised."

Ian handed Asher to Sierra. "And I'll back him up."

Malone hoped they were both overreacting, but she was thankful to have them there.

Reed reached the door and looked through the peephole. He let out a long breath. "Stand down. It's your mom and dad, Sierra."

Sierra sighed. "I should've known someone would've told her what happened."

Ian's shoulders relaxed, and he stepped back into the family room.

Reed opened the door, and Peggy quickly scooped Reed into a hug. "You or Sierra should've called me. I came as soon as I heard."

She released him and strode down the hallway. She wore jeans, a green turtleneck, and a lighter green cardigan. Her hair was short and spiky, a mixture of gray and silver. She was a stunning woman.

"Thanks for the escort, Drake," Peggy's handsome husband, Russ, said.

Malone heard the door close, and Russ, who was still fit

from his law enforcement days, stepped in carrying two shopping bags. He and Reed joined the others.

Peggy swept the baby out of Sierra's arms, put him on her shoulder, and kissed him until he giggled. She then turned her sights on Sierra and hugged her with her free arm. "I'm glad to see you're all right and staying home where you're safe."

"You didn't have to come, Mom," Sierra said, sounding both frustrated and grateful. "I know you had to get a babysitter for Logan and Sadie."

"Of course I had to come, and the kids are fine in Mrs. McWillis's hands." Peggy released Sierra after explaining about their younger foster children and set her sights on Malone. "How are you doing, sweetheart? You've had a tough time, and I didn't even know about it."

Malone wondered which of her sons had told her about the murder charges and the warning. Before she could ask, Peggy enveloped Malone and gave a careful hug that didn't smoosh the baby. She smelled like vanilla, just as Malone remembered her mother had when they'd baked cookies.

Peggy stepped back and ran a practiced eye over Malone. "What can I do for—?" She caught sight of Ian, and her eyes widened. "Now, who do we have here?"

Ian stepped forward. "Ian Blair. PPB homicide detective."

"You're helping our Malone out?" Peggy stepped closer to him, her inquisitive gaze running his entire body.

"I am."

Malone took a moment to enjoy hearing Peggy say *our Malone*. Peggy had basically adopted Malone, and it felt good. The woman had a bottomless heart that could encompass anyone in her circle and make the person feel special and included.

She shifted Asher. "And I hear Londyn Steele is working

with you too. We've known her parents for years." Peggy transferred her intense gaze back to Ian and slipped an arm into his. "Why don't we sit down and get to know each other before I put lunch on the table."

Ian looked like he didn't know what to do, but it wasn't like he had a choice. The steamroller of matchmaking known as Peggy tugged him to the couch and started peppering him with questions about his personal life.

Malone cast him an apologetic look but didn't know how she could save him.

Russ looked at his wife and shook his head. "Come on now, Peg. The food will get cold."

Sierra joined them and took Asher. "It's time for his nap, and these guys are starving."

Peggy held up her hands. "Okay, okay. I can take a hint." She stood and looked at Ian. "We can sit together at lunch. I hope you like chili. I made a big pot and a batch of my famous cornbread with honey butter."

"Sounds great," he said, but he looked wary.

Peggy tucked her arm in Russ's, and they went to the kitchen.

Malone joined Ian on the couch. "You don't have to stay. We can go through the files later if you want."

"I have to eat," he said. "And I do like chili."

"But you're worried about my mother-in-law's eagerness." Reed handed Ian the file he'd been reviewing at the dining table. "We can help run interference, but let me say this. If she has her sights set on matching you up with someone, there's no point in trying to fight it. You won't win."

Ian laughed, but Reed was serious, and Malone knew he spoke the truth. If Peggy set her sights on getting Malone and Ian together, they might well end up paired off for life. Something Malone didn't hate the thought of. Didn't hate it at all.

13

_____

Ian didn't know what he thought about the lunch. He sure saw where the Byrd brothers got their tenacity. Not just from Peggy. Russ was a sharp, intuitive guy too. One who could stop Peggy if he'd wanted to. Apparently, he hadn't, because he settled back and simply smiled at her with a fondness Ian had never seen in a married couple. And then there were times they shared a look that held the feelings Ian was having for Malone. They'd been married for over thirty-five years and were still in love.

Was it possible to have a successful marriage? It seemed possible to Ian right then. And it seemed like something worth striving to create.

The baby had Ian's heart filling with another feeling he'd never experienced before—protectiveness, but in a far more primal way than he felt toward anybody else.

Then there was the way Peggy's love surrounded them all. Not to mention Reed and Sierra added another point in favor of marriage. They hadn't been married for long, but they shared the same looks as Peggy and Russ. These older folks had been good role models for Sierra, and Reed had his parents in his life for two years longer than Malone did. He would have memories of good parenting and marriage skills. Their foster parents had set a good example too.

But what about Ian? He'd had no good role models. He not only hadn't seen a strong marriage with his own parents, but the majority of marriages with police officers failed too. Could Ian manage the kind of a relationship he was witnessing?

He wanted to. More than anything, right now. He felt comfortable with the Byrd family. As if he belonged. He had no desire to run, which he did with his parents, who couldn't bother to dredge up any emotion except over money.

Ian wanted to try. But first he had to make sure none of these people came to any harm and nab Olivo for the threat he'd sent. Ian needed to connect him to Junior's murder too. And maybe connect Olivo or Snipes to the older shooting.

He changed his focus to Malone, who was holding the baby and talking to Sierra in the kitchen. Asher hadn't slept long, and she'd swooped in to care for him. He loved seeing her with the child. Could even imagine her with his child.

Oh, man, he was smitten. More than that.

Focus.

He looked at the clock. He had an interview with the managing partner at Ground Floor Builders soon and needed to review a few things with Malone first. He held the folder up. "Mind if we get back to the investigation."

"Here, let me." Sierra dried her hands and reached out for her son. The baby smiled at her and giggled.

What must that feel like? Knowing you created and birthed a child, a child who adored you, who craved your attention? Magical, he suspected, but perhaps not something all parents felt. He never knew his mom and dad to be nurturing. They'd given that job to the various nannies he'd had over the years, and when he got old enough, to no one. Maybe Ian could be a good husband and father if he concentrated on doing the opposite of what his parents had done.

Malone joined him in the dining room, Reed hot on her tail. They sat while Sierra watched from the kitchen. Malone started looking through the file.

"If you're hoping to find something in that old case file," Reed said. "You're out of luck. I think our best bet is to talk to the detective who worked it."

"I talked to the head of our drug squad already. Got nothing from him, but I planned to interview the guy in my department after I reviewed the folder."

"What about Junior's phone list?" Reed asked.

"Haven't had a chance to even look at it yet." Ian grabbed the stapled papers and glanced at the spreadsheet that Londyn had created. She'd highlighted the calls that went to untraceable prepaid phones.

He skimmed the list. "Looks like calls to his parents' landline—quite a few the days before and the day he died. And his mother's cell. The parents didn't mention that. Give me a second, and I'll give them a call to ask about it."

He dialed the Flaggs's home phone and was happy when Karen answered.

"It's Detective Blair," Ian said. "Do you have time for a few more questions?"

"Of course," Karen said. "I meant it when I said, 'whatever you need.'"

"I'm going to put you on speaker so my colleagues can listen. Is that okay?"

"Sure."

"On the day Junior was shot and a few days prior, he

called your home and your cell quite a few times. You didn't mention that."

"I didn't, did I? Guess that's because I didn't think it mattered." She paused for a long moment. "Junior went through dark periods, and he called me a lot during those times. I was on a plane on my way back from visiting my sister in New York, and couldn't answer his calls. But I called him back the minute I landed."

"And what did he have to say?"

"He told me again that he was going to have to make things right, and he was sorry if it impacted me negatively. He was a sensitive guy, and he always cared about how I felt."

Malone shook her head, and Ian almost snorted. The Junior he'd known had never been sensitive. More like mean and demeaning. Maybe like his dad, but he could've been different deep down. Could've been the person his mother knew him to be when he was with her.

"But he never told you what this thing was that he had to make right?" Ian asked.

"No. And believe me, I asked. He said, when he had everything in place, he would tell me."

"Did you have a guess?"

"I thought he'd found a way to get out from under that Olivo guy's thumb. At least that's what I hoped. Maybe he planned to testify against Olivo. I worried he would have to go into hiding if he did, but at least he would be safe."

Ian knew that wasn't the case and looked at the list again. "One of the calls to the house was answered, and Junior had a conversation with someone for ten minutes."

"Had to be Gilbert, but he never told me about it." Anger rang through her tone.

Something for Ian to ask Flagg Sr. "Have you come up with anything else you think might be helpful?"

"No, and trust me. I've been thinking about it nonstop."

"If you do come up with something, please call me."

She agreed and ended the call.

Ian set his phone on the table. "That wasn't much help, but it seems Junior had two sides to his personality."

"Would be difficult to grow up with a dad like his," Malone said. "Has to form who you are, even if you don't want it to."

Ian worked hard not to let his mouth fall open. She as much as said he could be like his dad, no matter how much he tried not to be. Earlier, she'd suggested he could be a good husband. So, which did she believe?

"What about the other calls?" Reed asked.

"Restaurants, a drug store, and Tim Richardson, the friend Blake is interviewing." Ian turned the page. "More texts than calls, and they're the basic everyday things like arranging to hang out with the friend or about a woman they saw at a club. And ones to his mom that have the emotional tone she mentioned."

"Makes sense that, if he was conducting drug business, he would use a burner for that." Ian looked at Malone. "Is it possible the shooter took two phones that night?"

"If they were in the same pocket, it could be."

"Nothing was found in his car," Ian said. "Junior might not have wanted to be bothered with business at the reunion, and he left it at home. If Olivo wanted the work phone, he didn't toss Junior's condo to find it. Or maybe they didn't communicate by phone."

Reed arched his dark eyebrow. "Then how?"

"I haven't had a chance to mention that the neighbor across the street from Malone caught the package delivery," Ian said. "A drone dropped it off."

"Seriously?" Malone asked. "A drone?"

Ian nodded. "Olivo could've communicated by sending

messages that way too. Might explain how he and his guys have stayed clean."

"Not the craziest thing I've ever heard," Reed said. "We need to search ViCAP for any mention of drones in this area."

The Violent Criminal Apprehension Program was run by the FBI. Law enforcement officers could enter data about serious crimes, creating a database that other officers could search using any unique criteria like drones in their investigations.

"We don't have access from here." Ian picked up his phone. "I'll get Londyn on it." He texted her before Reed could offer to have one of his buddies do the search and took over an aspect of the investigation that Ian wanted to keep under his control.

Surprisingly, the guy didn't argue.

Londyn replied that she would do it right away, and he glanced at his watch. "If she finds anything connected, I'll get started on it. First, I have an interview with one of the executives at Ground Floor Builders."

"Good," Reed said. "If our dad uncovered any kind of corruption, he wouldn't have hidden it. And this sounds like a strong lead."

Ian stood and looked at Malone. "I know I don't have to tell you to stay put, but please don't leave the building. And even avoid the lobby."

"I'll behave." She cast a mischievous grin up at him.

If Reed wasn't sitting right there, Ian might have drawn her to her feet and kissed away that impish smile. "You can get me on my cell at any time, and I'll let you know when I hear back from Londyn on the drone."

Reed shoved a hand into his hair. "I feel trapped. I can't leave the building. At least not without Malone or Sierra trying to hold me down. What can I do from here?"

"Londyn is working on finding a current phone number and address on Detective Wisniewski. He seems to have fallen off the radar, and she'll have to set it aside to run the ViCAP search."

"The guy my parents might've been going to see?" Reed asked.

Ian nodded. "You could work on that and do a phone interview if you find him."

"Oh, I'll find him." Reed's eyes hardened. "You can bank on that."

Malone had been sitting at the small desk in Reed's guest room for over an hour and was going stir crazy. She had her work to do, but she couldn't focus. She just kept thinking about Ian and how she could help him realize what an amazing man he was. Remind him that he'd avoided becoming anything like his parents and that would give him great odds at becoming a good life partner.

But she knew from experience that people could tell you the same thing over and over. Didn't mean you could embrace the thing in your life and implement it. That took work to change. Hard work, and he'd believed this wrong notion about himself for years. If he continued to believe it, he could make it a reality.

A knock sounded on the door, startling her for a moment. She didn't even know she was this jumpy, but she still hadn't let go of the earlier threat. "Come in."

Reed opened the door and stepped in to sit on the bed near the desk. "I talked to Wisniewski. He remembered Mom and Dad."

"Were they on their way to see him that day?" she asked eagerly.

He gave a solemn nod.

"What about?" She held her breath.

"He didn't know. Dad had called him and said he located something they thought the police needed to know about, but he didn't want to talk about it over the phone."

She let out her breath. "The drywall?"

"Most likely, but I don't know why Mom was with him. Unless Dad wanted her to come along for moral support."

Malone gave that some consideration. "Doesn't sound like Dad, though, does it?"

"Not really. Maybe it was something in their personal life."

"But what? It's not like they were criminals or interacted with criminals."

"At least, as far as we know."

"Come on, now." She clutched his arm. "You know they were who they represented themselves to be. No deep dark secrets or past. Right?"

"Right." Reed's eyes narrowed. "But then, why in the world did they need to meet with a detective?"

"Maybe Ian will have more information after his interview at Ground Floor Builders."

"Maybe," Reed said. But just like Malone didn't believe her words when she'd said them, Reed obviously didn't believe her either, and they were no closer to figuring out why their parents had been murdered.

Oscar Newton was exactly like his name suggested to Ian. A starched-shirt, black-suit, pinstripe-tie kind of guy. Not a builder. Maybe he'd once been one when Ground Floor Builders first started, but now he was all executive.

Newton ushered Ian into his office and gestured at contemporary chairs ringing a round glass table. Ian sat in one of the upholstered chairs.

Newton took a seat across from him and put his leg over his other knee. He looked down and brushed something from his black pants as if he didn't know what to say. "Now, suppose you tell me what this is all about."

"I'm investigating the deaths of Joanna and Lewis Rice," Ian said bluntly in hopes of putting the guy on edge.

Newton dropped his foot to the thick pile carpet. "But they died, what? Twenty-five or so years ago in an accident. Why bring it up now?"

"Because we now have evidence that shows the crash wasn't an accident."

"Not an accident?" Newton tightened his eyes.

"That's correct," Ian said, not willing to tell him about the car tampering just yet. "Can you think of anyone who might have wanted to kill either of them?"

He sat back and clasped the arms of his chair. "I didn't know Joanna very well, but Lewis was a valued member of our staff. He worked hard and had exceptional skills. I can't imagine anyone wanting to kill him. Especially not anyone I know."

Okay. He wasn't going to mention the drywall, so Ian would. "Tell me about the Chinese drywall issues in the nineties."

Newton shot forward in his seat, and his face blanched. "Drywall? What on earth does that have to do with their deaths?"

"Didn't your company import the drywall and use it on projects?"

Newton gritted his teeth. "Where are you getting such information?"

"From Lewis Rice's files, which have been kept in storage since his death."

Newton's grip on the arms tightened. "I'd rather not discuss that subject without our attorney."

"Why's that?" Ian persisted.

"I'm sure such an issue should be handled with kid gloves, and I'm not always the best at doing that." He forced a laugh. "Don't let this office and my expensive clothes fool you. I started as a laborer and worked my way up. My finesse in these matters isn't always at the level it needs to be."

"Why does it need finessing?" Ian asked, hoping to get him to admit something he was doing his best not to say.

Newton stood. "Let me get with our attorney, and we'll schedule a meeting."

Ian had no choice other than to comply and hope the attorney was more forthcoming. Ian eyed the man. "You know your need to call in an attorney makes you look guilty."

"I sure didn't kill Lewis, and no one else here did either."

"Were you trying to cover up the drywall? Is that why Lewis had the information in his personal files?"

"No. No. We didn't cover up anything." He rubbed a hand over his face.

"Then why the attorney?"

"It's sensitive, like I said, but it has nothing to do with Lewis. I swear."

Whenever someone added *I swear*, Ian figured they were lying. He locked his gaze on the man. "Then get that appointment set and don't string me along. We need to do this sooner than later."

Newton gave a sharp nod and escorted Ian to the reception area. He said a hasty goodbye and fled back to his office. Ian had obviously rattled the man, but that didn't mean he had anything to do with murder. In fact, Ian wasn't liking him for it at all. The guy didn't react like a killer might when he was outed for a crime he thought he'd gotten away with for over twenty years. He did, however, act guilty when it came to the drywall.

Ian stepped into the brisk October day, the wind blowing multi-colored leaves across the parking lot. He'd no sooner settled behind the steering wheel when his phone rang. Seeing a call from Londyn, he eagerly answered.

"Searched ViCAP," Londyn said. "I found something interesting regarding a drone, but don't know if it's related."

"Go ahead," Ian said, his interest piqued.

"A ten-year-old girl who was walking home from school says she was followed by a drone all the way home on Thursday. She just told her parents about it, and they called the police. The detective posted it in case someone was stalking children with this drone."

Ian's lead radar started pinging, and he hoped she fit the studies today showing the average ten-year-old had a cell phone. "Tell me she got a picture of the drone."

"She did."

"Send it to me. I'll hang on while you do."

He tapped his foot and waited until he heard the ding then looked at the photo. "It matches the one that delivered Malone's package."

"Really?" Londyn asked. "I don't know much about drones, but I've never seen one like this one. Doesn't mean it was Olivo's drone that followed the girl. We've seen no sign he's into young girls."

Ian cranked his car engine. "True, but since the drones match, it's worth interviewing the girl."

"Agreed."

"Young girls often do better with female officers," Ian said. "I want you in on the interview."

"I was hoping you'd say that."

"I'll pick you up at the office, and we can head over there." Ian shifted into gear and offered a prayer as he flew out of the parking lot toward what he hoped was the lead that set his gut burning with hope.

14

The large two-story Tudor house where the girl, Nicole Thompson, lived was located in one of Portland's most affluent neighborhoods. And the home's inside décor spoke to the opulence he'd expected to find.

Nicole stood next to her mother, Ruth, who just finished introducing herself in their entryway that sported a soaring ceiling. The child had dishwater-blond hair woven in braids, and it was windblown as if she'd been outside playing before they arrived. Her powder-blue eyes were dimmed with worry, and she held her mother's hand and looked up at Ian and Londyn.

"I'm Londyn." She stepped forward and squatted to eye-level with the girl. "You look a little worried, but don't be. I'm a regular person like your mom here. No big deal. I only have a few questions. You think you're up to that?"

"Yeah." Nicole bit her lip.

"Sometimes if you're in the place you like best in the world, it's easier to talk. Is that your room? Or outside?"

"My treehouse." A half smile quirked up her lips.

"Do you want to go out there to talk?"

She nodded and looked up at her mom, who nodded too.

"Is there enough room up there for your mom and this big oaf I brought with me?" Londyn asked.

Nicole giggled. "I think so. At least me and all my friends fit."

"Then lead the way." Londyn got up.

"It's gonna be fun to see all of you up there." Nicole stared at Ian. "'Specially you. You're big."

She bolted from the room, and her mother mouthed *thank-you*.

"Nice work, Steele," Ian said as they followed the mother into a well-manicured yard with flower beds coloring the perimeter.

They crossed a patio flanked with an outdoor kitchen and gas grill that gave Ian grill envy, to three massive maple trees. The house was built among them. It had wide steps leading up to a twenty-foot platform holding a house that was styled to match their home, even down to the ginger-bread shingles at the peak.

"Wow," Ian said. "That's more like a mansion."

Her mother looked back at him and smiled. "My husband's an architect. He built the treehouse of his dreams."

Nicole had already scampered up and waited for them at the door. The other women climbed the ladder, and Ian took up the rear. He arrived in time to see Nicole scoot a box out of sight with her foot. Of course, that set off Ian's radar. The mom faced the other way and had her gaze fixed on Ian and Londyn, so she missed the action.

"Where should we sit, Nicole?" Londyn asked.

"The floor." Nicole dropped to the wood planks in the space with pink walls and big purple beanbag chairs.

Everyone settled with crossed legs on the floor, Londyn across from Nicole.

"So tell me about this drone," Londyn said. "Was it scary?"

"Not at first, but when it kept following me, I remembered all the things my mom and dad said about safety." Nicole shook her head. "They didn't say anything bad about drones. So I didn't tell them right away."

"And why did you decide to tell them?" Londyn asked.

"'Cause it came back the next day."

"Did it follow you again?"

She shook her head, her pigtails flying, and bit her lip.

"Where were you when it came back?" Londyn asked.

Nicole clutched her hands together. "In the family room. I heard it and looked out the window. It went to Ty's house."

"Our neighbor," Ruth said. "Nice family."

"And did the drone just fly up to the house and leave?" Londyn asked.

"Not exactly." Nicole clutched her fingers together.

"Exactly what did it do?" Londyn asked, her tone softer this time.

Nicole glanced at her fingers, then up at her mother and back down.

"It's okay, honey," Ruth said. "You can tell us what happened."

Nicole chewed on her lower lip. "You promise you won't be mad?"

Her mother's eyes tightened, but she smiled. "Promise."

Nicole looked at Londyn. "It dropped off a package on his porch."

"A package," Ian said, unable to keep quiet any longer. "Was it a special package?"

Nicole shrugged.

"Can you describe it to me?" he asked.

"Just a small box. Brown. About this size." She held her hands out to show the size.

"Is it sort of like the one you pushed behind the bench when we came up here?" Londyn asked.

Nicole's eyes widened.

Ruth locked gazes with her daughter. "Nicole, did you take the package? Is that what this is about? Is that why you didn't want to tell me what happened?"

"I just wanted to see what was so special that someone delivered it by drone. So I hurried over there to see. But I heard someone inside, so I took it and ran." She looked up at her mother. "I was going to put it back. Honest. I wasn't stealing. But then you came home and made me come help with dinner. So I couldn't do it without you finding out. And I couldn't tell you."

"Why not just put it back before helping with dinner?" Londyn asked.

"Ty was home, and I didn't want him to catch me."

"But you've had a few days to give it back," her mother said.

"He's been home all this time. So has everyone else."

"Can we see the box?" Londyn asked.

Nicole grabbed it and handed it to Londyn like she was passing off a hot potato. Londyn immediately held it out for Ian to see. The cardboard box sealed with packing tape had the neighbor's name handwritten in black marker, just like the way Malone's name had been written on her package. That wasn't what had Ian almost falling out of the tree-house. It was the name on the package.

Ian met Londyn's gaze and saw that her mouth was hanging open.

"Is there something we should know?" Ruth asked.

Ian shook his head, but there really *was* something they needed to know. The box was addressed to Tirone Olivo, whom Ian now assumed went by Ty with his neighbors. The box also had the word PROOF printed in big red letters across the top. Similar to Malone's package, but the handwriting didn't match the box she received.

Ian swallowed to calm his excitement and looked at Ruth. "I noticed you have security cameras around the property. I'd like to get a copy of any events it might've recorded to see if there are other drone sightings."

"I can get that for you," Ruth said. "But I've never gotten an alert that included a drone."

Despite Malone's neighbor catching the drone on camera, Ian knew whoever flew the drone would try to avoid cameras, and if Nicole hadn't been watching, no one would ever have known about the delivery.

Ian handed over his business card. "Send the picture and video to this email address. Do it immediately if you can."

"Yeah, we can do that." Ruth turned the card over and over in her hands, studying it with eyes that were wide with concern.

"Thank you for telling us about the box, Nicole," Londyn said. "We'll take it with us and make sure your neighbor gets it back."

"Will you tell Ty I took it? He'll be mad when he finds out. He pretends to be a nice guy, but I've seen him be mean to his kids and to other people too."

Ruth's gaze shot to her daughter. "You never told me that."

"I couldn't." Nicole scooted away from her mother. "I was watching him in his backyard from up here. You told me not to."

Ruth studied her daughter's face, her hands clenched in her lap. "Sounds like we have some things to talk about."

"You should do that," Ian said, eager to leave and find

out what the box contained. "And if there's anything we need to know, give us a call."

Nicole looked at him, her eyes wide. "Am I going to get arrested for stealing?"

"Not this time, but in the future, don't take things that don't belong to you. And don't worry about telling Ty about this. We'd prefer to keep this information quiet for now," Ian said, but deep down he was glad she took the box. She might've taken something that would break this investigation wide open, and for that, he couldn't fault her.

Ian was desperate for a lead, and he was sure he'd held one in his hands. He'd wanted to rip the box open and ignore the legal ramifications. But before Londyn even got a word out telling him not to do it, he'd come to his senses and put the box in the back seat.

Still, as he raced for the office, he kept looking in the rearview mirror to be sure he hadn't imagined the child turning over the box.

They'd nearly reached downtown when his phone dinged, and he glanced at the screen. "Text from Ruth. Go ahead and look at it."

Londyn grabbed his phone, and he had to share his password so she could unlock it.

"Ruth didn't find any videos with a drone," Londyn said. "She'll keep looking for older footage that might show a drone."

"Still seems like the photo will give us the connection we need to Malone's delivery."

"Photo's not clear enough to read the serial number," she said. "It'd be better if we had matching numbers, but it's the same model."

"Send it to Nick at Veritas, along with the video from the delivery at Malone's house. Ask him to compare the drones, and tell him it's urgent. His number's in my contact list."

She tapped the screen, and when she'd finished, she placed the phone back in the holder.

He sped to the office, and the second he reached his desk, he applied for a warrant to open the box and reveal its contents. The warrant was taking too long, and Ian was too anxious to sit. He jumped up and started pacing, mentally willing the judge to give his approval.

Londyn got up from her desk where she'd been researching the drone company and crossed the room. She stopped in front of him. "Pacing won't make the warrant come in any faster."

"What if we don't get one at all?" he asked, feeling like the mere thought was strangling him. "What if we have to give the box back to Olivo unopened?"

Londyn tilted her head and took a breath, then slowly let it out. "We have probable cause. The picture Nicole took showing the drone matched the one that delivered Malone's package. And my research says it's not a common brand. Add Junior's association with Olivo, that the packages were delivered in the same manner..."

"It seemed good going in, but when you list the reasons, it doesn't seem like enough."

"It was enough for the LT to sign off on the request. He wouldn't do that if we didn't have enough to request it."

"Then why is it taking so long?" Ian looked at his watch. "It's been a couple of hours already."

"You know crime's up and warrants are taking longer."

He did know. Their murder rate had skyrocketed this year, as had other crimes. His desk phone rang, and he snatched it up.

"Your warrant's on the way to your fax machine, and I'm also sending an electronic copy," the judge's clerk said.

"Thank you." Ian ended the call and looked at Londyn. "We got it."

He charged across the room to the fax machine. He tapped his foot until it started humming and spitting out the pages. He snatched them up and hurried back to his desk. "You want in on this?"

She nodded.

"Then let's go." He'd arranged for Sierra at Veritas to X-ray the box before he opened it, just in case it held a dangerous powder. Now he could take it over there.

He and Londyn nearly jogged for the elevator and raced to his car in their secured lot. He put the package in the trunk so he didn't keep looking at it but kept the warrant in the car with him.

Londyn clicked on her seatbelt. "I keep wondering what we're gonna find."

Ian cranked the engine. "It's such a small box, but heavy for its size, so who knows. Not likely a picture this time, unless he tossed a brick or two inside the box."

"A photo could hold proof of something, which would explain the word written on the outside of the box."

"But proof of what?" Ian's phone rang from the dash, and he used his car's infotainment system to answer the call from Nick on speaker.

"I finished analyzing the photo you sent and comparing it to the video," Nick said, his voice deep and concise. "When I enlarged and enhanced them, I discovered you're looking at two different drones."

Ian cast Londyn an uncertain look. Good thing he didn't know that bit of information when he'd asked for the warrant. It might've stopped him from getting it.

"Good news. The picture the kid took has such clear

resolution that we got a fingerprint from the drone, and Reed said he would run it through the fed's database."

"Good. Have him do that. And please have Sierra compare it to Junior's prints. We're on our way over there now." He hung up.

"You think Junior could've sent the package to Olivo?" Londyn asked.

"He was alive at the time it was delivered. Who knows, whatever's in the box could've been the thing that got him killed. I hope there are prints on the package too, but I'm guessing whoever sent it would've worn gloves."

"Did you tell the LT that you were going to have Sierra print it?"

"No," he answered. "Depending on what we find inside will depend on who I have do it. If the item makes me think we need to move fast, then I'll have her process it. If not, we'll drop it at the state lab."

"You'll go into a long queue at the lab. Would be good to avoid that if possible."

"If we can prove Olivo ordered a hit on Junior, I'll take the slow boat for sure so we don't bring the evidence into question."

"Sometimes slow's not a bad thing." Her tone had darkened.

He glanced at her. "Sounds like you're speaking from experience."

"The breakup I mentioned. I should've taken it slower with him. Then, I would've known a whole lot more about him before becoming so invested."

"Not the guy you thought he was, huh?"

"Not at all." She curled her hands into fists. "Turns out he could hide who he was for a little while, but then it all started coming out. His home life growing up wasn't so great, and he carried a lot of baggage from that."

"Maybe he could've changed," Ian said.

She studied him. "After being in law enforcement as long as you have been, do you really think people change?"

"Not most of them, but I've seen it happen." Was he just saying that because he was wishing if he discovered he was like his parents that he could change? "Do you think people survive dysfunctional childhoods and live normal lives?"

"Depends on the dysfunction," she said, "but yeah, I *do* think that happens. The odds are against them, but none of us grow up in a perfect household."

"I don't know," he said. "I've been spending some time with the Byrd family, and their childhood seems pretty sweet."

"They're family is great. At least that's what my parents say. I still promise you each one of them has an issue or two that they've had to overcome. For one, there's always sibling rivalry if you're not an only child."

"That's me. An only."

"Really?" Her eyes flashed open. "You don't have that spoiled center-of-the-universe vibe that many onlys have."

"Hey." He grinned. "Onlys have good traits too."

"Oh, I know. Maybe I'm just jealous. There were many days when I wished I was one." She laughed, but suddenly sobered. "But then you lose a sibling, and you know you're blessed to have each and every one of them."

"I heard about your brother's murder," he said. "I'm sorry for your loss."

"Thank you." She fell silent and looked out the window.

He'd killed the good mood, but then they were almost to the center anyway. He turned into the parking lot and chose a space as close as he could in the lot filled with cars. Londyn grabbed the warrant they would need to show Sierra to prove they had the legal right to open the box, and he picked up the box from the trunk.

He approached the front desk. "Detectives Blair and Steele to see Sierra Rice. She's expecting us."

"Let me call her." The receptionist, a cute blonde with the name Lily on a tag pinned to her print blouse, smiled at him.

He listened to Lily make the call and looked at Londyn, who was glancing around the lobby with all the chairs and sofas filled with clients.

"Been here before?" he asked.

She nodded. "How about you?"

"First time was this week. Quite a setup."

"I'm impressed." She looked at him. "And it's nice to have contacts here in case I need their services."

"Yeah, it's great."

"Detectives," Lily said drawing their attention again. "Reed Rice is on his way down to get you." She slid an iPad across the counter to each of them. "Just fill in the form while I prepare your passes."

They tapped information into the screen, and by the time they'd finished, Lily was holding out the same white plastic passes on blue lanyards that held the Veritas Center logo that he'd gotten on his earlier visit. "I see you've both been here before, so you should know the security routine."

"Wear this at all times." Ian dropped the lanyard over his neck. "And don't go anywhere without an escort."

Lily gave him a beaming smile. "If only every law enforcement officer was so accommodating."

"I can imagine you get some blowback."

"Some?" She chuckled. "But it's all good. They're just passionate about their investigations and usually want things done yesterday."

Ian laughed, knowing the feeling. But he'd seen his dad be rude to too many people like Lily that Ian made it a practice to do the opposite. One of the little ways he worked hard to be different from his father.

Reed opened a door on the back wall and quirked a finger.

"Thanks for your help," Ian said to Lily then followed Londyn over to Reed.

He led them past a glass-walled conference room and down a hallway to an elevator. Inside, he selected the fourth floor. "Sierra's in her lab with Malone and has the X-ray machine all fired up."

"Perfect." Ian had thought he might have to wait to see Malone, if he saw her at all, and having her waiting for him was icing on the cake today. He didn't want to act anything but professional in the lab and would have to be careful to control his emotions when he finally laid eyes on her.

"I found Wisniewski," Reed said. "He knew our parents and remembered they were coming to see him. My dad had called and said he had something the police needed to know about."

"Did he say what?" Ian asked.

Reed shook his head.

"Could be about the drywall," Ian suggested.

"Yeah, but why bring my mom along? Makes no sense for her to be involved with that."

Good point. Ian pondered the development until they reached Sierra's trace evidence lab, and Malone greeted him with a smile that said *welcome back, I missed you.*

A warm feeling blossomed in his heart, and he released an involuntary smile. He knew Londyn and Reed had to be picking up on the vibe she was sending his way, and as much as he was trying, he was likely firing the same emotions right back at her.

"I'm ready to do the X-ray." Wearing a protective apron and gloves, Sierra held out her hands for the box.

Ian passed it to her. "Before we do this, were you able to compare the print from the picture of the drone to Junior's print?"

Her eyes lit with enthusiasm. "It matches."

"You're sure?" Ian clarified.

"Positive."

Ian looked at Malone then shifted to Reed. "This gives us an official connection to Olivo."

"Not that it will prove anything other than that they knew each other," Reed said. "But it's a first step."

Ian wouldn't let Reed's practical statement dissolve any of his joy at proving a connection between the two men.

Sierra picked up the package. "Our X-ray machine is in a protective room. Hold on while I shoot it. I'll be right back."

She went to a door in the corner that was holding a yellow sign with the radiation symbol, stepped inside, and closed the door behind her.

Ian had texted Malone about the box after they'd interviewed Nicole, but he now gave her additional details Nicole had provided.

Malone's eyes narrowed. "I sure hope Olivo doesn't find out she took this box and target her and her family. They would have to move. Maybe go into witness protection."

"I suppose it all depends on what's in the box," Ian said.

"I've been thinking about it, and I wonder if it's proof of some action Junior took against Olivo. And even if Olivo didn't get this package, maybe another one was successfully dropped off. Whatever was in it caused Olivo to have Junior killed."

"Could be," Ian said. "Nicole's mother is reviewing additional security footage, but so far her cameras didn't capture anything."

The door to the X-ray room opened, and Sierra came out

carrying the box like it was one of Asher's dirty diapers. Her face had paled, and her eyes were narrow.

"What's in it?" Reed demanded.

Sierra took a long breath. "A human finger. A severed finger."

15

Malone had to swallow a few times to curb the nausea rising in her stomach. She'd expected something like the picture she'd received. Never did she imagine the box would contain a human body part. Never. Especially when Ian said the box was heavy.

"Whoever sent the finger took care." Sierra set the box on the nearest stainless steel table. "It's in a foam cooler surrounded with a lot of ice packs. If it'd been delivered on time, it might've been able to be reattached. But now? I doubt the finger is viable and reattachment isn't possible."

Malone's stomach churned just thinking about it, but at least she now knew the many ice packs made the box so heavy.

"If Junior sent it, it's odd for a major drug dealer like him to be concerned about saving a finger," Ian said. "Unless he had a sentimental connection to the person he snipped the finger from."

"We'll need to get this to the ME to examine," Londyn said.

"Might I suggest we take one step before doing that?" Sierra asked.

Reed shifted his focus to his wife. "What do you have in mind?"

"You're authorized to open the package, so I suggest we do and have Kelsey look at the finger to see what she can tell us." Sierra looked at Ian. "Kelsey is our forensic anthropologist. She could give us an idea of who the finger might've come from. Maybe we can even get a print."

"Great idea." Ian took out his pocket knife. "Go ahead and call her, and I'll open the box."

"I'll call," Sierra said, "but there might be other prints on the box. Let me process it."

"I assume you'll leave powder behind," Londyn said. "We'll have to explain that to the LT, and he won't like it."

"She's right," Ian said. "We'll stick with examining the finger in any capacity that doesn't change it."

"I can take a DNA sample and print the finger without altering anything," Sierra said, taking her phone from the pocket of her lab coat.

"Then do that after you make the call," Ian said.

She tapped the screen and lifted it to her ear. "Kelsey, good. Glad I caught you."

Malone half listened to the conversation, but most of her attention was on Ian slipping on gloves then slicing the box open. She'd never seen a severed finger before and suspected it would be gruesome, but she wouldn't fall back and ignore it. If this finger helped convict Snipes, and as an added bonus, Olivo too, she would suck it up and do whatever was needed of her.

Ian reached into the box and lifted the lid on the Styrofoam cooler. "Wow, the ice packs are still cold."

She braced herself for seeing the finger.

He pulled out a piece of paper. "Note says, You wanted proof, here it is. Pay up or I'll start sending you one body part at a time until you do."

Malone gasped. "A ransom note."

"That's harsh," Londyn said.

"We'll need to have this processed for prints and DNA." Ian gritted his teeth and set the paper down to lift a clear plastic zipper bag from the box.

Malone took a quick look to confirm a finger from the knuckle up dangled in the bag, but her stomach churned, and she had to look away.

"Seems like it's from a male," Ian said. "But what do I know?"

"Kelsey's on her way up." Sierra shoved her phone into her pocket and stepped up behind him. "If you want to know gender, I can tell you from a print. I'll do it electronically, and it won't alter the finger by adding ink."

Malone turned back. "You can really tell gender just from a fingerprint?"

"Yes. There are two ways actually. First, females have significantly higher ridge density. Meaning a finer ridge than males for both radial and ulnar areas. And eighteen-year-olds and younger have higher fingerprint RD than older males."

"And the second way to tell?" Ian asked.

"Fingerprints contain certain amino acids," Sierra replied. "The levels of these amino acids are twice as high in the sweat of women as in that of men."

"So the first is visual and the second a lab test," Ian clarified.

Sierra nodded.

"Then if you don't change anything, go for it." He held out the bag to her.

Malone watched to see if Sierra seemed at all squeamish, but she just took the bag, set it down then got out a small electronic print reader. She cleaned the screen and picked up the bag.

Sierra took the finger out of the bag, but the lab door opened, and Kelsey entered, giving Malone something else to focus on.

Malone was always struck by the fact that Kelsey didn't at all look like the kind of woman who might unearth decaying bodies and deal with their bones. She had nearly black wavy long hair, pinned back today with an intricate metal clip, and green eyes that sparkled like emeralds. She wore a lab coat, but underneath she had on a frilly patterned blouse and a pleated navy skirt. She clipped across the room in high heels that Malone envied.

"Hi all." She smiled at the group then she peered at Ian. "And you must be Detective Blair."

"It's Ian." He shook hands with her.

She looked at Malone, cut her eyes toward Ian, and gave a firm nod. Was she approving him for her? Had Sierra been telling her partners that Ian and Malone had a thing?

Kelsey stepped to the table, her professional look in place. A look Malone thought Kelsey probably needed to get through the things she saw. At least Malone needed a stone face when battered children and women and dirty homeless teens showed up on her doorstep needing help. And not just anyone's help, but Malone's help. To give it, she had to remain objective and not let her emotions take over.

Kelsey put on gloves and waited for Sierra to finish taking prints from her reader.

The silence in the room was getting to Malone, and she had to end it. "I had no idea prints could be taken from a finger that was severed days before."

Kelsey glanced her way. "Fingerprints are very durable. Especially when on ice and kept cold like this finger. When you die, they're one of the last things to disappear."

Malone shook her head. "I had no clue."

"Okay, you're up, Kelsey," Sierra said.

Kelsey laid the finger on the clean paper. "It's an index finger from a right hand. No question about that."

Malone didn't interrupt to ask how she knew that but watched with nearly closed eyes as Kelsey measured the finger and studied it, turning it several times. "Longer than a typical female's index finger. But, as I say, typical, so could still be a female with a long finger. Honestly, the way the nail is cared for, I would say male. Plus, it's meaty and blunt. And the skin hasn't aged, so I'd say young male."

"I concur," Sierra said looking up for a microscope. "The ridge details match a male, and the amino acid concentration say male as well. Eighteen or under."

"So, a young male is missing his index finger," Ian stated.

"A Caucasian male," Kelsey added.

Sierra held up a swab in a labeled plastic container and looked at Ian. "I swabbed for DNA, which we can get to Emory, but we'll need your approval to run it in CODIS."

Malone had clients whose prints were in the Combined DNA Index System, another database managed by the FBI and contained DNA profiles for criminals and law enforcement officers.

"I'll get your formal approval," Ian said.

"You think the LT is going to approve an outside agency running the DNA?" Londyn asked.

"The ransom note makes it a case for this being proof of life. It's possible we have someone who's been kidnapped and needs to be rescued before he's killed," Ian said.

"But who?" Londyn asked. "Not one of Olivo's thugs, as I can't see him caring enough to pay up."

"What if it's his son?" Malone asked. "They said Olivo had hunkered down with his family in their house. What if they did that because someone kidnapped the boy, and they're trying to get him back and make sure no one takes the daughter?"

"How old are his kids?" Kelsey asked.

"Daughter's sixteen. Son's eighteen."

"Could be the son's finger for sure," Kelsey said.

Ian looked at Londyn, and the look in his eyes raised Malone's concern. She was worried he was going to suggest some crazy plan or idea. One that might get him and Londyn hurt or killed.

Ian took a deep breath. "I think it's time to go to Olivo's house and ask to talk to the son. Maybe Olivo knows about the package, maybe not. But one look at the kid's hand will answer a lot of questions. And if Olivo can't produce his son..." He narrowed his gaze. "Maybe this could lead us to something that can put Olivo behind bars."

Ian and Londyn delivered the finger to the medical examiner's office before visiting Olivo, and Dr. Albertson concurred that they were looking for a young male. So the visit to Olivo was inevitable. They pulled up to the house to see all the blinds closed, just as Nix had told Ian he would find.

Ian shifted into park, his eyes on the house. "Wonder if anyone will even answer?"

"We have Olivo's phone number. We can try that if he doesn't." Londyn released her seatbelt. "Besides, I have this obnoxious voice I can use when I knock that usually gets them to answer just to make me go away." She laughed and got out.

Ian chuckled to himself. She was fun to work with, though he suspected this was a nervous laugh, and yet she was also committed and dedicated. He had to wonder why she was still single. She was a beautiful woman, confident, and had a pleasing personality. Maybe she was too confident. Lots of men had a problem with that. Maybe this last guy was like that.

Ian joined her at the door.

"Ready?" she asked, her hand already raised to knock.

He nodded.

"Let's give him a chance to answer before I get annoying." She grinned and knocked.

Turned out he was spared of hearing her annoying voice, as Olivo came to the door right away.

They displayed their IDs.

"Detectives Steele and Blair," Londyn said as they'd agreed she would lead the questions. Men like Olivo were often macho and condescending to women, underestimating their abilities, which might allow Londyn to ask questions Ian could never ask.

"Your son, Carlo, has come up in an investigation," she said. "We'd like to have a word with him."

"What's he supposedly done?" Olivo asked.

"He's eighteen, so we'll need to talk to him about that." Londyn smiled, but there was an edge of steel in her voice that said it wasn't optional.

He stood back. "Come in, and I'll get him. He's in his room."

Surprise. The boy had not been kidnapped.

They entered the house, which had Roman columns in the entryway with a wide hallway leading into a sunken family room with a two-story fireplace. But Olivo led them to a formal living room, where the furniture was traditional with fancy carvings and the lampshades were finished with fringe on the bottoms.

He gestured at the sofa. "Can I get you something to drink?"

"Thank you, but no." Londyn gave him another smile.

"Nothing for me," Ian said, trying not to sound too gruff and disapproving.

"I'll be right back with Carlo." He spun and strode out of the room.

Ian watched him until he turned into a doorway. Ian faced Londyn. "I don't know how you can smile at him like that."

"Took lots and lots of practice in front of a mirror." She shook her head. "I started out trying to be a tough guy, hoping men would take me seriously, but half the time they didn't. One day I figured out I could get more with a smile. Not all the time. I have to judge the guy first, but the first time it worked was the day I started practicing."

"Whatever works for you," he said. "You think he's really going to produce the boy?"

She shrugged. "Not sure how he can get out of it, but he's a slimeball, so I figure he'll try something if his son isn't here."

Ian heard footsteps heading their way on the Italian marble floors and bit back his comment.

Olivo entered first, a nervous teen behind him. The boy wore faded jeans with ripped knees, a black-and-white striped button-down shirt, and black-and-white sneakers. He had his right hand in his pocket when he strode into the room.

Ian needed to get a look at that hand. He stood and held his out to shake. The kid looked back at his dad, who took Carlo by the shoulders and directed him away from Ian and into a chair. The boy sat and kept his hand in his pocket. But then he picked up a pillow with his left hand, and shielding his right hand, he slipped his hand free of the pocket.

Not exactly subtle.

Olivo was frowning at him. Ian glanced at Londyn, who hadn't missed anything. Ian nodded at her to begin.

"Carlo, I'm Detective Steele, but you can call me Londyn." She gave him a more sincere smile than Olivo had earned.

Carlo nodded but didn't speak.

"I have to first ask if you want your father present while we talk to you."

Carlo glanced at his dad, who was sitting rigidly in a chair across from Londyn.

"It's okay if you don't want him here," she said softly. "But I wanted to ask because, in my experience, most eighteen-year-old men like you prefer to stand on their own and not hide behind their daddies."

Ian wanted to high-five Londyn. She'd just made it hard for Carlo to say he wanted his daddy there.

"Of course you want me here, son," Olivo said, his tone hard as steel. "We don't have anything to hide from each other, right?"

"Right," Carlo said, but he didn't sound all that convincing. "It would be good if he stayed."

The kid was either smart enough to recognize that his dad would help him through the interview or too afraid of his dad to send him away.

"Okay, then let's get started." Londyn sat back, crossed her legs, and smiled at Carlo again, coming across like she was there for a family visit. "Perhaps you can tell me where you've been the last four days."

He shot a look at his dad, sheer terror in his eyes.

"The family has had kind of a lock-in the past few days," Olivo answered. "I even took time off of work. Sort of a time to unplug and get to know each other better."

"Sounds nice," Londyn said, her focus still on Carlo. "What kinds of things did you do?"

"Um, played video games?" It was said like more of a question than a statement.

"I did give him and his sister some gaming time." Olivo gave his son a patronizing look. "But we also played cards and board games. Did puzzles."

"You like all those games, Carlo?" Londyn asked.

He shrugged.

"I'm more into sports than sitting around," Londyn said.

Like Ian, she'd read the report Nick quickly put together on Carlo, which said the boy was an athlete. "You like sports?"

He nodded, and his eyes lit up. "Baseball."

"Any good at it?"

"All star," Carlo answered, and he and his dad both straightened their shoulders.

Londyn reached out to the table, grabbed a decorative ball from a metal bowl, and tossed it to him. The boy knocked the pillow down and caught the ball with a bandaged hand. He winced when contact was made, though from pain or fear, Ian couldn't tell. The bandage covered the spot where the end of his index finger had been.

"What happened to your finger Carlo?" she asked.

The kid looked panicked and glanced at his dad. "I can't do it. Not after what I've been through."

He jumped to his feet and fled from the room.

Olivo got up and stepped into the hallway. "Carlo, come back here."

Ian's phone chimed, and he looked at the text from the ME. *Fingerprint for the finger matched a juvie record for Carlo Olivo.*

He held the screen out to Londyn.

She narrowed her eyes and lowered her voice. "We press the son if he comes back. If not, we lean on Olivo."

Ian nodded. "You keep taking lead."

Olivo returned and directed his focus on Ian. "I'm sorry my son was rude. He's had a rough time."

"I would imagine so," Londyn said. "Since someone cut off his finger and sent it to you as proof that he'd been kidnapped."

Olivo whipped his gaze to Londyn. "What?"

"You heard me," she said. "We intercepted the package containing his severed finger."

"When? Where?"

"It was delivered by drone but wound up at the wrong address," she said. True, though perhaps not the full truth.

"You have it? You have his finger? You must give it to me so we can see if it can be reattached."

That would never work, but now that they'd confirmed the finger belonged to Carlo, they would return it to the family. "We'll be glad to arrange for you to pick it up at the medical examiner's office."

Olivo gave a quick nod, his lips pressed so tightly they were white.

"Must make you mad to see the way your son was tortured," Ian said.

Olivo curled his fingers but didn't speak.

"And you would want to get back at the person who took him," Londyn added. "I know I would."

"That would be human nature." Olivo stared at her, his gaze hooded.

"And if you knew who cut off his finger, perhaps you even ordered a hit on that man's life."

Olivo scoffed. "You must be nuts if you think I have those kinds of connections."

"Not nuts," Londyn said quietly, making the man lean forward to hear her. "But we do know you run the biggest drug operation in the area and have for years. That kind of position gives you all sorts of resources to take out the person who harmed your son."

"Even if what you're saying is true, which it is not, you're assuming I know who kidnapped him."

"Of course you do," Ian said. "It was one of your lieutenants. Gilbert Flagg Jr. Known to all as Junior. The man you had killed four days ago."

16

Ian didn't like having to grill the kid after what he'd gone through, but after peppering Olivo with a string of questions, the father didn't confess to killing Junior. That would've been too easy. So, Ian was going to take the kid down to the precinct and separate him from his dad to see what they could learn. Ian would then interview Olivo. Except Olivo called his attorney as they stepped out the door. Ian figured the lawyer would tell them both to clam up. Didn't matter. Ian would still try.

He gritted his teeth and escorted the pair down the sidewalk. Nearing Ian's car, a woman popped up from behind the bushes that lined the far side of the driveway.

She raised a gun and fired.

Olivo dropped to the concrete.

Ian grabbed the kid and tugged him to the ground behind the car. Londyn dove in after them and quickly called for backup.

"My dad." Carlo struggled to get up.

"Too dangerous." Ian held him down. "If you promise me you'll stay here, I'll go after him."

"I promise," he cried out. "Go! Go!"

"No additional gunshots." Ian looked at Londyn. "Ready to move?"

She nodded.

They popped up above the hood. The woman, who Ian could now identity as Karen Flagg, stood over Olivo. He lay on his back, his eyes open. Blood gushed from three chest wounds. Looked like there was nothing they could do for Olivo.

But they did need to take Karen into custody without anyone else getting hurt. The gun dangled from her hand, and her focus was on Olivo.

Ian raised his gun. "Put the gun down, Karen."

She looked up at him, her eyes glazed with pain.

"Put it down slowly," Ian directed when she didn't move. "On the ground right beside you."

Her gaze fixed on Olivo again, she set the weapon on the concrete. She never took her gaze off Olivo when she stood back up, her eyes almost as fixed and lifeless as Olivo's.

Ian and Londyn made their way around the car slowly, carefully. Ian reached Karen first, and he kicked the gun out of the way. "On your knees, Karen."

She dropped down silently, continuing to stare at Olivo.

"Now on your face, hands behind your back," Ian said, following protocol, though he likely didn't need to be so cautious with her. She'd done what she wanted to do and was more than finished emotionally.

She complied, lowering her body and bringing her face-to-face with Olivo. "You deserved it. You killed my son."

She started weeping, and her pain saturated the air. Ian felt bad having to cuff her, but murder was murder, no matter a person's motive.

He secured cuffs on her wrists with a quick snap and signaled for Londyn to search the woman. Londyn took control of Karen, and Ian felt for a pulse on Olivo. Nothing. No surprise.

The door to the house opened, and a woman Ian assumed was Olivo's wife came out. She took one look at Olivo and screamed.

"Tirone!" she called out. "No. No."

Carlo ran to her, and she swept him into her arms, covering his eyes to keep him from looking at his father.

Despite Olivo's criminal behavior, Ian's heart broke for his family. He had no idea if they knew about his criminal ways, but regardless, they were grieving.

Ian stepped up to them. "I'm sorry, ma'am, but he's gone."

She screamed again, the anguish piercing Ian's heart and bringing the teenage daughter outside too. She looked at her dad.

"No!" she cried. "No." She turned to her mother. "First Carlo's finger, now this. What's happening?"

Was it really possible that these people didn't know who Olivo really was? What he did? Maybe the kids had been protected, but Ian figured after all these years that the wife knew or, at least, suspected Olivo was a drug kingpin. If she did, it didn't lessen her grief.

A patrol car siren broke the quiet, and the vehicle soon screamed down the street. When the officer bolted toward the driveway, Londyn got Karen to her feet and turned her over to the officer to secure in his car.

"Who is she?" Carlo drew away from his mother to watch Karen being loaded in the cruiser.

"Let's not talk about that now," Ian said as more sirens blared on arriving vehicles. "It's going to get a little crazy out here. Let's go inside."

He signaled for Londyn to take charge of the scene and escorted the distraught family inside and closed the door.

They went into the formal living room. The mother and daughter huddled together on the couch. Carlo sat in the same chair as before, and Ian took the chair where Olivo had stonewalled them in the interview.

"I'm Detective Ian Blair with the Portland Police Bureau."

The older woman looked at Ian, but her gaze was unfocused. Grief stricken. "Vittorio. Tirone's wife."

"I'm sorry for your loss."

"Why?" She eyed him. "You brought this to our house."

"I didn't. Your husband and his business dealings brought this on you."

She clamped her mouth closed and lifted her chin, but it trembled as did her hands.

Ian wasn't going to get anything from her. He looked at Carlo. "You knew your kidnapper, didn't you?"

He nodded. "Junior. He came to parties at our house. He was a lot of fun, before. I think he might've worked for my dad."

"Gilbert Flagg Jr.," Vittoria clarified.

"How did your dad free you?" Ian asked, ignoring the mother for now. "Did he pay a ransom?"

Carlo shrugged. "He just appeared one day when Junior was gone." He held up his injured finger, his face anguished. "After Junior did this. How could he do that to me? We were friends."

Ian wanted to tell the boy that friends didn't exist in the drug world, but that wouldn't help him.

His mother tightened her grip on the daughter's hand. "Tirone figured out where Junior would take Carlo—a cabin where he'd gone hunting last year with Tirone. When Junior left Carlo alone, Tirone moved in and brought our boy home."

She sounded so proud of her husband, and Ian had to

wonder again what she knew about where their money really came from.

"What did you know about Junior?" he asked instead.

"He was an associate and wanted to move up in Tirone's company," she said. "But Tirone didn't think Junior was ready, and he told him no. That was when Junior took Carlo out for a drive and never brought him back. He demanded ten million dollars. Tirone wouldn't pay it unless he had proof that Junior had Carlo. We never got it but it didn't matter. Tirone had located our son."

"Do you know Mickey Snipes?" Ian asked.

She nodded, looking more wary than when he'd mentioned Junior.

"He's been charged with Junior's murder, but we believe Tirone ordered Snipes to take Junior out."

"No," the daughter said, a defiant look in her eyes so reminiscent of her father. "Daddy wouldn't do that."

Ian knew better, but he wouldn't share details. He would wait until they were over their immediate shock and question them individually. Who knows, each of them could have information about their father's illegal activities.

Malone sat on Reed's sofa next to Ian. She couldn't quit shaking her head. She couldn't grasp that Karen Flagg had shown up at Olivo's house with a gun and killed him. But a mother's wrath was something to behold. Malone had seen the fierce protectiveness and need for vindication in her work with battered women. She just never experienced it going to this length.

"Did you interview Karen?" Malone asked.

Ian nodded. "She said she left home on a whim and built up her courage on the way."

"But she couldn't know that Olivo ordered the hit on Junior, right?"

"She said he'd sucked her son into his drug organization, and that was enough for her."

Malone thought about what it meant to have Snipes behind bars and Olivo dead. "So, will you wrap up Junior's investigation now?"

"Pretty much. Londyn is at the cabin where Carlo had been held in case there's any evidence that could help us prosecute Snipes, but I would assume Olivo had the place cleaned of anything incriminating."

"That makes sense."

"Now that Olivo is dead, we'll lean on Snipes to see if he admits Olivo's involvement for the record. We're still searching his computer, so that might tell us more about his organization. We came up empty on searching Olivo's house and business both. Forensics is still looking at his home and work computer, too, but he had to be hiding things elsewhere. Maybe a central storage area that they all used. We might never find the location."

"But if Snipes talks," Malone said, "it might help to further dismantle Olivo's organization."

"One thing is for sure." Ian locked gazes. "If Olivo sent the photo to your house, you and your family should be safe now."

"Right. I didn't think of that." She mulled it over in her brain. "I wonder if it'll be enough for Reed to let me go home alone."

"It's not enough for me. Not yet." He took her hand and held it tightly. "We should give it some time to see if you receive another threat. I don't think you need an entire Nighthawk team detail, but someone should be with you at all times."

"Do you really think someone other than Olivo is trying

to warn me off? I mean, Snipes could've done it, but I doubt he did from behind bars."

"Agreed. But you mean too much to me to let you go home without knowing for sure that Olivo was behind the threat." He continued to hold her gaze.

"Then I guess it's easiest for all if I stay here with Reed and Sierra."

Asher's cries rang out from his bedroom, and Malone stood to get him, as Sierra was in the lab and Reed was working in the other room, but Ian held tight to her hand. He looked up at her. "Promise me you'll still be careful and not go out on your own."

"I promise."

"Good." He lurched to his feet and took her shoulders. He kissed her hard on the mouth then abruptly let go. "Because I can't lose you."

She didn't know what to say. She was overcome with emotions she couldn't even put her finger on, so she bolted down the hallway to Asher's room. She opened the door to find he'd rolled over on his tummy and was beaming a big smile up at her, looking proud of his accomplishment.

"Hi, precious." She scooped him up and cradled him against her shoulder, savoring the feel of his soft cheek against hers.

If life were only as simple as the tasks Asher was learning. She remembered her childhood, wanting time to fly by so she could get older and achieve new skills. When did things change? When had she started to want life to slow down? To take each moment and savor it? Like picking Asher up and smelling his delicious baby scent. She wanted to cling to him, but he was squirming to get going. To master those new skills.

She took him to the changing table and unsnapped his romper. As much as she loved being with Reed, Sierra, and this new precious nephew, their family only reminded her of all she didn't have. Tears stung her eyes. She was alone. No child to cuddle. No man to hug in a long-term relationship. Alone. Except for her family. She could come over here anytime, but it wasn't the same as having her own family. Her own husband.

She took off Asher's wet diaper and put on a fresh one.

Loud voices sounded outside the door. Peggy and Russ. They were bringing dinner tonight, and all the siblings were coming over too. Not to celebrate Olivo's death but to celebrate that the immediate threat to their family had been eliminated.

Asher cooed and smiled up at her, drool dribbling from his mouth. "You'll soon have a tooth. Then what?"

He babbled at her, shoving his fist into his mouth, and her heart melted.

She wanted a family for herself. Her feelings for Ian had brought the longing to the forefront. And she didn't want the family with just anyone. She wanted it with Ian.

But that wasn't going to happen.

She sighed and shook her head. What was with this sudden sentimentality? She needed to nip it in the bud right now or Peggy would pick up on it, and Malone would have a lot of explaining to do.

She turned her full attention to Asher and cooed at him until he laughed. That bolt of longing sharpened, but she ignored the emotion and finished snapping his romper then left the room.

Peggy was in the kitchen with Sierra, who had returned from her lab, and Russ was sitting on the couch with Ian. It looked like they were in a deep discussion, but when Malone entered the room, their talk stopped, and Russ stood.

"There's my little man." He held out his hands for the baby, and Asher went willingly to him.

Ian kept a solid eye on Asher, perhaps wondering what it took to be a dad. Dare she hope, with the way he'd just kissed her, that he was considering such a thing?

Nah, he wasn't even ready for a relationship. The thought of fatherhood would likely send him running.

~

Ian stepped away from the Byrd clan and Malone. They were all chattering too loudly around the dinner table for him to hear the call he'd just received from Londyn. Besides, he didn't want to talk about homicide in front of the family.

"What's up?" he asked, walking toward the hallway, plugging his free ear to block out the still boisterous conversations.

"I nagged the tech staff to review Olivo's computer, and they fast-tracked it for me."

"What did you have to promise to get them to do that?"

"Don't ask." She chuckled. "Anyway, they forwarded all the photos from his drive to me, and the pictures of Reed, Sierra, and the baby were on it. He even had pics of Malone."

"So, Olivo *was* behind the threat," Ian said, not sure if he was glad to hear the news or not. He *was* glad she was out of danger.

But that meant Malone could go home and walk out of his life. He still didn't think he was a suitable mate for her, but he sure didn't like the thought of not seeing her again after tonight. Or worse, running into her in public while she was on the arm of another man. That thought cramped his gut.

He wasn't sure what it said about him that he was happy

he hadn't closed her parents' murder case. They'd at least talk again a little.

"Yeah, they also found an email where he received the photos from a PI, and Olivo made a bitcoin payment to the PI for his services."

"Any mention of Malone's parents?"

"The files didn't go back that far, but there wasn't anything on the computer related to Malone other than the pictures."

Ian took a moment to process the news. "Don't you think it's odd that Junior encrypted his computer and Olivo didn't?"

"There's nothing else incriminating on the drive. It's all personal or related to his legit company. I suspect he was handling this at home due to his self-imposed lock-in. And I figure he would've gotten rid of these pictures once he knew his threats worked."

"Makes sense, and I doubt he expected to be arrested. Our detectives never had anything to talk to him about until Nicole swiped that package."

"It was a lucky break that she did."

He agreed. "Anything else I should know?"

"I asked them to spend more time on breaking Junior's encryption, but they said they were doing all they could."

"Now that Olivo's dead, let's plan to meet in the morning to interview Snipes again. We can then review the Rices' murder investigation and set a game plan on that too."

"You want me to keep helping on that?"

"Absolutely. If you want to, that is."

"Sure thing. See you at eight." She ended the call.

On his way back to the dining area, he paused at the mouth of the hallway and watched the family laugh and enjoy each other's company. Peggy and Russ were the glue that held them all together. Glue his parents never had. He wanted what he was witnessing. Wanted to be a part of something real. But he was a big chicken. Too afraid to try and fail. To fail and hurt Malone. He watched her, smiling, laughing, leaning back in her chair looking relaxed and beautiful. Gorgeous.

She caught his gaze and smiled. She got up and joined him. "The family is something to take in."

"Kind of overwhelming, but in a good way."

She kept her gaze pinned to him. "Do you have extended family who gather like this?"

"We have family, but my parents never see them. My mom and dad only invited a person to a get-together if they could do something for them." He shook his head. "Just the opposite of what I'm looking at here. Each and every one of these people will give anything and everything for their family members."

"Nice, right?"

He nodded.

"Why the frown?"

He didn't know if he should answer, but she deserved the truth from him. "I can't do it. Be like them. I'm just not cut out for it." He reached for her hands, then changed his mind and shoved them into his pockets. "I've really come to care about you. A lot. We'll still be in touch because I'll keep working your parents' murder investigation. But I think we need to keep things platonic between us from now on."

Her eyes closed for a moment. She opened them and looked at him for the longest time, her lips pressed together and her eyes darkening. His answer disappointed her. He hated that look. Hated to disappoint her in any way. She was too special, and she'd had a million disappointments in her life already. She didn't need the rejection. He'd kissed her. He'd led her on. But better he let her down now than later, when they were deep into a relationship that wouldn't work.

"I should get back to the family," she said.

"Before you go, I need to tell you that was Londyn on the phone. Our computer techs found the pictures that were sent to you in the package on Olivo's computer and an email and payment to the PI he hired to take them."

"That's proof he was behind it, so I can go home."

He nodded.

"Perfect," she said. "I'll go right after dinner's over."

She gave him a long look, maybe waiting for him to restate his feelings and tell her he'd changed his mind about a platonic relationship, but when he said nothing, she strode across the room.

He needed a minute to ready his mind before joining the family again. He'd noticed Peggy watching him with Malone from where she was standing behind the oldest of three children they were fostering. Her hands were on Willow's shoulders, but Peggy looked over the child at Ian. She kissed Willow's head and marched across the room toward Ian.

Uh-oh. Looked like he was going to be on the end of something he would rather avoid, but he wouldn't run. She meant well, and she had raised six incredible children, so maybe he could benefit from whatever she was going to say.

"You and Malone don't look too happy with each other," she said, her gaze locked on him. "Not like you're mad, but not happy either."

"I was telling her we have proof that Olivo delivered the picture to her, and she can safely go home now."

"And she doesn't want to go?"

"No, she does."

"You're not going to tell me what's going on, are you?"

He took a breath and let it out. "It's kind of personal."

"Regarding why you don't want to be with Malone, right?"

"It's not that I don't want to be with her. It's that...I can't."

"Are you married? In love with another woman?"

"No. Nothing like that." For some reason he couldn't even begin to fathom, he told her about his parents. "I want to believe I'm not destined to be like them, but I'm afraid I am, and I don't want to hurt her by leading her on. Or worse, be with her and then turn out to be like my parents and hurt her even more."

"Just because you had bad role models doesn't condemn you to be a bad father or husband."

He shook his head. "If you met my parents, you might change your mind."

She rested a hand on his shoulder. "I'll tell you what I'd tell one of my sons if they were having this problem. Your argument is very logical. Right up here."

She tapped her brain and studied him. "But this isn't some abstract situation. This is you. Your future. Your potential wife and family. This is about the connection you'll share with them. There's nothing logical about it. Nothing."

She paused and took a breath. "It's like your faith in God. That's not logical, and yet you believe. Believe in yourself, Ian. Believe God is with you. Believe your past doesn't make you who you are today and that you deserve a future. Then, you will be the man who God made you to be. Only then."

Malone had watched the miles pass by while riding in the Nighthawk SUV with Aiden and Erik until they finally turned onto her street. She was nearly home. She called it that, but did it really feel like home? Like it had felt when she was a child? That was something she needed to do some thinking about.

The whole situation with Junior's death, her arrest, and

most importantly, her time with Ian had taught her so much about herself and revealed what she wanted. She needed to consider that too.

For now, she was free to go back to her normal life. The Byrd brothers could stop camping out on her doorstep and planning her every move outside of her home. And Ian? She would still talk to him, but he didn't want more than a professional relationship.

She'd seen Peggy go to him, and right after that, he'd shared with the family the information about the pictures on Olivo's hard drive. Ian had done so in a sensitive way so the children wouldn't pick up on what he was saying, and then he'd departed. Quickly, like whatever Peggy had said to him was the final straw, and he had to flee.

Aiden pulled into her driveway. It *did* feel good to see her own car and know she could go wherever she wanted on her own and be safe.

She leaned forward. "Thank you guys for everything. I owe you all even more than I do when I call you in the middle of the night for one of my clients."

"No worries," Aiden said. "Just glad Ian proved the murder had nothing to do with you and Olivo can't hurt you or anyone else anymore."

She shuddered but wouldn't comment on how terrified she'd been when she'd thought Olivo might have her in his sights. "Let me know if there's ever anything you need." She reached for her door handle. "Of course, it goes without saying that you each get free legal advice and representation for life."

"You know, with the way we like to push the limits, we'll take advantage of your offer." Erik grinned over the seat.

She chuckled and got out, feeling odd to be walking up her sidewalk by herself. She wished she had Ian at her side, but that wasn't meant to be.

17

Ian stifled an early morning yawn and crossed the bullpen toward Londyn's desk, feeling kind of odd being without Malone. He'd spent so much time with her of late that he was missing her. Had been missing her since he'd fled last night after his talk with Peggy. The woman made sense. So much sense, and after tossing and turning all night, he'd come to realize that he'd be a fool if he let someone as wonderful as Malone go. But just because he was willing to risk failing didn't mean she was willing to invest her emotions in a relationship that had strong odds of not surviving.

"Glad you're here." Londyn leaned back in her chair, a spiky black shoe dangling from her toes. "You'll never believe what I found."

"I'm all ears," he said, thinking now he could forget about Malone and focus.

"Gilbert Flagg Sr. owned Malone's house before her parents bought it."

"Seriously?" He perched on the edge of her desk.

"It was listed under a subsidiary to Flagg Contracting, but I tracked it back to Flagg Sr."

"Why a subsidiary company?" Ian asked.

"Looks like he uses the company for all the properties he's owned over the years," Londyn said. "Not sure of his reason. Most likely taxes, but I'll dig a little deeper. As to Malone's house, the records reflect permits and improvements right before they bought it, so it looks like Flagg remodeled the house before selling it."

"It's since been remodeled again, and I can't tell you if he did it or not. But we can ask Malone if she knows anything about it. I do know she's changing it back to the way it was when she lived there."

"Did you ever hear Junior say anything about Malone living in his old house?"

Ian shook his head. "I have to think he didn't know."

"Why's that?"

"I can't see him missing the opportunity to tell her that she was slumming it while he was king of the hill in their big house. I know he had a field day with the fact that she was in foster care, and he wouldn't miss the opportunity to rub the house in."

"Maybe the house and her parents' deaths are connected," Londyn said. "Maybe Flagg Sr. scammed them somehow when he sold the house to them."

"And then killed them?" Ian shook his head. "Seems odd to kill someone over something like that, but I'll ask Senior and Karen about the property. Malone too. When I last questioned Flagg, he denied having known Malone's parents."

"With the house belonging to a subsidiary company, his lawyers might've handled everything except his signature, and he may not have paid much attention to who it was sold to." Londyn leaned forward. "I already scheduled an interview with Karen in lockup in five minutes. We'll talk to Snipes afterward."

He stood. "Let's get to it."

Londyn grabbed her notepad and followed him down the hall. He thought about Malone's house during their walk to the detention center, where they secured their weapons in gun lockers. Once in the interview room, a deputy brought Karen in to see them.

She dropped onto the metal chair. Her face was haggard, her eyes red from crying.

"I can't believe this." She lifted her handcuffs. "I never imagined I'd be jailed for anything. Especially murder. Something in me just snapped, and I couldn't stay in my house any longer. I had to take charge. Make something happen."

She placed her hands on the table and looked at them. "Not that Olivo was the only person to blame. Living with Gilbert hasn't been easy. He has to have his way all the time. No matter the cost. Even belittling our son and making him turn to dealing drugs. I was a fool to stay with him. If I hadn't..." She started to cry.

"I'm sure the jury and judge will take all of that into account," Ian said, honestly wishing he could help her. It seemed as if she'd been abused all her married life. Not physically but mentally. Or she could be putting on a show for them. He was a good judge of character, and her grief and regret were sincere.

He waited for her to gain composure again and look back up. When she did, he leaned toward her. "When I visited your house, I'd mentioned about the parents of one of Junior's classmates dying in a car accident. We now know it wasn't an accident. I didn't tell you that they bought one of your old houses." He gave her the address.

"That place." Her eyes lit up. "I loved that house, but Gilbert had to have something bigger. Something grander. Each time I'd get settled in and really feel at home, he would announce he had a new house for us, and we'd move. Now he's building an even grander place. Well, he'll be living in it all alone. Six thousand square feet to himself. Probably what he wants. Or he'll find some young thing to be by his side for all the business dinners. That was pretty much my only value to him." Karen's sigh turned into a shudder.

"Could this couple's murder have anything to do with the house or even your husband?" Londyn asked.

Karen swiped a hand under her eyes then sniffed. "I doubt it. Gilbert isn't a nice man, and he's a shrewd businessman. He might cheat someone or swindle them, but he wouldn't kill anyone." She suddenly broke into hysterical laughing. "He probably would've said that about me a few days ago too."

"Was there anything unusual about that house?" Ian asked.

She tilted her head. "After we moved out, Gilbert spent some time remodeling the place. He didn't do as much remodeling with all of our houses, but he always had some work done to get top dollar for the property. Guess then he must've sold it to your friend's parents, but there was no other connection to us that I know of and nothing odd about the house itself."

"Would Junior have known that Malone's parents moved into this house?"

"He was so little—preschool age—so I doubt it."

Ian was disappointed, especially since it was Junior who led them to the fact that the crash wasn't an accident. "Can you think about it, and let us know if you remember anything?"

"Sure," she said, looking at her hands again. "It's not like I have anything else to do."

Londyn stood and called in the deputy.

"Thank you, Karen," Ian said as the deputy took her to the door. "Again, I'm sorry for your loss."

She gave a sad nod, her head hanging as she walked away.

Londyn took her seat again. "The deputy will bring Snipes in next."

"Hopefully, he'll be more helpful."

"Karen was sincere enough."

"I don't expect Snipes to be genuine unless there's something in it for him."

"I wish his computer had given us some evidence, but he's just like Olivo and Junior. Hiding his work elsewhere. But we'll keep digging until we find where."

The guard brought Snipes in, and he tried to shrug free of the guard's hands. His face was haggard, and dark circles hung under his eyes. Obviously, jail wasn't agreeing with him.

"You don't look so good," Ian said. "Not liking the accommodations?"

"Not so bad," he said as the guard urged him to sit, cuffed him to the table, and left the room. "You're wasting your time. I still won't say anything without my attorney present."

"You sure your attorney is still representing you now that he doesn't have anyone footing the bill?" Ian asked.

Snipes's cocky smile slipped, and a flash of unease darkened his eyes. "No reason he'd stop representing me."

"Maybe you haven't heard the big news," Londyn said.

He eyed her. "Not sure what you mean."

"Your boss was gunned down outside his house," Ian said. "He didn't survive."

A muscle twitched in Snipes's jaw, but that was his only reaction. So maybe his attorney had told him about the shooting, or maybe word had gotten around the prison.

Snipes tried to cross his arms, but the cuffs stopped him. He leaned back in his seat. "I don't have a boss, so not sure who you're talking about."

"Come on, now. We all know you're one of Olivo's lieutenants. Junior was the other." Ian leaned forward. "Or should I say you guys *were* his lieutenants? He doesn't need one anymore. And Junior? Seeing as you're the one who shot him, you know what happened to him."

Snipes shook his head. "You've got some imagination, man."

"I do, but this is fact." Ian tapped a finger on the table. "One we will prove in court, and if you want things to go easier for you, you'll start talking."

"You might as well," Londyn said softly, drawing the man's attention. "Olivo can't hurt you anymore. And with Junior gone and you inside, Olivo's organization is collapsing as we speak. Do yourself a favor and admit that Olivo ordered you to kill Junior in retribution for abducting his kid and cutting off his finger."

A flicker of unease flashed in Snipes's eyes.

"Naming Olivo as the mastermind and telling us where he kept the records and other things he used for his illegal business could make the judge go easier on you," Ian said, though honestly he didn't know if it would or not. Still, even though Olivo was dead, Junior deserved justice, and that would only happen if the older man's part in the murder came out.

"We're done here." Snipes looked at the door. "Deputy! I'm through."

"Just think about what we told you," Londyn said. "I want to make things easier for you, but you have to help me do that."

He arched an eyebrow. "You're pretty to look at lady, and I know you want me to focus on that and forget who you are.

But you no more want to help me than this clown does. If you want to waste your time sitting across the table from me, letting me take my fill of looking at you, be my guest. But anything else? Nah. That's not going to happen, and you might as well stop trying."

Malone woke to birds chirping and a decided chill in the air. Winter was coming, and she wanted to get a jump on the renovations so she could relax in front of the fire. She dressed in ragged jeans—not the pre-torn kind that were popular these days—along with an old college sweatshirt. Perfect attire for ripping into that wall by the front door. But as much as she was eager, she had work to do first. She had calls and emails to return and several urgent motions to file.

She grabbed her computer and went to the kitchen, where she made a full pot of strong coffee. She plopped down at the counter while it perked. Not thinking about Ian at all. At least, not letting herself think about him when he came to mind, which he'd done several times an hour when she wasn't sleeping.

"Argh. Stop." She focused on her work and took breaks to refill her coffee. She sipped and stared at the modern flat front cabinets. Did she really want to return this room to look like her past? Could she even get materials that would match? Did they make honey oak cabinets and the same pattern Formica countertops as her parents had? And what about the beige-and-powder-blue vinyl floors her mother had loved?

Probably more important to ask herself was, would she be spending a large chunk of change and devaluing the property in the same stroke? Likely. And what would it accomplish other than lowering her bank balance? The remodel wouldn't bring her parents back. Nothing would. And she didn't want to be stuck in the past like she'd been since that first night she learned she was an orphan.

Nothing could erase that searing pain.

Well, nothing but God's love. He could do anything. Everything. He'd shown her that. He'd cared for her every day since she'd lost her mom and dad. She still didn't know why she'd had to lose them, but she did know the gut-wrenching anguish prepared her to help others.

God probably didn't want her living in her past. Maybe that was what the situation with Junior was meant to teach her.

She opened her computer and searched for Bible verses about living in the past. Over one-hundred verses came up on the subject. She'd been so focused on her losses that she hadn't stopped to see how God was at work in her life. Sure, she'd cried out to Him over the years. So many times, and He'd been there. Caring for and helping her. But she still resented losing her parents, and she could see now that her bitterness had blinded her to possibilities.

I'm so sorry. I didn't realize. But now I do. Forgive me. Thank You for putting Ian in my life, drawing me away from what I thought I really wanted. Even if he doesn't want me. I'm glad for our time together. Let me remember the past for the good that it's brought to my life. For what it's taught me. And let me use it all to help other people who are suffering.

Feeling like years of heaviness were starting to lift from her shoulders, Malone went to the family room and grabbed a hammer. Rage funneled through her arm and into her hand, nearly sending the hammer through the other side of the wall.

Wow. Where did that anger come from? Maybe the last week of stress?

Maybe years of unresolved issues.

She hit the wall again and again. "If you want to leave your past behind, why are you still doing this remodel? Why do you need to make it exactly like you remembered? Or like Dad wanted?"

Yeah, why?

If she were one of her clients leaving an abusive spouse, she would tell them they were stuck in the past. Was she stuck too?

She settled down on the floor and began pulling the drywall away from the studs.

She was caught in the past. Sure, she was. Time to admit it. But did she want to stay there or do something about it? To have a life like the one Reed and Sierra were building? To have children and live her life to the fullest?

That was what she wanted. Exactly what she wanted. No doubt anymore.

She dug her phone from her pocket and dialed her real estate agent. The call went straight to voicemail.

She waited for the beep. "It's Malone Rice. I've decided I want to sell this house. Give me a call when you can so we can draw up a contract. I want to get it sold quickly."

Yes, perfect. She would move on just as she said. Beyond Ian, because he didn't want her. And she would find the man God had planned for her life.

18

Ian wanted to call Malone. Badly. Maybe ask her out to dinner to talk about a potential future, but he didn't know if he could live each day with the fact that, if they got together, his true colors might fly. What if he started exhibiting his parents' tendencies. He would only hurt the person he was now coming to believe he loved. And wasn't it love to walk away when that was best for the other person?

But what if Peggy was right? What if he wasn't toxic to Malone?

Is Peggy right? Can I pursue this? Become the man You made me to be?

He wasn't ready to talk to Malone about it yet, but he had to question her about the house.

His best course of action at the moment was to text her.

He typed, *Did you know Gilbert Flagg Sr. once owned your house?*

My parents place? Really? When?

They moved out right after remodeling it before your parents bought it.

I had no idea. Any thoughts on what this might mean?

He wanted to pick up the phone and call her. Not send characters through the phone. He wanted to hear her voice.

Still not the best move.

No idea, Looking into it with Londyn.

I'll go through the boxes in the garage again. See if we missed something.

He'd like to join her, but he needed to go talk to Flagg Sr. so Ian typed. *LMK if you find anything.*

I will.

And just like that, their brief communication was over, and he was left wanting more. He shoved his phone into his pocket and joined Londyn at the bullpen door.

"Malone didn't know about Flagg owning the house." He opened the door for Londyn.

She stepped into the hallway and started for the elevator. "Just as you thought."

He held the elevator doors for her. "She's going to go back through the garage boxes to see if she can find anything we missed."

"Do you think you missed something?" Londyn tapped the first floor button.

"Not likely," he said. "But it's possible."

"I still wonder if her parents might be connected with the Chinese drywall fiasco, but there was nothing in her dad's notes to suggest that."

"Doesn't mean it didn't exist," Ian said. "Too bad Nick hasn't found anything in his drywall search. I'll check in and see if he can add Flagg as a search parameter."

On the street, he typed the message and wound his way among pedestrians. His actions weren't lost on him. He was doing exactly what he warned others not to do. Not paying attention to their surroundings. Leaving himself vulnerable to attack. But Londyn walked with him, and should an issue arise, she had his back. He knew that about her now and could trust her.

Malone would have his back too. And support him in everything else in his life. That he knew with certainty.

He thought about her and her amazing personality all the way to Flagg's large home where he had to stow his thoughts, but even more he knew they needed to talk.

Help me to say the right things when I do talk to her.

More eager than ever to solve the mystery of who killed her parents, Ian parked in the driveway.

Londyn opened her car door. "I can't believe Flagg needs a bigger place than this one."

Ian got out. "Maybe with Junior gone and Karen likely to spend a long stretch in prison, he'll forget about the new house."

They took the walkway to the front door, and Ian rang the bell. As he enjoyed the cool temperatures and soft breeze, the birds chirping in the trees and the scents of flowers, Ian tried to imagine that he was at this door for any reason other than to question a man whose son was recently murdered, his wife turned into a killer. Just didn't fit the neighborhood, but criminals lived everywhere, even in pricey Portland neighborhoods. Olivo was proof of that.

Ian rang the bell again and heard the chime reverberating through the house. Footsteps quickly approached, echoing off the tile. They paused, and Ian imagined Flagg on the other side of the door looking out the peephole. The door jerked open.

Flagg made eye contact with Ian. "Detective." He changed his focus to Londyn and a broad smile crossed his face. "And you are?"

She held out her shield. "Detective Londyn Steele."

"Londyn," he said. "Interesting name."

"Our parents named all of us girls after cities in England

236

in honor of our family heritage." She smiled back at Flagg, and he preened, likely what she was hoping to accomplish. "I'm working with Detective Blair on winding down Junior's investigation. Mind if we come in and ask a few more questions?"

"My house is your house." He swept his arm out gallantly.

Ian could easily see how he might be charming to women who didn't know him.

Londyn went past, and the older man's gaze tracked her every move. He didn't seem to be grieving his son or lamenting his wife's situation. But then, people dealt with grief in different ways. Maybe enjoying watching a beautiful woman walk down his hallway was Flagg's way. Ian found that kind of smarmy. He should look into any affairs Flagg might have been having. Maybe he'd been seeing someone back when he sold the house to the Rices, and this potential woman might know something important.

Ian followed Londyn and was glad Malone wasn't with him. He'd deck Flagg for looking at her the way he looked at Londyn. Londyn was likely used to it from working in a predominantly male field, but that didn't mean she liked it.

She sat on the sofa in the same seating area where Ian had talked to Flagg and Karen a few days earlier. Ian made sure to sit next to Londyn so Flagg wasn't within touching distance.

He perched on the arm of a modern leather chair, his focus pinned to Londyn, though his gaze was professional now. "What can I answer for you?"

"Why didn't you tell us Junior called you the night before he died and talked to you for ten minutes?" Ian asked.

The man seemed disappointed to have to tear his gaze away from Londyn. "Oh, that." He waved a hand. "It wasn't important enough to mention. The kid wanted his mama and settled for me. Dumping all kinds of feelings over the phone. I'm surprised I lasted ten minutes."

Ian figured it was something like that, but he had to confirm. "I wanted to ask again if you knew Joanna and Lewis Rice. Maybe you remembered them since we last met."

Flagg tilted his head. "Can't say as I can place them."

"The house my classmate bought, the one we talked about before? You sold the house to her parents." Ian shared the address.

"That place?" He tilted his head. "We did an extensive remodel on the house and made a nice chunk of change, but I don't remember the details."

"But you would've had to sign the sales paperwork," Ian said.

"Yeah, sure. I'm positive I did, but we've bought and sold nine houses since then. I can't remember every buyer's name." He shifted his attention to Londyn. "When you reach a certain level of success, as I've done, you have people to handle the details. All they do is bring a summary of the terms to me, and I accept or decline. Then they shove the final documents under my hand to sign. It's wonderful having minions." He chuckled.

If he was trying to impress Londyn, her blank expression told Ian that he'd failed.

"If she's interested in sprucing the place up, let her know about my company," Flagg said.

"She's already begun remodeling."

He shook his head. "DIYers who think they can do the same work as professionals are the bane of my existence. Can't tell you how many times we've had to rescue them."

"Would you still have copies of the paperwork from that sale?" Londyn asked.

"Somewhere, sure. The minions probably stored it in one of our warehouses." He grinned again, but when Londyn didn't respond, a quizzical look crossed his face. Perhaps he wasn't used to women not reacting to his charm.

"Warehouses?" she asked. "How many do you have?"

"Four. Two for building materials. Another for tools and a workshop. One for miscellaneous company things. That's probably where the records are stored."

Ian couldn't believe how out of touch this man was from his business. "Can you get one of your staff to locate the file for us?"

He narrowed his eyebrows. "Don't see what you hope to find. What does this have to do with Junior?"

"Probably nothing," Ian said as casually as he could manage. "It's just that he's the person who alerted us to the Rices' crash not being an accident. Maybe we can find information like addresses, phone numbers, et cetera, on such documents, which might help us locate other people who remember the Rice family."

"Oh, okay. Sure. We can get the records for you." Flagg pulled his phone from his pocket. "I'll call my assistant right now and get her moving on it."

He was surprisingly courteous to the person he was talking to, even thanking them. He might call them minions, but at least he seemed to respect this minion.

Flagg balanced his phone on his knee and looked at Londyn again. "I'll let you know when my team locates them."

She gave a swift nod. "Is there anything unusual about this house that we should know?"

"Unusual? Not really. I think Karen liked it the best. She didn't want to leave." His forehead creased. "Maybe if we'd stayed there, she wouldn't have cracked up the way she did."

"Speaking of Karen," Ian said. "She told the patrol officers at the scene that the gun she used was yours, and she'd never fired a gun before."

"True. We had a break-in at our last house. Kind of spooked me, so I bought a gun. Can never be too safe."

"Did you keep it locked up?"

He shook his head. "Kept it in the nightstand. No kids around. Figured it wouldn't be a problem. Guess if I'd locked it up, she couldn't have gotten to it, but who could predict she would lose it."

"Is there anything else she told you about Junior and his connection to Olivo or Snipes?" Ian said.

"Not that I can think of." Flagg shook his head. "I still can't believe everything that's happened. Losing Junior and Karen."

"You haven't lost Karen."

He looked confused for a moment. "Well, sure, but she won't be in my daily life anymore. Might have to get a live-in housekeeper."

Yeah, this guy was about as deep as a kiddie pool, but it didn't seem like he had anything to do with the Rices' deaths. It was time to move on.

Malone was tired and dirty from digging through boxes. And she was sad. Looking at things from her past had brought back memories. When she'd reviewed the items with Ian, fond memories played in her mind, but today, a lot of the items seemed like anchors weighing her down. Trying to keep her in the past instead of letting her move forward.

Before she put this house back on the market, she would have Reed spend a day with her to review every item. They needed to decide what to do with the contents of the boxes. She would make four piles. Trash, give away, keep for her, and keep for Reed. Her pile would be small, the items that made the cut significant.

She didn't need all her old toys. All the stuffed animals. Or even the Barney sheets for her twin bed. It all had to go. The mere thought of a fresh start helped replace the sadness.

She dug into the next box and lifted out a hardcover journal in a fresh mint color with a large silver cross in the middle. She didn't remember this book. Hesitant but eager to see one of her parents' personal thoughts, she sat on a stack of boxes and opened the cover. She immediately recognized her mother's penmanship. Her beautiful cursive letters had swirly flourishes on some of the capital letters.

Malone remembered running her fingers over the letters as a child, hoping someday she could write as beautifully. She'd traced her mom's signatures on school permission slips, report cards, and other items signed by her mom and placed them safely in her backpack to return to school. All next to Malone's Barbie lunchbox that held a daily handwritten Bible verse tucked inside and an I love you note from their mom.

Tears threatened again, but she shook off the memories and flipped through the book, that was dated the year her parents had died. Malone turned to the last entries, hoping they would shed some light on what had happened at the end. Her mom had written each day, and it was in diary form. She'd started the entry on the day they died with a Bible verse, *2 Corinthians 5:17. So whoever is in Christ is a new creation: the old things have passed away; behold, new things have come.*

The verse was exactly what Malone needed to see. The old things were gone. New things had come. She was new. So was Ian. They were both believers. Surely they could work things out and pursue a relationship. She had to tell him about this. It was almost as if God was speaking the exact words they needed to hear.

She would call Ian, but first she would finish these boxes in case she located anything he needed to know about. She read down the page that talked about Reed and Malone heading off to school and their father starting the demolition on the wall. It ended there, so Malone turned the page. But a ragged edge told her a page had been ripped out, and the next one was torn off at the bottom. There were indents in the page from whatever was written on the missing page. She flipped another sheet. Nothing.

She went back to the entry. The very last words her mother had written. Malone could see her sitting in the fluffy chair she'd always chosen for making notes and paying bills. She would've had a pen braced between her teeth as she thought about what to write, her legs tucked under her.

How I miss you, Mom. More than words can say. I want to talk to you. See you. Hold you. Let you hold me.

Malone couldn't stop her tears now and let them flow.

She could almost hear her mom say, *I'm in a wonderful place, and I will see you again. Hold you again. Now move on and thrive. Live like there might not be another opportunity, because we aren't guaranteed tomorrows.*

Malone swiped away her tears and looked at the book again. The torn page was the right size and shape to be the paper found in their car. Could what had been written on the missing page tell them what had happened? Why they were in the car?

She knew forensic staff could process the indents to reveal words. They could also compare the torn page to this one. She took out her phone and looked at the photo Ian had taken of the note in the car and sent her.

Yes, it looked like it would line up.

She had to send Ian a message. She typed a text. *I found a diary where my mom might've written something about where they were going the day of the accident. I think you'll want to see it. Call me ASAP.*

She stared at the screen, waiting for a reply, but it went black.

"Come on. Answer. Please." She kept watching, willing her phone to light up. One minute. Two. Three. Five. Ten.

Okay. She couldn't just sit there. He was a busy detective, and she had no idea when she might hear back from him. She jammed her phone into her pocket and set the journal aside, then dove back into the box.

Her phone chimed, and she nearly jumped to her feet. The text was from Ian.

Londyn is on her way over to pick up the journal. She'll get it to forensics, and we'll let you know what they find.

That was it. Nothing personal. Nothing asking how she was doing. And he was sending Londyn instead of coming himself. Malone's heart hurt, but he was just doing what he'd told her he was going to do. Keep things platonic. She was the one who'd changed her mind. She needed to tell him what she'd discovered and how it might help him consider entering into a relationship. But that needed to be an in-person conversation.

She typed a thank-you, finished the last box, and carried the journal into the kitchen, where she set it on the counter to free her hands to wash up. It was cold and gray outside, so she brewed a pot of tea. The doorbell rang just as she finished putting out mugs and honey.

Londyn stood on the front stoop as Malone had expected. She wore a brown coat with a fake fur collar, not at all practical in the rainy Oregon weather, but she looked very fashionable, and Malone could appreciate that.

"Thanks for coming." Malone stepped back. "I just made some tea. Would you like a cup?"

Londyn smiled. "That would be great."

"Then follow me. We can put your amazing coat on the sofa if you'd like."

Londyn slipped it off, revealing a lovely eggplant-colored suit with a white blouse underneath. She took an evidence bag and gloves from the pocket.

"Love your coat, and the color of that suit," Malone said. "I think we could be fashion friends real easily." Malone waved a hand over her attire. "If you don't take this outfit into account."

"I don't dress like this all the time." Londyn draped her coat on the sofa arm. "In fact, I prefer your attire. This is more of a uniform for me."

"The prettiest uniform I've ever seen."

"I work in a man's world. I can try to fit in and hope they don't notice me or stand out and make sure they remember me." She mimicked a model pose. "Obviously, I chose the second one."

She laughed, and Malone joined her.

She led Londyn to the kitchen and motioned at the stools. "Have a seat, and I'll pour the tea."

Londyn sat near the journal. "Is this what I've come to pick up?"

Malone nodded and set a mug in front of Londyn. She didn't pick it up, instead slipped her gloves on.

"The torn page is about two-thirds of the way into the book." Malone set down her own mug, poured honey into it, and stirred. "I think it matches the torn page Ian found."

"Me too." Londyn held the book up to one of the garish pendant lights hanging over the island. "And you're right on the indentations. You might really be on to something here."

Londyn put the book in an evidence bag and took off her gloves.

"Would you like milk or honey?" Malone asked.

She shook her head. "I'm a purist." She laughed again, and Malone was coming to see that this woman had a nice sense of humor.

Londyn took a sip of the tea. "Odd that Ian didn't want to come get the journal."

Malone didn't answer right away and considered what she might say. She didn't want to get Ian into trouble for mixing his personal life with business.

"Ah," Londyn said. "I thought there was something between you two."

Malone blinked at her. "How did you know?"

"Your expression speaks louder than your words. You got this dreamy look in your eyes." She waved a hand. "Relax. I don't care if he has feelings for you. He's doing his job, and that's what matters to me."

"Oh, good." Malone appreciated Londyn's straight talk.

"You two going to go for it?" Londyn picked up her mug. "Not that it's any of my business, but when you have two sisters, you learn to get nosy about things like this."

"We decided to keep things platonic."

Londyn's perfectly plucked eyebrows rose. "I don't know Ian all that well. This is the first time we've worked so closely with each other. But you become a detective, and you learn to read people. He's a great guy. Committed. Compassionate. And he still wants to make a difference when a lot of law enforcement officers become jaded after the years of service he's put in. He's one of the most hard-working detectives in our department."

"Sounds like there's a but coming," Malone said.

"But I think he works so many hours to forget how

empty his life is outside the job. I can recognize it because I do the same thing."

"You're not in a relationship?"

Londyn shook her head, her eyes clouding over. "Was until recently. But this job is hard on relationships. I hate to tell you that and add another reason for you and Ian not to get together. But often the job has to come first, and you have to find a partner who can handle that. I haven't, and honestly, I've given up."

Malone didn't know Londyn well, but she squeezed the detective's hand. "I'm sorry about that."

Londyn shook her head. "Listen to me. This is so far from professional. I don't know what's come over me."

"Must be that we share the fashion connection." Malone grinned and pulled her hand back. "And maybe the fact that Ian and I can't have a relationship either."

Londyn cupped her mug and looked at Malone. "Don't let what I said deter you. I think Ian has the strength and determination to overcome whatever is put in front of him. Plus, his faith is strong, and that helps us all set priorities, right? So don't give up hope."

Malone sipped her sweet tea, letting the warmth coat her throat. She wouldn't lose hope, even if Londyn pointed out that she had more strikes against a relationship. But Londyn reminded her, Malone and Ian had God on their side. She just needed to help Ian see that.

19

Ian stood in Junior's apartment with Londyn and tried not to yawn. He'd spent a sleepless night, his dreams filled with Flagg Sr. coming on to Malone and attacking her as Junior had done so many years before. The kid probably learned the behavior from his dad. More proof for Ian that children could become just like their parents. But then the Flaggs didn't believe in God. Didn't seek to be better people because of their love for God. They did as they wanted, exactly like his parents. If not for having gone to a church youth event to get away from his family one night, he could've become them.

Had he really escaped a lifetime of living decadently like Flagg Sr. and his son did? The shallowness of it all still twisted his gut. Like this condo. Ostentatious. Money spent on every expensive furnishing, but what good did that do anyone? Didn't help Junior or Karen.

Ian had lived years on a police officer's salary, and he had everything he needed. More than he needed, and unlike his parents, who lived for gaining additional wealth, he was content being who he was and with what he had.

Yeah, he could be the man Malone needed him to be. The man God wanted him to be. He'd left his past in the past. The only thing he'd carried with him was the fear of letting the past take over his life. Now he could leave that too.

Resolved to talk to Malone in person as soon as possible, he took a deep breath and let it out slowly to return his focus to work. In the few days since Ian's and Londyn's last visit to the condo, the air had turned stale, and a hint of mustiness permeated the space.

"Exactly what do you hope to find here?" Londyn asked as she snapped on latex gloves.

"I don't know. I just have a feeling Junior hid something that will explain how he learned about the Rices' accident."

"He could have a storage unit or used a storage facility paid for by Olivo."

"But you wouldn't want to go to a storage unit every time you needed something to do your job, would you? A cell phone, for example. I know we have no proof he communicated with Olivo and think they may have used drones, but if he really was Olivo's lieutenant, he had to talk to someone to move the product, right? Plus, where's the drone he used to deliver the finger?"

"You'd think so." She glanced around the room that had black fingerprint powder on most surfaces. "I figure once they crack his computer, it might tell us about where he kept things, but this place has been searched as has his storage locker downstairs. They could've communicated by email, but I doubt they'd put their actions in writing."

"Humor me and let's look for hidden storage."

"You mean like floorboards that come up?"

"Like that, but not in the floor. Condos are built on concrete slabs, so unless the entire floor is raised—which I doubt—there's no room underneath the wood." He looked around. "Check cabinets for false drawers, hidden spaces behind pictures. Stuff like that. You take the living area. I got the bedroom again."

He headed down the hallway, tapping the walls along the way and looking behind pictures.

In the bedroom, he went straight to the walk-in closet. The space was the size of a small bedroom. Deep brown closet organizers filled all the walls, and a small island sat in the middle. Ian remembered the drawers of the island held expensive watches in one of the drawers, socks and under-wear in another. The others were empty. He pulled out each one and felt for false bottoms. Nothing.

He went to the hanging racks. The clothing varied but was mostly T-shirts and jeans. Ian went to the hamper to check pockets again but came up empty. He ran his hands over the cabinets, feeling for a hidden or trap door. He searched the inside of closed cabinets. Slid clothing out of the way and felt the walls behind. Felt in pockets of the hanging clothes and folded items. Dumped out shoes to look for hidden objects like a key for a storage unit as Londyn had suggested.

Nothing. Not one hint of what Junior did for a living or how he learned about Malone's parents.

How had he done such a good job of hiding his occupation? In Ian's experience, the guy wasn't that smart.

Ian went to the bedroom and dumped out nightstand drawers and checked under the mattress and bed. He gave the bathroom a thorough search.

Frustrated, he went into the hallway to rip things out of the linen closet he'd passed on the way in and check the back wall. He felt every inch. No hidden crevices.

He thought about the condo layout from an elevated

view. This closet backed up to the main closet, but there wasn't a bump-out in the main closet to accommodate this one. The builders would've had to build out the wall in the main bedroom and put the closet in front of it.

Had they created a hidden storage area, or had they been lazy, not wanting to deal with the extra framing cuts that a bump-out required?

Eager now, Ian ran back through the main bedroom to the closet and estimated where the void would be located.

A unit with slanted shelves holding a variety of colorful sneakers took up the space. He shook it, and the wood under his hand moved a fraction. The other cabinets had felt more solid. This section could simply be poorly installed, or he could be on to something.

He swept all of the shoes onto the floor and felt around and over the shelves. He tugged on the middle shelf, and the wood rose in his hand.

The unit slid out and pivoted, revealing a door. Holding his breath, he pressed the top corner. The door popped open.

"Got something," he called to Londyn.

He heard her hurrying down the hallway to the closet, and he felt around the wall for a light switch.

"A secret storage area," he said, still feeling the inside wall for a light switch. "Flagg Sr. gave the condo to Junior. He remodeled it so his dad could've built this in. Gotta wonder what the old man hid here."

Ian couldn't find a switch. Frustrated, he tapped the flashlight on his phone and ran the beam over the room.

He sucked in a breath, and Londyn gasped behind him.

"This can't be real, can it?" she asked and moved closer.

"It's real, all right." Ian's gaze roved over the items pinned on the wall. "And it looks like we had things wrong. All wrong."

As the sun made a dash for the horizon outside Malone's big picture window, she contemplated making dinner, but she grabbed a utility knife from her tool bag instead. She'd finished the boxes in the garage, and she needed to fix the half wall before she could put her house on the market.

After all, there was no point in taking the wall down now. She had to remove and replace the section of drywall she'd already smashed. She'd never done drywall, but she'd watched tons of home improvement shows. How hard could it be? She would need to take down the entire piece of sheetrock to get a nice straight edge to affix the fresh piece against.

She found the seam and sliced the board.

Satisfied she wouldn't damage the abutting piece of wallboard, she jerked off a large piece. It released quickly, and she fell back. She laughed at her clumsiness and got back on her knees to assess her work. In the corner of the cavity, she spotted a zipper storage bag.

What in the world? Maybe her dad put a time capsule in the wall before he closed it up.

She tugged out the bag and held it up. She spotted a knife—a knife glistening in the light with what looked like dried blood.

She lurched back, keeping her gaze on the knife as if it might free itself and harm her.

Taking a deep breath, she looked in the cavity again and drew out a woman's bloodied blouse in another bag, and a yellowed newspaper that was folded beside it.

She read the headline. *Woman Brutally Murdered on Running Path.*

A photo of a path wandering through a park accompanied the story. She recognized the path. The trail ran through a park less than a mile from her home.

Stomach clenching, she read the details. Twenty-one-year-old Sarah Anderson had been viciously stabbed in the mid-nineties. Less than six months before the brutal murder, Malone's family had moved to this neighborhood. She'd never heard anything about it, but she'd been six at the time.

She did remember her parents telling her and Reed not to go to the park alone. The warning was always accompanied with a stranger-danger message.

Junior's dad had owned this place before her parents. Had he or his wife murdered Sarah Anderson? Had her father found these items when he opened the wall, and was that why he'd been going to see the detective? But then, why would he have closed the items back in the wall? Why not just take them to the detective? Maybe he didn't want to touch or disturb anything like she'd done. Or he could've closed it up so she and Reed didn't see what he'd found.

The skin on her neck prickled, and she dropped the newspaper to grab her phone. She dialed Ian. The call went to voicemail.

"What are you doing? I need you." She left a message for him to call her right back.

She tapped her foot, waiting for nearly thirty minutes for him to call, each minute her heart racing faster and faster until she thought it would explode if she had to wait any longer. She had to go to the precinct. Hopefully either Ian or Londyn or even their lieutenant were there.

She jumped to her feet and left everything as she found it. She grabbed her purse and a jacket and ran for her car. A heavy mist was falling, and she quickly got the door open on the old car and slid in.

Inserting the key in the ignition, she vowed to get rid of the Mustang too. How many times had she gotten wet while trying to unlock the door with the key? Too many to count. She'd buy something with remote entry.

She backed out of the drive, waving at her neighbor across the street, who was coming out to get her mail. Beatrice was a very nice older woman but kind of a busybody. If something was going on in the neighborhood, she was the first to know about it and share it with everyone she could waylay at the community mailbox on the corner.

Malone left Beatrice in her rearview and focused on her driving. It hadn't rained for days, and the roads in the winding hillside community would be slick. Despite the desire to get downtown and see Ian, she was extra careful, braking slowly at curves and stop signs. She soon climbed to the main road and turned toward the city. She accelerated, and the steering wheel began to shake under her hands.

She flashed back to her conversation with Freddie Peck, and her pulse shot up. He described what her father might feel before he crashed. Peck had called it the death wobble.

Was that what was happening? The death wobble? Had someone tampered with her car too? The same person who'd killed her parents?

Ian's phone vibrated in his pocket, but he would hold off answering until he and Londyn figured out what to do with the closet lined with photos, newspaper articles, and a map.

Londyn's eyes were narrowed, pain and disbelief fighting to gain purchase in her expression. Ian didn't blame her. The newspaper clippings told of six murdered women who'd been sexually assaulted, and the map linked them all to locations within a mile of where the Flagg family had lived at the time. Listed next to each woman was the date they'd been murdered, pictures of the Flaggs's houses, and the date that the Flagg family had moved on to their next home. They'd left within a week of the murders of all six women over the course of thirty years.

Also posted were pictures of their current home and the one Flagg Sr. had under construction. In the photo, large equipment surrounded the half-built home on one of the hills in west Portland. Photos of Flagg Sr. from around the dates of the murder were posted too.

"Why hadn't Junior reported his dad before another woman was killed?"

"Do you think Junior put this here?" Londyn asked. "Or did his father keep it as some sort of a shrine and Junior just discovered it?"

"If his dad did, he risked Junior finding it. And I don't think Flagg Sr. would post his own photos." Ian moved closer to read about the death of Sarah Anderson. He pointed at the picture. "This murder occurred when they lived in the Rices' house."

"Flip up the newspaper," she said. "There's something else there."

He lifted it, revealing another newspaper story about the Rices' accident and their obituaries. He glanced back at Londyn. "Maybe they found out about Sarah's murder, and the killer took them out."

"Sounds like a possibility, but how?"

He shook his head. "Are we in agreement that this information points to Flagg Sr. as a killer? A serial killer?"

She stared at the wall. "Could be Karen but the sexual assault rules her out so there's no other conclusion. Problem is, we don't have any actual proof."

"When I think about his behavior in our interviews," Ian

said, "I can see him fitting sociopathic or psychopathic tendencies."

"Yeah. He's charming, but his ego puts you off once you talk to him a bit."

"And he didn't seem to have any feelings about losing his son or wife. And no empathy for his son being short. He was more concerned with his property, his wealth."

"He would fall under the "successful" psychopath type. They have a tendency to perform premeditated crimes with calculated risk, which these murders seem to fit."

"We need to get forensics in here. And with this now being a potential serial killer investigation, we need to call Reed to bring the FBI in." Ian's mind raced with the possibilities and consequences of their discovery.

Malone! She was in the house her parents lived in. Was she in danger?

His heart nearly stopped pumping. He had to find out. He grabbed his phone to call her. Saw a voicemail from her. It had been almost an hour since her call.

He pressed the icon for her voicemail and put her on speaker.

"What are you doing?" she cried in the message, terror riding through her tone. "I need you."

His heart sank, and he pressed her phone number. It rang and rang. "Answer. Come on, answer, Malone. Please. Please."

His phone rang. It was an unknown number, but it could be about Malone. "Ian Blair."

"Hi, Detective, it's Beatrice Paulson. Malone's neighbor."

"Is this about Malone? Is she with you?"

"No, oh no. In fact, I just saw her drive off a little while ago. We even waved at each other."

If Malone was waving, she was probably all right.

"How can I help you?" he asked.

"Remember you told me to let you know if there was anything else?"

"Yes."

"Well, my hubby said there was video of someone repairing Malone's car on Monday."

The day they'd gone to Peck's place. Ian's gut tightened. "Did your husband keep the video?"

"He deleted it from his iPad, but he downloaded it from the security company, and I emailed it to you just like you taught me." She sounded very proud of herself. "My hubby also said he saw a similar pickup sitting up the road by a neighbor's house for the last few days, including this morning."

That didn't sound good. "Did he catch a license plate?"

"I asked, but he said the guy wasn't in the truck, and he didn't know if it was the same one. We're usually real careful about strange vehicles on our street, but the Olsens are remodeling, and workers' vehicles are coming and going all the time. We don't pay much attention to them."

"Thank you for the information." He disconnected and shared what he'd learned with Londyn while he opened his email and held out his phone. He and Londyn watched the video together.

A man pulled up in a black Ford F-150 and parked in front of Beatrice's house. The license plate was out of view.

"Too bad we can't see the plates," Ian said.

"Such a common truck it could be anyone."

He sat in the truck for a while, glancing around.

"C'mon, C'mon, C'mon. Get out. Show your face."

"I can't make out who it is either," Londyn said.

The guy finally climbed out and carried a bag of tools across the road, his back to the camera the entire time. He got down on the ground by Malone's front tires and did something that took only a few minutes, then scooted out and marched back across the street.

As the man neared the camera, Ian's heart sank to his stomach. "It's Flagg Sr."

"He wasn't fixing her car," Londyn said. "He was tampering with it. Maybe like he'd done to her parents' car."

"And Malone just drove off in that vehicle."

20

The rain picked up, spitting on Malone's windshield, and she could barely see the road ahead in the dusk. But she couldn't let go of the wheel to turn on the wipers. She gripped with all her strength and tried to apply the brakes, but the car had a mind of its own and pulled the vehicle toward the embankment.

She whipped the wheel the opposite direction. Nothing changed. Her trajectory continued toward the edge of the road.

Please, protect me. Please.

A loud thump sounded under the car. The wheels squealed, the high-pitched sound eerie.

The wheel grabbed the gravel shoulder, and she lost total control. The vehicle shot over the edge of the embankment and plunged down the steep terrain toward a granddaddy of a pine tree.

She couldn't stop the car from careening closer, the speed blazing fast.

No. No. No. Ian had been right. She only had a lap belt and no airbags. Lap belts had killed her parents.

Was history about to repeat itself?

Ian had failed Malone, and he didn't know where she was. If she was safe. Or hurt. Dying or even dead. He dialed Reed, who answered right away.

"Is Malone with you?" Ian snapped.

"No. Why?"

Ian explained, the words rushing out of his mouth like a geyser.

Reed muttered something under his breath. "I can find her. I have a tracker on her phone."

Ian didn't ask why Reed was monitoring her, just waited for him to share her location.

"I've got the coordinates," Reed said. "The map doesn't show her on the road. She's located in the wilderness area."

Ian's gut cramped so hard he thought he might hurl. "Send me the coordinates."

"Coming your way," Reed said, fear taking his voice higher.

Ian's phone dinged and he looked at the text from Reed. "I'm headed there now."

Ian heard footsteps in the background of his call. "Meet you there."

Ian hung up and tapped the coordinates, his hand shaking so hard he could hardly accomplish it.

"She's here." He showed the screen that revealed the same road Malone's parents had been killed on to Londyn. "I'm going for her."

"I'll come with you."

"You need to stay here and protect the scene." He dug out his keys, his hands trembling.

She took them from him. "You can't drive in your state."

"But Flagg could figure this out like we did and destroy

everything in the closet. We can't let a serial killer get away with what he's done."

"We've taken pictures. Besides, there's nothing here we can't find again." She headed for the door. "And I can order the guard on duty to stand outside until forensics and a patrol officer arrive."

Ian raced for the door. Arguing was a waste of time, time that could be the difference between saving Malone's life and losing her forever.

~

The passenger side of the car crashed into the tree. Metal bent. Screeched. Rasped. The safety glass cracked and webbed, a large chunk falling into the passenger seat. The side window shattered, and glass peppered Malone's arm like tiny thumbtacks piercing her skin.

She screamed, a deep wrenching sound from her throat, a sound borne of terror.

Her body catapulted forward, and her head smashed into the steering wheel. Pain radiated through her skull, and stars danced before her eyes.

The steering wheel shifted. Pressing in, close to her chest.

The vehicle reverberated, rocked back and forth, then settled with a thump.

It was over.

She'd survived.

But how well? Was she hurt?

She took stock of her injuries, starting with her head. A large lump ballooned out of her forehead, but no bleeding. Glass had salted tiny cuts on her hand, but they were just minor abrasions.

She moved her arms. Hands. Fingers. Her legs, ankles, and feet. They all worked.

Her heart lifted.

Thank You! Thank You!

She searched the passenger side for her phone, but couldn't see it in the dark and the crumpled car made it impossible for her to reach the floor on that side. She would have to get out and go around the car to feel for it.

She shifted to open the door. It groaned and popped, but she forced it open.

Good. Good. She could get out and find her phone to call for help.

She squirmed out from under the steering wheel, planted her feet outside, and pushed to stand. Her legs collapsed under her, and she fell to the needle-covered ground. She took a deep breath and inhaled the rich humus smell. It smelled like life.

She was alive.

Oh, thank You!

The heavy mist wetted her face. She pushed off the soaked ground before her clothing became saturated and cold. Her legs remained weak and wobbly. She used the car as a support to walk around the back of the car to the passenger side, where she'd set her purse holding her phone. The window was gone, only sharp shards remaining.

Her purse lay on the floor, spilled out. Her phone had come to rest a foot away.

She grabbed the door handle and pulled on it. No movement at all. The front end of the car had collapsed around the door, leaving it jammed. Her only way to get the phone was to crawl through the window.

First, she needed to clear the remaining glass shards. A tree branch would safely do that.

She turned to find the wood. A figure loomed behind

her, and she screamed, but the sound was cut-off when the man's hand came over her mouth. He wrapped his other arm around her and dragged her up the embankment.

She kicked. Fought. Bit his hand.

He cursed and released her mouth.

"Help!" she screamed, but she knew it was futile. No one would come to save her. It was up to her to save her own life.

Londyn was speeding well beyond the legal limit, but Ian kept pressing his foot to the floorboard as if he could somehow make her go faster. He wanted to be driving. Should be driving, but she was right. His hands trembled, and his mind was tortured with thoughts of Malone at the bottom of some ravine, her car wrapped around a tree or flipped on its back.

He'd called for a patrol deputy to head to the scene, but with the rain, there were several accidents in the county, and there wasn't a nearby deputy.

"You need to stop imagining the worst," Londyn said, her eyes still on the road.

"You're a mind reader, now?" he snapped.

"I know how I would be feeling in your situation. But she could've broken down. Maybe the car is parked on the shoulder."

"Then why did it display on GPS as in the scrub?"

"GPS can be off a bit."

Ian wanted to believe that was what happened, but he couldn't. Not when the woman he'd come to love might have died in an auto crash. Yeah, he loved her. That was clear now. And losing her forever? He couldn't bear it. If she was safe, he would tell her how he felt, then let God take care of the rest. It seemed as if God had brought them together again. If he was wrong about that, about everything? Well, then it wouldn't work. Sure, they could both be hurt. A plane that never left the tarmac couldn't crash. But it would never soar, either. He wanted to soar. With Malone at his side.

They crested the final hill.

"Just ahead five hundred feet," Ian told Londyn as he leaned forward to search for her car. "A truck. What's it doing there?"

"If she was in an accident, maybe he stopped to help."

"It's a match for Flagg's truck," Ian said.

"Could be, but there are hundreds of Ford F150s in the county."

"There's another person in the cab with him. Could be Malone." Ian strained to get a better look, but the truck took off, spitting gravel from the shoulder. "Can you make out the plate?"

"No." Londyn sped up.

They gained on the truck, and Ian read the plate out loud.

"Do you want me to go after the truck or stop at the coordinates?" she asked.

"No way to know if Malone was in the vehicle. We have to stop."

She hit the brakes, and the rear skidded before she regained control.

Ian looked out the window as they approached the location. "Tire marks. Skids. Heading for the embankment."

The car rocked to a stop. Ian shoved his door open and charged for the edge of the road. He spotted the cherry red Mustang wrapped around a tree. He dropped to the ground and slid down the hill, leaves and needles scattering around him. At the bottom, he raced for the car. He heard Londyn at the road calling for a patrol deputy as he searched the car. It was in rough shape. Nearly as bad as her parents' car had been. The driver's door stood open.

Malone wasn't there.

"Malone!" he shouted. "Malone!"

No response.

She must have gone in that truck. Or she was walking the other direction from where they arrived.

He dialed her phone. It rang from the floor of the car.

No, oh, no. They could no longer track her via GPS. They had to follow that truck, and fast. It was their only hope of finding her.

21

Every part of Malone's body ached, her head most of all, and drowsiness kept dragging her toward sleep. She must've suffered a concussion when she hit her head. Nothing else could explain her nearly falling asleep after Gilbert Flagg Sr. dragged her up the hill and shoved her in his truck. He tied her wrists with rope and fastened them to the door. The truck smelled strongly of musk cologne, and that didn't help with the nausea that was building in her gut.

He flicked the wipers on a higher speed, and they scraped across the window with irritating screeches, hurting her head more. The tires whisked over the wet pavement, and miles flew past under his maniac driving. Maybe he had a death wish, but she didn't.

The tires slid on the curve, the truck fishtailing. Adrenaline pumped through her body waking her up.

"You won't get away with this, you know." She glared at him. "I left the information for Sarah Anderson's murder right where you hid it all those years, and Detective Blair was on his way over to see me."

"Already taken care of."

"You were in my house?"

"Right after you left. Been watching the place for days to see if you started ripping apart that wall." He looked at her. "You really should get some drapes or blinds. Nice try with the detective thing, but if he was on his way over, you wouldn't have left."

He had a point, but she wouldn't acknowledge it. "I can understand you hiding the souvenirs of your heinous crime in a wall when you lived there, but why not take things with you when you left?"

A smug grin lit his face. "The thrill of it, baby. I've left prizes in five other houses, just waiting for discovery. But it couldn't be pinned back to me. We had construction workers at every house, and they could've hidden the items."

Malone gaped at him. "You killed five other women?"

"You'll make number seven," he said matter-of-factly, as if they were talking about taking out the trash. "Of course, you'll be a little different. I can't leave mementos at my house now. But maybe I can put them in the new house I'm building, and it'll be like you're with me every day. With Karen locked up, that will be nice. I won't be alone."

Malone couldn't stop herself from shuddering.

He frowned and stroked her hand. "Now, come on, honey. Don't worry. You should be happy to be chosen as one of my girls. I'm very picky."

His tender tone said he really believed what he was saying. He had to be insane to think that way.

It creeped her out, and she had to move on. "Why did you kill my parents?"

"They forced the issue."

"How?"

"Your dad knew my company had renovated their house before they moved in. He called to say he was going to remove the half wall and wanted to know if we had more of

266

the wood flooring. I told him a good flooring guy could piece in hardwoods. He thanked me for the info, but *I* should've thanked *him*. After all, he'd given me a heads-up that it was only a matter of time before he found Sarah's things. I had no choice." Flagg shook his head. "But what a rush. Learning I could've been found out. That the news media would speculate on who killed her. It was a rush when her murder was reported in the paper, but that? That was closer to home. More thrilling. Much more."

She could hardly look at him. "Junior found out about you somehow, and that's what he was going to tell me."

"Seems like it, but he never told me or my wife. He was probably too afraid to confront me. Instead, he ran to you like a tattletale. Big baby." Flagg's lip curled up. "He's my one regret in life." He glanced at her, gaze hardened, and she could easily imagine him standing over her with the knife in hand. "My one and only."

~

Ian held the rifle he'd retrieved from his trunk and outfitted the weapon with his night vision scope. Maybe today was the day he would actually use the scope. Maybe God had prepared him by encouraging him to carry the right equipment.

He glanced at Londyn who kept the speed above the limit, but it didn't feel fast enough.

He sat forward in his seat and peered out the front window deluged by a sudden downpour, the wipers furiously trying to keep the glass clear. The vehicle was cool, but perspiration beaded on his forehead. At every turn, he hoped to catch up to the pickup. He would use his rifle's telescopic sight that magnified the subject and focus on the truck to confirm that Malone was in the vehicle and Flagg was driving. The vehicle was registered to Flagg's construction company. Not a surprise, but it could be one of Flagg's workers in the truck.

"Hopefully, a patrol officer will spot them soon." He'd requested an alert be put out by the county sheriff's office, which would go to the entire metro area. The officers had the truck's description. The plates. And the fact that the truck had been on this road. But the big question, the one burning a hole in Ian's gut was, had Flagg turned off?

The map he'd pulled up on his phone didn't show any side roads to this point, but a major intersection was coming up in another mile.

He'd turned the radio to the sheriff's channel and periodically switched back and forth to PPB to listen in, praying for news of the truck.

"Where do you think Flagg's taking her?" Londyn asked.

"If he follows his pattern, he'll want to kill her somewhere close to his house. Of course, this is nothing like his other murders."

"Criminals often commit crimes within a narrow radius around their homes."

"He won't kill her at his house now. Not when he knows he's already on our radar."

"What about the house he's constructing?" she asked. "It's secluded and workers would've gone home by now."

"Would be a good place to commit murder." Ian got out his phone to look at the pictures he'd taken of Junior's closet. "I'll call in and get an unmarked car out to his current residence to tell us if they arrive so we can head to the construction site."

He called dispatch on speaker and made his request.

"Please hold," the dispatcher said.

He tapped his foot as he counted down the time. "C'mon. Hurry up."

"Good news, Detective," she said. "One of the detectives on the drug squad already has the house under surveillance. Flagg isn't home, and they'll remain in place for as long as you need and will notify you if he arrives."

"Roger that," Ian replied and hung up.

"So what do you want to do?" Londyn asked him.

Yeah. What? Think, man. Think.

If he made the wrong decision, Malone could die. Even if he made the right one, they could already be too late.

"Ian," Londyn said.

He racked his brain. "If we don't catch up to them by the intersection and they haven't been spotted by an officer, we'll head over to the house Flagg is building."

"Too bad we can't get eyes on the place from overhead," Londyn said.

Ian nodded, but neither PPB or Washington County Sheriff's office had helicopters. PPB had a surveillance plane, but it would take too long to get approval for take-off on a non-tactical situation, if he even could get approval with the limited information he possessed.

He lifted his gun and ran his scope over the area. No truck. No Malone.

His hopes sank, and he lowered the rifle. They were entering a more populous area, and he didn't want someone to spot the gun and report him.

He craned his neck to see ahead, his pulse pounding loudly in his brain.

C'mon. C'mon. C'mon. Where are you?

Londyn approached the intersection.

Ian brought up the address of Flagg's new house in a map program on his phone. He zoomed in on a photo of the Flagg's new place that was on Junior's closet wall. "Junior wrote the date on the pictures he'd taken of his parents' new house. They were dated just a few days before he died. All the walls are framed, but only the front is sheathed. No approach from the back due to a steep hill and trees."

"Then he's likely watching for us to come after him from the only way in," Londyn said.

"He might even have security cameras on the property and get alerts on his phone when anyone gets near. We'll have to be careful of that."

"I'll call for backup and tell them to hold at a distance until we give them the signal to move in. Don't want them spooking Flagg." Ian made the call and gave specific instructions.

After he ended the call, Londyn glanced at him. "Any rear access? Could we surprise him if we came from that direction?"

"Not with the steep hill. We would need heavy equipment to lift us up to the house." He enlarged the picture even more. "There's an articulating boom lift below the house. It can reach the house and might still be there."

She flashed him a wide-eyed look. "You're not thinking of going up in that, are you?"

"Absolutely. If there's someone on site with keys or even forgot the keys in the machine." Ian considered the plan and believed it was their best chance in saving Malone. He glanced at his watch. "The workers would've likely just gotten off work so maybe someone is still there."

"Wouldn't Flagg hear the boom?"

"There's an off chance that he might hear the diesel startup, but he won't hear the boom since it's much quieter. He shouldn't hear it. Especially in this downpour." At least, Ian hoped that with his limited experience with these kinds of booms that his opinion was right.

Please. Please, let me be making the right decision. Malone's life depends on me, and I can't lose her. I just can't.

Malone kicked and scratched as Flagg hauled her from his truck up the steps of his giant new house. Rain pummeled them, and heavy Oregon clay soil sucked at their feet. But Flagg kept his footing, even with her fight. She gave up for a moment to catch her breath and noticed four houses were being built on this new street, all in various stages of construction. The street had one temporary light pole, but the houses were dark and silent. The workers would've just gone home for the day.

Flagg could kill her and dispose of her body. The foundation was already in place, but he could pour a concrete patio. Maybe his other victims were buried in concrete in his prior homes. If she got free, she would make sure Ian searched the properties.

If she got free. That was the obstacle. Her hands were tied in front of her, the end of the long rope in Flagg's hands. His eyes glazed with a craziness she'd never witnessed, not even in crazed fathers and husbands who wanted their wives back. Never in her wildest dreams did she guess Junior's father was a serial killer.

He dragged her across the plywood floor to the back of the house, where the framing had been completed but was still open to the elements. A large patio abutting the house was also framed with two-by-fours. Rebar crisscrossed half of the area just waiting for the concrete pour. The other half still needed the rebar.

Flagg spun to look at her, a gleam in his eyes. "What do you think of this as a resting place? You'll be overlooking the Portland skyline, and there are glorious sunrises and beautiful sunny days."

She could easily imagine him digging a hole there,

dumping her in, and covering her up. Workers would rebar over her, and the concrete would seal her grave.

She shuddered, and tried to swallow, but her mouth was too dry to manage it.

His eyes narrowed. "Not that it matters much to me what you think. It's what *I* think that's important. Always has been. Always will be."

She searched the darkness for a way to escape, but she found only a sharper ravine than the one her car had plunged over. Scrub, bushes, and trees covered the steep drop-off just beyond the patio. She could hurl herself over the framing, but that would mean certain death. Remaining where she was standing meant certain death too.

The only question she needed to contemplate now was which way she wanted to die?

22

Ian grabbed his rifle and earbuds from the glove box so he could keep in contact with Londyn as she put on the brakes at the small clearing by the boom lift. He burst out of the car, ignored the rain and lifted his rifle to search the back of the house. A man and woman were standing there. Their backs were to Ian, so he couldn't identify them, but he had to assume it was Flagg and Malone. His heart soared at seeing her alive. He'd arrived on time.

Maybe.

Ian had to act now. He couldn't just shoot the man. A police officer's job was to maintain life at all times, even if the life he was maintaining was a serial killer's.

Ian had to get up there and fast.

He spotted a truck parked in the clearing. A man sat behind the wheel, the light from his phone glowing on his face. Ian dug out his credentials and charged for the vehicle. The guy was so involved in his phone he didn't look up. Ian pounded on the window, and the man startled. Ian held out his creds, and the man lowered his window.

"Do you have a key for that boom lift? Do you know how

to operate it?" Ian's words tumbled out fast as he took in the name Vern embroidered on the man's denim shirt.

"Yes and yes."

"I need to be lifted up to the Flagg house as quickly as possible."

"I'd need Flagg's permission to do that." Vern burned his gaze into Ian. "'Sides, you can easily get into the place from the road. There's a security gate up at the end of the street for vehicle access, but you can hoof it over there."

Ian didn't have time to waste, but the guy wasn't budging. "I need to surprise him."

"He's up there?"

"Yes, and he's about to kill a woman. We have no more time to talk. Either help me or I'll arrest you for impeding an investigation."

Vern crossed his arms. "Flagg's no killer."

"You'll have to take my word for it." Ian jerked Vern's door open. "Let's move."

Vern picked up his hat and slid out slowly. Ian had had enough. He grabbed the man's shoulder and catapulted him toward the lift.

Ian dug out his phone and earbuds from his pocket then looked at Londyn, who remained by the car. "Keep in touch with our back up. Call me, and we'll stay connected so I can update you."

Vern put his key in the control panel on the side of the machine. The diesel fired up, running loud by the lift's base, but Ian hoped the distance and rain prevented Flagg from hearing it.

Vern turned the key. "We're good to get into the basket and take control from there."

Ian raced to the metal-framed basket and jumped in. Vern joined him. The machine was in the right location and didn't need to be moved.

"Fast as you can," Ian said to Vern and swiped the rain from his face.

He pressed his foot on a pedal and shoved the joystick control forward, and they headed into the dark night sky. Ian's view of the house was blocked by trees, but he lifted his rifle and waited for the basket to crest the top of tall pines. He searched the back of the house. It was dark, but his scope cut through it and gave him a clear view again.

Flagg and Malone hadn't moved much. What were they looking at inside the house?

Ian couldn't focus on that now. He had to plan his approach as they rose higher. "Does Flagg have security cameras on the build site?"

"A few, but they point toward the road."

After Vern's reluctance, Ian didn't know if the guy was telling the truth, and Ian couldn't be too careful with Malone's life. He would check. He ran his scope over the building. If Flagg had cameras facing the hillside, they would light up like a spotlight in his night vision.

Nothing flared. Good. They were clear.

He focused on the house. There. Finally the pair turned and jumped down to the ground. Ian could make out their faces. Malone and Flagg. Ian was sure now. Malone was moving normally. A large goose egg on her head but no other visible injuries. Flagg wasn't brandishing a weapon, but he'd tied Malone's hands and was holding the rope.

Ian had to get up there before he hurt her. "Faster."

"Going as fast as I can in this rain," Vern said.

Ian raised his rifle, wanting to shoot. There was no evidence that Malone was in immediate danger, and Ian couldn't shout.

But what could he do?

He couldn't jump Flagg unless Vern maneuvered the basket into position right next to Flagg. That wouldn't work.

If Flagg saw Ian's approach, he'd have time to harm Malone or take her hostage.

No. Ian couldn't let either of those happen.

Flagg faced Malone and pushed her to the ground. A knife came up in his hand, and he bent over her. His arm started down.

"Stop, police!" Ian shouted.

Flagg spun, but Ian didn't know if the knife had hit home before he turned.

Ian sighted his scope on the man's chest, the red dot over his heart.

Flagg looked down at his chest, and his mouth dropped open. He threw down the knife and ran, charging up to the house. Ian wouldn't shoot a fleeing man in the back, but he couldn't go after him either. Not from the basket.

"Bring in the cavalry!" he said into his mic to Londyn.

"Roger that," Londyn said, and he heard her give the order for the others to move.

Sirens sounded from the road. Ian prayed the officers or Londyn arrested Flagg. Because right now, Ian had only one thing in mind. He had to get to Malone.

Had she been stabbed? Was she bleeding out?

Malone was alive. Flagg didn't stab her.

Thank You! Thank You!

So close. It had been so very, very close.

She wanted to get up but her legs lost all strength. Her heart was racing, and she panted to catch her breath and blow out her fear. Her clothes were saturated from the rain that was now receding, making them heavier.

The second she felt stronger, she climbed to her feet.

She'd heard Ian's voice come out of the sky. But how? On her feet, she spotted the lift carrying him up to the patio.

Ingenious. And even more impressive that Ian figured out how to find her.

The basket came up close, and he jumped out the door onto the ground by the deck, his rifle strapped to his back.

He climbed over the framing to get to her, his gaze alert. "Are you hurt?"

"No, but another minute more, and I might've been dead." She shuddered.

Ian let out a long breath and enveloped her in a hug. She clung to him, inhaling his unique scent, reveling in his touch. Her legs felt like rubber, and she wanted to sit, but she needed his touch more than a chair.

"I'm alive because of you," she whispered, barely able to get the words out.

"Flagg could circle back once he sees the officers," he said, when all she wanted was for him to hold her. "I need to get you into the basket. We'll continue this when he's in custody."

She nodded her understanding. She would agree to anything, but she was too overwhelmed with gratitude to continue talking.

"I'll update Londyn."

"Malone's unhurt," he said in his mic. "Report when Flagg's in custody."

"Roger that."

Ian escorted Malone to the basket that the operator had settled on the patio framing, the door facing them. Ian helped her climb aboard with a tight hold on her arm and a gentle hand resting on her back.

His touch ignited her ability to overcome the weakness in her legs and keep going. She moved to the back of the basket and held on while Ian climbed in.

Her eyes widened. "I thought you would go after Flagg."

"I wouldn't leave you unprotected." Ian closed the basket. "We'll be down before you know it."

He motioned to the guy operating the lift, and he lowered them. "Full speed again."

The man got the lift moving. The jolt unsettled Malone, and she hung onto the cold rail. The basket backed up and lowered faster than she'd have guessed it could move. Ian stood, rifle in hand, scanning the area.

"Flagg was really going to kill you?" the construction worker asked.

Now that Malone's adrenaline was subsiding, anguish over her near death clogged her throat, and she nodded. Her leg muscles nearly failed, and she worked hard to stay standing until they reached the ground.

Ian continued to search the area with his scope. "Okay. Stay by my side, and we'll move toward my car."

He stepped out, and she marveled at his concentration and commanding presence in such a dangerous situation. He was her hero. She would tell him that, but not now. When this was over, she would thank him in every way she could think of.

They stepped across the thick gravel. He kept his rifle up and unlocked the doors with his key fob.

"Back seat, please," he said not looking at her. "And on the floor."

"You really think Flagg is coming down here?"

"I can't take a chance with your life, Malone." He took a long tortured breath, the first hint that he was upset. "Never with your life."

The intensity of his conviction made her heart swell with a feeling she never knew before. Love for a man. Not just any man but this special man. The one who seemed uncertain in many ways, but when it came to life-or-death matters, he showed up. Showed up big time.

She climbed into the back and lay down on the floor.

He closed the door and stood guard. Time ticked by, the only sound was trees swaying in the strong wind that had kicked up. She focused on the sound to keep from giving in to the weakness invading her body.

She didn't want to fall apart.

She had to focus. To think clearly. Not be a weak, sobbing woman who made things harder for Ian. The man she owed her life to.

To Ian, but mostly to God. He'd brought Ian into her life. Her protector.

She closed her eyes and lifted her face.

Thank You for saving me, Father. Thank You. Let someone arrest Flagg so he doesn't hurt anyone else. And protect those who are going after him.

She heard Ian talking to someone. Probably Londyn again.

Through the glass, she watched his shoulders sag, and he lowered his rifle. She waited for him to let her out of the car, but he ran a hand over his head, then took another of those breaths he'd taken earlier.

He opened the door and offered her a hand. The man who'd only a moment ago looked so strong and confident now had a gaze filled with pain that she couldn't explain. "Flagg's in custody. Londyn will go to the precinct and process him. I'll take you home, if that's where you want to go."

She clasped his hand and came to her feet. She expected him to reach out for her, but he went to his trunk and placed his rifle inside. What was with this professional approach? Was that still what he wanted, even after what they'd just gone through? If he cared about her as she cared about him, he wouldn't be able to remain so impassive, would he?

She followed him, and the moment he secured the trunk, she slid her arms around his neck and drew his head down for a kiss.

His lips went from cold and resistant to insistent and demanding in an instant. He crushed her body to his, his arms holding her firm. She reveled in his touch and slid her hands into his hair to hold him close.

The kiss intensified.

Oh, wow! She wished they were anywhere else but near this place that had almost become her grave.

"Ah, Detective," the construction worker said. "You still need me, or can I get going?"

Ian lifted his head and looked dazed for a moment. "Do you have a card with your contact details, Vern?"

"In the truck. Let me grab it." Vern walked away.

Ian put his focus back on her. "I guess we'd better hold off for a few more minutes."

She traced his rugged jaw with her finger.

"Keep doing that, and I'll make a spectacle of myself." He laughed and caught her hand and kissed it.

Ah, yes. That was more like it.

Vern came back and shoved the card into Ian's hand.

"Thank you for your help," Ian said, keeping his focus pinned to Malone.

"Glad to do it." Vern started to walk away, the gravel grinding under his boots, but then he stopped. "Guess this job is a total loss now."

"Looks like it," Ian said.

Shaking his head, Vern headed for his truck.

When he was gone, Malone peered at Ian. "Speaking of holding off, I don't care what issues either of us might have about starting a relationship. I know how I feel. I love you. So even if you want to argue, I—"

He pressed his finger on her lips. "No argument from me. When this investigation is closed, I plan to pursue you with the same intensity."

"Well then, Detective Blair." She slid her hands around his neck again. "Let's get this new pursuit going as fast as you can."

EPILOGUE

The midday sun beat down on Ian's truck as he parked in front of Malone's house. He checked his hair in the mirror, still wet from the shower. He was there to pick up Malone for Thanksgiving dinner at Peggy and Russ Byrd's house.

He pushed out of the truck and jogged up the sidewalk, moving past a big For Sale sign posted in the ground. Malone had delayed putting the house on the market while she looked for a new home, and it had just gone up for sale the day before. Her Realtor would hold an open house that weekend. He'd accompanied her to look at a bunch of houses in the past few weeks, until she found the perfect one. He loved that she wanted him to come along and offer his opinion. They'd even talked about a future where they could share the home she bought.

His shower after being called in to investigate a homicide made him a few minutes late, so he hurried to the door.

Malone was waiting at the door for him, holding out a casserole dish. "Can you take this? I'll grab my purse."

"No."

She cast him a confused look, but he let his gaze rove over her black skinny jeans. She'd paired with crazy high heels and a black-and-gray plaid shirt topped with a tailored version of a leather motorcycle jacket. Her hair was down, tumbling over her shoulders in soft waves, and she was wearing a deep red lipstick.

All of which he found insanely attractive.

"Can you set the casserole down for a minute?" he asked, remaining on the front stoop.

Her eyes narrowed. "Is something wrong?"

"Not at all. It's very right."

A puzzled look on her face, she placed the casserole on the hall table and turned to face him.

He swept her into his arms. "You'll need to replace that lipstick that's driving me crazy. Maybe a different color even."

He lowered his head and kissed her, their lips melding together, and he couldn't care less about the homicide he'd had to investigate that morning. About the fact that Beatrice was probably watching from across the street. About the rest of the world.

All he wanted was *now*. This moment with Malone in his arms. He could deal with the rest later.

He tightened his hold, careful not to seem too desperate. But he was desperate for her. He wanted her in his life. He was desperate for a normal life, whatever that might be. He didn't know the future, so he was taking things one day at a time. That was all he could do.

She pushed back and dragged in a deep breath. "I'm not complaining, but what was that all about?"

"I had a tough morning, and I missed you."

"I missed you too." She rubbed her finger over his lips, removing the lipstick he assumed, but all it did was make him want to kiss her more.

She was decent. Honorable. Honest. A woman a man

could get lost with forever, and he hoped he could be that man.

He couldn't commit to that yet. Not until they'd dated for some time, not until he judged his fitness for being her partner in life. If he passed, then yeah, he was going to ask her to marry him.

"How about we get going," she said, "and you tell me about your morning on the way? You can get it all out so it won't trouble you at the Byrd's house."

"Sure." Not that the lingering disquiet from the scene he'd cataloged that morning would go away that fast. "But first, one more of these."

He swooped in for a kiss before she could react, but when she did, it wasn't to push him away. She slid her fingers into the hair he'd just straightened in the mirror and messed it all up. He didn't care. He loved her touch. The way it made him feel human and whole.

He slowly let her go and looked deep into her eyes. "Okay. Now we can go."

She rubbed her thumb over his lip again. "This color doesn't look so good on you."

"I'll clean it off in the truck." Before her touch urged him to kiss her again, he slid past her and grabbed the casserole dish. "What did you make?"

"It's called corn pudding. Sounds kind of odd but if you like cornbread, you'll love it."

"If you made it, I will love it."

"Or, at least, you'll say you do." She giggled and closed the door.

They walked through the cool autumn day toward his truck, a crisp feel to the temps, but the sun was warm, a welcome change when it more often than not rained on Thanksgiving in the Portland area. He opened the door for her, and after she buckled her seatbelt, he handed her the casserole dish.

When he got behind the wheel, he used the mirror to look at his lips and laughed. "You're right. Not my color."

She already had her purse open and lipstick out. "Then it'll have to be lips off for the rest of the day."

He gave her a grin. "Maybe it doesn't look so bad after all."

She laughed, and he loved the sound of it bouncing around his truck. Bouncing around his life. He could surely get used to hearing it every day. He started up his truck and backed out of the driveway. "You ready for the open house?"

"I've already had a few showings. Lots of comments about how it needs remodeling, and it still makes me shiver when I hear that. And then there's the whole part about a serial killer hiding his murder weapon in the wall while he was living here."

"I assume both of those things will devalue the home."

She nodded. "But taking a loss to move on, especially now that I know the history before I lived here as a kid, is worth it." She swiveled to face him. "What's the status on the other items Flagg hid in his houses? Have you finished the last place yet?"

"He's still not talking, and we're having to use wall finders and take X-rays. It's slow going, but we're confident we'll find what he hid there without having to tear into all the walls."

"It's so odd that he did that. It's like he wanted to get caught. Maybe it shouldn't surprise me. I'd heard that was true of some serial killers."

"Not so." He glanced at her, and she was twisting her hands together in her lap. "That's a false notion. They simply relax a bit with each murder they get away with, get cocky, and make a mistake that allows us to catch them. He really played Russian Roulette with hiding those things. It was just a matter of time before the items were found in one of the houses. Once that happened, it would have been a matter of how well he kept his prints and DNA off the items."

"I know you're not supposed to tell me, but have you found DNA or prints?"

"All I can say is, we've built a very strong case against him for the murders of the six women and your parents."

She gave a solemn nod. "What about the women's bodies? Have you found them?"

He shook his head. "Kelsey at Veritas is using ground penetrating radar to search the properties, and she's found three women so far."

She cringed, and he didn't want her to keep thinking about the murders.

"So tell me," he said. "What can I expect at the Byrd's place today?"

"Chaos." She chuckled, as he'd hoped she would, but the dark look lingered in her eyes.

Just like the darkness lingered in Ian's heart, but this woman washed it away when he was with her. She replaced it with goodness and warmth. "How many Byrds are there?"

She tilted her head. "Well, the parents and six kids. Then each one has a spouse or significant other, so six more."

"Fourteen adults and how many kids?"

"There's Asher and Brendan's adopted daughter, Karlie." She held her hand out and ticked off on her fingers. "And, of course, the three children Peggy and Russ are fostering. So five kids."

"A grand total of nineteen. Twenty-one with us." He shook his head. "Wow. Coming from a family of three, twenty-one is a lot to take."

She clutched his arm. "Maybe for some families, but the Byrds are all warm and welcoming, and I know they'll open their arms for you too."

"Or spread their wings." Ian laughed.

Malone rolled her eyes.

"No matter what happens, it'll be better than the incident I was called in for this morning."

She released his arm and rested her hands on the sides of the casserole. "Families can be the hardest to deal with." He knew she spoke from all of her experience with battered women and her time as a prosecutor.

"Worse than everyday fights are when families get together for the holidays," he added. "We get so many more calls on holidays. Which was the case this morning. The large family started arguing over politics, and one guy grabbed the turkey carving knife and stabbed the cousin, killing him."

"Oh, no, really?" She gaped at him. "That poor family."

"When I got there, two guys were still arguing about the same political issue, and I had to break up a fistfight on top of the homicide call." He shook his head. "Political views and holidays don't play well together."

"You won't experience anything like that at the Byrds," she said adamantly. "I promise."

He hoped she was right. Putting sixteen adults together who might get into a fight wasn't his idea of a good time. But then, sitting home alone or working on a holiday wasn't his idea of a good time either. Right now in his life, he didn't know what was a good time, but he hoped Malone would show him what God intended for families to be like, because it certainly wasn't like the family Ian had seen that morning. Of that, he was certain.

$\sim$

Malone led a shell-shocked Ian to the couch. She'd warned him about the numbers, but not about how loud and lively the Byrds could get. Especially around the football game that was playing in the family room. She loved all the noise. The warmth from the fireplace. The smell of Peggy's turkeys cooking in two big roasters. But most of all, she liked Ian's hand holding hers as if he was afraid one of the Byrds might abduct her. How fast her near death had caused the two of them to change their priorities. God brought them to the end of themselves and then gave them the mercy to survive and realize what was important in their lives.

Ian shifted on the couch, then shifted again.

She looked at him. "Everything okay?"

"It's a lot to take in," he said. "You said I should expect chaos, but it's way more than what you described."

She slid closer to him so their legs touched in hopes of giving him some comfort. "I know you don't have much family, but your parents had big parties, right?"

He looked down at their legs and eased even closer to her. "Yeah, but our house was bigger, and the people were more reserved. Plus, I didn't hang out with them much."

She didn't like that her big, strong detective felt vulnerable, but she was glad she was there to help him. "Do you want to go?"

"No. I'm fine. I just need to adapt to it." He smiled at her, that smile that had a hint of a secret and promise just for her. "Besides, you want to be here, and I'll do anything you want. Though I probably shouldn't admit that."

"You say that now, but I'm sure there's a line somewhere."

He shifted to face her and took her other hand. "Honestly, I'm so glad that we're together that anything that's not illegal or immoral—and I can afford without going into debt —it's yours."

"If only we were alone right now." She held his gaze. "I would be kissing you senseless."

"Okay, changed my mind. I want to go." He laughed.

They must've drawn Peggy's attention because she came straight across the room to them with purpose in her step as she was drying her hands on her apron. "I wanted to take a moment to say how happy I am to see you two holding hands. I knew it was a match the moment I saw you together." She pointed her focus at Ian. "And I'm especially glad you worked out whatever was in the way."

"Me too," Ian said, sounding so sincere.

"As am I." Malone smiled up at Peggy. "So your work is done. All your children have found their life partners, and me too."

"Is it?"

"What do you mean?" Ian asked.

"I was thinking about the Steele girls. They're all still single, and each of them are such a catch. They might need some help in that area." A timer buzzed in the kitchen. "Their parents probably have that in hand, but you never know. I'll give Iris and Rose a call next week." Peggy wrinkled her nose. "Dinner's almost ready. Got to get that pie out of the oven."

She hurried away.

Malone chuckled. "She does love matchmaking."

"I should probably warn Londyn."

"I would if I were you."

They sat in silence for some time, just watching the family interact. Malone's heart overflowed with the happiness in her brother's life. He loved being a dad and being married to the amazing Sierra. God had given him his dream, even though Reed hadn't known that a family *was* his dream.

God could be doing the same thing for Ian. Maybe next year at this time, they would be married.

Four-year-old Karlie came out of the kitchen and marched across the room, her adorable focus pointed their way. She tossed back her blond pigtails and fixed her big blue eyes on Ian. "I'm Karlie, and Nana said you were new here, so I'm s'posed to take you to the table." She tilted her head. "It's my 'sponsibility today. I'm almost five. How old are you?"

Surprise flashed on Ian's face. "Thirty-three."

Her eyes widened. "Wow! You won't take my drumstick, right? The big kids say they get to have it, but Nana says it's for me. She didn't tell me if the old people would want it."

Ian held up a hand. "I promise not to touch it."

Karlie looked at Malone. "You promise too?"

Malone gave a serious nod. "We'll stay far away from it."

"We're going to have pie too. Punkin with whip cream. I helped whip it. Nana says I'm going to be a good cook like her. I love Nana and want to be just like her when I grow up." She lifted her arms above her head and stood on her tip-toes. "Then I'll be this big."

Her expression turned serious, and her arms fell to her sides. "Nana wants you to find your places first 'cause you're new. But don't be afraid. I love all of my new family. Even if we keep getting new people. They're nice, and I love them. I'll love you, too, soon as I know you. C'mon." She spun and skipped across the room.

"Please tell me I don't have to skip," Ian whispered to Malone.

She laughed. "That child is destined to have a job that involves public speaking and diplomacy."

Ian took Malone's hand, and they crossed the room. Karlie skipped over to Brendan and grabbed his hand.

He smiled at her and ruffled her hair. "What are you up to, little bit?"

"Nana told me to bring them to dinner." She pointed at Malone and Ian, then fixed her big eyes on Brendan. "He's old, Daddy. Your age. That's *really* old, right?"

Ian snorted and looked like he was struggling to curtail a laugh.

"It is." Brendan chuckled.

Karlie turned her focus on Malone and Ian again. "He's my new daddy. He married Mommy. I love him too. Lots and lots."

Brendan scooped her up in his arms and planted a kiss on her cheek. "I love you, too, little bit."

She cupped the sides of his face and kissed him back. "He's the best daddy. Even when he has to punish me 'cause I did something wrong. But I try not to. Sometimes it just happens."

Brendan opened his mouth to say something, but Peggy entered the room carrying a golden brown turkey on a large white platter. "Okay, everyone. Let's get seated. Just look for your name card on the turkeys the children and I made."

Karlie squirmed down. "We get our own table with the turkeys we made from leaves. Not the ones from outside. Nana said those would be dirty, so she bought leaves from the store. They look real. I like them."

She bolted toward the card table set up with four place settings on an autumn tablecloth and colorful gourds in the center. Each setting had a small turkey with leaves for the plumage, an acorn head with googly eyes, and a walnut body. They held small name cards. A few other touches with felt and ribbon made them look very realistic. At least the ones at the grownup table did. The kids' turkeys were much more free-formed.

The Byrds' three foster children scurried from the

kitchen and took their seats too. Eight-year-old Willow helped two-year-old Sadie into a booster seat. Their brother Logan took a seat between them and Karlie. He was about the same age as Karlie, and Peggy had once said they were great friends. Malone smiled at how happy the Gentry children looked. She'd had a part in getting them away from their dysfunctional parents and bringing them together with the Byrd family a few months before.

Thank You. What a blessed day that was. And thank You for Peggy's and Russ's big hearts for these children.

Brendan looked at the kids' table. "Our little chatterbox loves just about everything and expresses her love very vocally. I only wish kids came with a user manual. I'm either winging it, asking my wife, Jenna, or calling my mom. But I guess I'm doing okay. Karlie's been with me for nearly a year, and I haven't broken her yet, so there's hope for me. Might even mean we're ready for another one."

Jenna came up from behind him and slid under his arm. "Another one of what?"

Brendan secured his arm around her shoulder. "I was just saying we might be ready for another child."

She cast a dreamy look up at her husband. "Definitely worth discussing."

"Maybe we should bail on dinner and discuss it in detail." He winked at her.

"And risk your mother's disappointment. No way." Jenna laughed.

"Come on, people," Peggy brought in the second turkey just as golden brown and perfect as the first. "Have a seat before the food gets cold."

"Yes, ma'am." Brendan saluted his mom, and she laughed.

Brendan poked his thumb over his shoulder and looked at Malone. "I saw your name tags in the middle on the other side. My mom put you next to Drake and Natalie. I heard her say you'd likely be more comfortable since you've known Natalie for a while."

"Your mom really tries to think of everything, doesn't she?" Ian asked.

"Sometimes too much." Brendan chuckled and took his wife's elbow to direct her down the side of the long table.

Ian, still clasping Malone's hand, led them to their places. They passed Reed, who was holding Asher, and Malone gave the baby's head a kiss.

"Happy Thanksgiving," she said to her brother and Sierra.

Reed nodded, a contented look on his face. "We have a lot to be thankful for this year."

She squeezed Ian's hand and looked up at him. "More than I could ever imagine."

"Mom's giving me the stink eye," Sierra said. "We can catch up after dinner."

They split up, and Malone made quick work of introducing Drake and Natalie after giving Natalie a hug.

"The social worker," Ian said to Natalie.

"Correct." Natalie smiled. "I bet it's been a challenge to learn who everyone is."

He nodded.

"Don't let it overwhelm you. I thought it was going to be hard at first, but every single person in this family is welcoming. Even if the guys do still fight and tease like little boys."

"Hey now," Drake grabbed her into a hug. "We just discuss things. Loudly."

Natalie rolled her eyes.

"Sit!" Peggy called out again. "Please! You can catch up while eating."

Ian pulled Malone's chair out. The Byrd boys had

impeccable manners, so there was a lot of that going on around the table. Malone would expect nothing less from Peggy's and Russ's children.

Russ stood to offer a prayer of thanks and a blessing for the food and for Peggy's hard work in preparing it. The moment the prayer ended, he looked down the table. "I think it's time for the youngest to get to carve the other turkey. Erik, will you do the honors?"

Erik gave his fiancée, Kennedy, a smile, then hopped up to grab a knife and serving fork and held them up in triumph. "About time the second turkey is decently carved."

Clay rolled his eyes. "You might do better than everyone else, but no one will top my mad skills."

"I'm sorry I missed seeing that." His wife, Toni, kissed Clay on the cheek.

Clay grinned at her. "It was epic."

Drake snorted. "Says you and only you."

The brothers laughed and spouted off good-natured wisecracks.

Peggy tsked. "You'd think no one taught you boys table manners. You can go ahead and eat."

The brothers shot out hands for serving bowls and plates. Instead of taking food for themselves, they offered it to their significant others first. Peggy and Jenna helped the children get their food, and Karlie reminded them twice about the drumstick.

Once Russ had removed one from the turkey he was carving, Peggy put it on the child's plate. "Think you can eat all of that, sweetie?"

Karlie gave a solemn nod. "My other daddy never let me have it. He said my lame hands couldn't hold it. But I can. See." She picked up the drumstick and took a large bite.

Malone leaned close to Ian. "Karlie has juvenile idiopathic arthritis. Her dad used to mock her when the poor thing couldn't control her autoimmune disease."

"That's cruel."

Malone nodded, tears wetting her eyes over how that man had treated this sweet little child. She was glad he was no longer in the picture. Not that she was happy he'd died, but at least Karlie had been spared that cruelty all her life. Karlie reminded Malone of how she'd always believed she had something to prove growing up. Hopefully, with Brendan on Karlie's side, she would outgrow that need.

Natalie held out a bowl of creamy mashed potatoes, and Malone took a generous helping. Plates were soon overloaded with food, and the room was quiet, save silverware clinking against china and the children giggling.

"Ah," Peggy said, still standing at the head of the table. "This is what a mother wants to hear. Her family enjoying their food."

"It's great, as usual, Peg," Russ said.

Everyone murmured their agreement.

"Anyone need anything before I sit," she asked.

"Just for you to enjoy your own food." Russ got up and pulled out her chair, then kissed her cheek.

"Before I do, it's time to share what we're thankful for this year. And what a year it's been, so I'll start by sharing my thanks for all the lovely young women who have joined our family. Some not officially yet, but I know it will happen. And for the faithful husband Reed has been to Sierra. And the blessing of children added to our family. All five precious little babies. Wow. My heart is full."

"I'm not a baby," Willow called out, giving Peggy a fond look. "But I know what you mean."

Malone understood some of what this child was experiencing today. As a foster child, though it was clear Willow already deeply loved this family, she knew it was temporary.

The Byrds couldn't adopt the children, and neither could Natalie and Drake, who'd helped rescue them. No one could, not without their parents' permission. Even though they were both in prison, neither would relinquish rights to the children.

"I really can't top Peg's speech," Russ said. "Except that I'm thankful for my continued health, and for my son's generous gift of a kidney, which keeps me moving along."

Wine glasses with sparkling apple cider were raised to that and clinked.

Peggy sat at the table. "Ian and Malone, since you are the newest members of our family, why don't you go next?"

Malone's heart was full to brimming at having a family to call her own again, and she was too choked up to talk. She gestured at Ian to speak.

"I...well...I've never done this before."

"Not once?" Karlie's question came from the other table.

"Not once." He looked around the table, but no one seemed surprised or judgmental.

Karlie hopped up and came to stand by Ian. "I can help if you need it 'cause we have something to be thankful for every day. That's what Mommy says when we pray."

"I think I can handle it on my own, but thanks for the offer."

"See, you can be thankful for me." She spun and rushed back to the table.

Brendan and Jenna shared a what-are-you-gonna-do look.

Ian cleared his throat and set his fork down. "I'm thankful for the beginning of a relationship with an amazing woman. And for God, showing me how wrong I'd been for years."

"God doesn't care if we're wrong," Karlie said. "You just gotta ask for forgiveness and really mean it."

The table erupted in laughter, and Karlie looked baffled. Jenna got up and went over to whisper something to her daughter, and that smile was back in place as Karlie sat. "Sorry, everybody. I gotta be quiet now and eat so I can have pie."

This time the others held their laughter, but smiles abounded, and Malone felt her throat closing even more.

Ian sat quietly for a moment, then added, "I'm thankful for the invitation to dinner and for being welcomed by such a wonderful family." He looked expectantly at Malone.

She had to get over herself and rescue this man again. "I'm thankful for the warm welcome too. And a great sister-in-law and for Reed and Sierra's precious child. For their marriage, too, which I hope to emulate someday." She looked at Ian. "And I'm thankful that God pointed out my wrong thinking. I can now look forward to building a strong relationship with this guy." She tucked her arm in his and rested her head on his shoulder as cries of *aw* came from the women.

"That was very special." Peggy paused with a forkful of turkey held midair. "Who's next?"

"I'll go," Sierra said, and started talking about Asher.

"This family really sets a great example," Ian leaned close and whispered to Malone. "I still don't know if I can live like they do, but it'll help to see selfless love in action like this."

"They're not like this all the time," Malone said. "They have their differences and squabble like all families do. But their faith and love always win out. Or Peggy does." Malone giggled quietly.

Ian turned toward Malone. "We've never talked about having kids."

"Something we need to do."

"But you want them?"

"I do." She looked at him. "What about you?"

"I didn't think I did, but now, with you? Yeah, I think I do. I just wish what Brendan said earlier was true. You know, about a user's manual." He stared at Reed, who was holding Asher. The baby was too young for a high chair, and he was grabbing for everything on the table. "I think it'd be helpful."

"But look at Reed," Malone said. "He never had any experience with children before Asher. And the baby might be challenging Reed right now, but look at the peace in Reed's eyes. He loves being a dad, and he had a lot of reservations at first. You just have to take it one day at a time and have Google, or better yet, Peggy on speed dial."

Malone laughed, and Ian smiled.

"Reed does look pretty content." Ian leaned closer. "So I guess it's one day at a time. I can do that. Especially with you and God by my side."

"And don't forget, when things get difficult, we can fly the coop for a few hours. We'll have a whole flock of Bryds to babysit."

~

Thank you so much for reading Night Prey. If you've enjoyed the book, I would be grateful if you would post a review on the bookseller's site. Just a few words is all it takes.

And you'll be happy to hear that there is a new series coming soon!

STEELE GUARDIANS SERIES

STEELE GUARDIANS

Intrigue. Suspense. Family.
Six Steele women.
Five years in law enforcement under their belt.
One security business inherited from their fathers.

Join the Steele Guardians as they investigate stories that include a baby kidnapped from a hospital, a jewelry heist, a man who can't remember who he is, an abducted socialite, smuggled antiquities, and murder. And in every book, God's amazing power and love.

Meet the Steele Guardians –
Book 1 – Tough as Steele – February 1, 2022
Book 2 – Nerves of Steele – May 1, 2022
Book 3 – Forged in Steele – August 10, 2022
Book 4 – Made of Steele – November 1, 2022
Book 5 – Solid as Steele – February 1, 2023
Book 6 – Edge of Steele – May 1, 2023

For More Details Visit -
www.susansleeman.com/books/steele-guardians

Susan Sleeman

Searching for an abducted woman...

Detective Londyn Steel is thrown into the deep end when she's assigned to find an abducted socialite. Problem is, her family's company, Steele Guardians, was supposed to protect the family matriarch at her seventieth birthday party when she disappears, and Londyn fears her investigation will expose problems in her family's company and bring them down. Especially when County Detective Nate Ryder declares jurisdiction over the scene, and Londyn must take a back seat in one of the most important cases she's ever investigated.

Could put them in a deadly killer's crosshairs.

Londyn has no choice but to work with Nate and bristles at

his interference at first, but soon forms a working truce so they can combine forces to locate this missing woman before it's too late. As they search for leads, emotions he hasn't felt since before his service as a Navy SEAL come to the surface. He credits Londyn for unearthing the guy he used to be before his military service, and Londyn can barely fight her attraction for him. But when they fear the socialite was murdered and the killer is still hunting, seeking another prey, their feelings for each other have to be put on hold to stay alive.

For More Details Visit -
www.susansleeman.com/books/tough-as-steele

NIGHTHAWK SECURITY SERIES
Protecting others when unspeakable danger lurks.

Keep reading for more information on the additional books in the Nighthawk Security Series where the Cold Harbor and Truth Seekers teams work side-by-side with Nighthawk Security.

A woman plagued by a stalker. Children of a murderer. A woman whose mother died under suspicious circumstances.

All in danger. Lives on the line. Needing protection.

Enter the brothers of Nighthawk Security. The five Byrd brothers with years of former military and law enforcement experience coming together to offer protection and investigation services. Their goal—protecting others when unspeakable danger lurks.

Book 1 Night Fall   –   November, 2020
Book 2 – Night Vision – December, 2020
Book 3 - Night Hawk   – January, 2021
Book 4 –Night Moves   – July, 2021
Book 5 – Night Watch – August, 2021
Book 6 – Night Prey – October, 2021

For More Details Visit -
www.susansleeman.com/books/nighthawk-security/

THE TRUTH SEEKERS

People are rarely who they seem

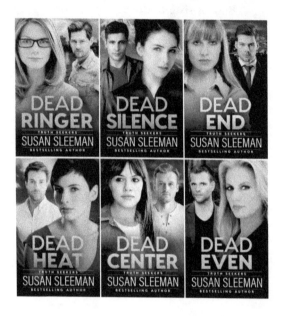

A twin who never knew her sister existed, a mother whose child is not her own, a woman whose father is anything but her father. All searching. All seeking. All needing help and hope.

Meet the unsung heroes of the Veritas Center. The Truth Seekers – a team, that includes experts in forensic anthropology, DNA, trace evidence, ballistics, cybercrimes, and toxicology. Committed to restoring hope and families by solving one mystery at a time, none of them are prepared for when the mystery comes calling close to home and threatens to destroy the only life they've known.

For More Details Visit -
www.susansleeman.com/books/truth-seekers/

BOOKS IN THE COLD HARBOR SERIES

Blackwell Tactical – this law enforcement training facility and protection services agency is made up of former military and law enforcement heroes whose injuries keep them from the line of duty. When trouble strikes, there's no better team to have on your side, and they would give everything, even their lives, to protect innocents.

For More Details Visit -
www.susansleeman.com/books/cold-harbor/

HOMELAND HEROES SERIES

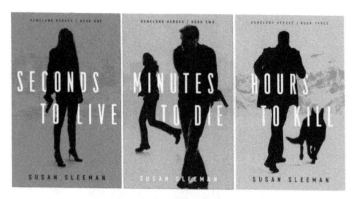

When the clock is ticking on criminal activity conducted on or facilitated by the Internet there is no better team to call other than the RED team, a division of the HSI—Homeland Security's Investigation Unit. RED team includes FBI and DHS Agents, and US Marshal's Service Deputies.

For More Details Visit -

www.susansleeman.com/books/homeland-heroes/

WHITE KNIGHTS SERIES

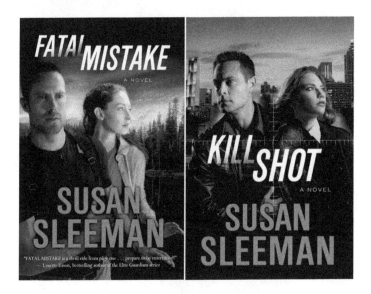

Join the White Knights as they investigate stories plucked from today's news headlines. The FBI Critical Incident Response Team includes experts in crisis management, explosives, ballistics/weapons, negotiating/criminal profiling, cyber crimes, and forensics. All team members are former military and they stand ready to deploy within four hours, anytime and anywhere to mitigate the highest-priority threats facing our nation.

www.susansleeman.com/books/white-knights/

ABOUT SUSAN

SUSAN SLEEMAN is a bestselling and award-winning author of more than 40 inspirational/Christian and clean read romantic suspense books. In addition to writing, Susan also hosts the website, TheSuspenseZone.com.

Susan currently lives in Oregon, but has had the pleasure of living in nine states. Her husband is a retired church music director and they have two beautiful daughters, a very special son-in-law, and an adorable grandson.

For more information visit:
www.susansleeman.com

CPSIA information can be obtained
at www.ICGtesting.com
Printed in the USA
LVHW032330221221
706957LV00005B/722